Praise fo

"Yates weaves surprises
about strong and nurturing female family bonds."
—*Booklist* on *Confessions from the Quilting Circle*

"*Secrets from a Happy Marriage* is a beautiful, emotional, tender story with a gorgeous setting and characters I adored. Maisey Yates always writes stories that stay in your heart long after you read the last page."
—*New York Times* bestselling author RaeAnne Thayne

"Fans of Robyn Carr and RaeAnne Thayne will enjoy [Yates's] small-town romance."
—*Booklist* on *Secrets from a Happy Marriage*

"[A] surefire winner not to be missed."
—*Publishers Weekly* on *Slow Burn Cowboy* (starred review)

"Multidimensional and genuine characters are the highlight of this alluring novel, and sensual love scenes complete it. Yates's fans...will savor this delectable story."
—*Publishers Weekly* on *Unbroken Cowboy* (starred review)

"Fast-paced and intensely emotional.... This is one of the most heartfelt installments in this series, and Yates's fans will love it."
—*Publishers Weekly* on *Cowboy to the Core* (starred review)

"Yates's outstanding eighth Gold Valley contemporary...will delight newcomers and fans alike.... This charming and very sensual contemporary is a must for fans of passion."
—*Publishers Weekly* on *Cowboy Christmas Redemption* (starred review)

Also by Maisey Yates

Secrets from a Happy Marriage
Confessions from the Quilting Circle
The Lost and Found Girl

Four Corners Ranch

Unbridled Cowboy
Merry Christmas Cowboy
Cowboy Wild
The Rough Rider
The Holiday Heartbreaker
The Troublemaker
The Rival
Hero for the Holidays

Gold Valley

Smooth-Talking Cowboy
Untamed Cowboy
Good Time Cowboy
A Tall, Dark Cowboy Christmas
Unbroken Cowboy
Cowboy to the Core
Lone Wolf Cowboy
Cowboy Christmas Redemption
The Bad Boy of Redemption Ranch
The Hero of Hope Springs
The Last Christmas Cowboy
The Heartbreaker of Echo Pass
Rodeo Christmas at Evergreen Ranch
The True Cowboy of Sunset Ridge

For more books by Maisey Yates, visit maiseyyates.com.

Cruel Summer

MAISEY YATES

CANARY STREET PRESS

CANARY
STREET
PRESS™

Recycling programs
for this product may
not exist in your area.

ISBN-13: 978-1-335-47145-1

Cruel Summer

Canary Street Press
22 Adelaide St. West, 41st Floor
Toronto, Ontario M5H 4E3, Canada
CanaryStPress.com

Printed in U.S.A.

To Megan and Nicole—for being there on the hardest day.

To Jackie—for all the late-night phone calls from my pantry.

To Haven—for being the best husband and giving me all the space and understanding I needed.

To writing—for letting me work out all the grief.

To my dad—for being strong for me, but soft when you need to be.

And to my mom, who isn't here physically,
but who made me the person I am.

one

"I think we should see other people."

Samantha Parker dropped her fork, right onto the salad she was eating, and looked across the table at her husband of twenty-two years.

At that familiar face saying the most unfamiliar words.

Will Parker was her soulmate. She'd known that since she was sixteen years old and he'd kissed her on a school field trip to the Rock Museum.

She had never cared much about rocks.

But she'd cared a lot about whether or not the boy she considered one of her best friends *liked her* liked her, like she did him. She'd only had to wait a breath between her confession and his kiss—her first kiss and his—to get the answer.

That they felt the same.

They had felt the same every day since then.

She'd written *W + S 4 Eva* on her binder. So had he. He'd taught her to drive a stick. And well…he'd…taught her to *drive a stick*.

When they'd guiltily broken all the rules of their churchy

upbringing and had sex for the first time at seventeen, they'd both owned that choice. They'd both wanted it.

When they'd found out at eighteen that their passion had actually been recklessness and Sam found herself pregnant, they'd been united in knowing what choice had to be made.

They'd had a small wedding with only family, and at their high school graduation, they were a married couple with a baby on the way and a mountain of small-town gossip and disapproval buzzing around them.

But they were together, so it had never mattered.

Every choice, every fork in the road, every moment, Samantha and Will had been one. Because they were soulmates.

When Will had said he wanted to go to dinner tonight, she'd been certain it was an affirmation of sorts. Their youngest child, Ethan, had told them he wasn't coming home this summer because he was doing a study abroad program. Sam had been sad about that, initially. There was something…good about it too. Ethan was launched. They'd done it. She and Will were empty nesters. They'd crossed a finish line, and they'd done it at forty, because that was what happened when you did everything early.

It had been hard sometimes, no doubt about that. But they'd been fine with it because they'd weathered it together.

Together.

Like always.

So why wouldn't she think they were going out to celebrate a job well done? A life well lived? Finally going on an extended vacation like they'd planned to do when they'd graduated, but hadn't because they were having a baby, and they were young and broke anyway.

Then they'd been raising three boys and growing businesses and organizing life.

They were *still* young, and *not* broke, and didn't have kids at home to worry about, so it was the ideal time to travel, and she'd been absolutely sure that would be the topic of discussion for the evening.

Not…

That.

She…laughed. And laughed and laughed. She didn't mean to, but what else was there to do? It was a joke. It *had* to be a joke.

She decided then and there that it was, and that was how she would respond.

"Yeah, sure. Seeing other people. How about Elysia? She might be ready to date again by now."

He did not laugh. He looked…worried. Her stomach went so tight she could hardly breathe.

"Sam… I'm serious."

He could have just punched her. She would have been less shocked. But Will would never punch her. He would never hurt her.

This *hurt.*

It made her feel like she didn't know anything. About herself or about the man she'd been sure she knew better than anyone else on the planet.

She cleared her throat for something to do and looked at her salad. "Why… *What?*"

"Sorry, it didn't come out right."

She tried to imagine a way it could mean something wholly different if he rearranged the words, or it came out *right.*

"I hope it came out in all the entirely wrong words."

"Not…entirely wrong." He closed his eyes and let out a hard breath, and she couldn't remember her husband ever making exactly that face before. "We've had that perfect life." Well, she agreed with that. "We raised our boys, and we had a stable home for them. We transcended all the…the shame people tried to heap on us when you got pregnant in high school. We made a life so normal and so conventional the kids never faced any kind of scrutiny." He let out an uncomfortable-sounding breath. "But have you ever thought about why we did it?"

She couldn't answer his question with sincerity. "Why we went to Texas Roadhouse? Because I like the rolls, Will. I thought that was why." Except right now she just had a salad, and she really needed bread and butter.

"No, why we got married."

She felt like she'd been doused with a bucket of ice water. "No. I have *never* wondered that. I *know* why we got married."

"That isn't what I mean. Why marriage? We did that be-cause it was the only thing we could do to avoid being shamed. To make our *mistake* right. Why did it even feel like a mistake? Because we were told it was by our youth pastors and by our parents. We didn't think we were making a mistake." He let out a hard breath. "We did it to please everyone around us."

She rejected that. Hard. "No, Will, I married you because I *loved* you." Oh, God. She was that woman. That forty-year-old woman who didn't have kids left at home and whose husband didn't want her anymore. They weren't special at all. They were cliché and terrible and...and... "Are you... Is this a midlife cri-sis? Are you asking me for a divorce?"

"No." He put his hand out across the table and rested it over hers. A wave of calm washed over her. She felt safer, just like that. His touch had always done that for her.

She looked at him, at his light brown hair, pushed back off his forehead. His face, lined now and not as boyish as it had been. But there was still something in his smile that would always be sixteen-year-old Will to her, no matter their ages.

She could breathe again.

He was Will. He wasn't a stranger.

That reminder, that mantra, helped her get through the next few seconds at least.

"I love you," he said. "I love you as much now as I always did. But I... I'm not happy."

She picked up her iced tea and tried to take a drink, but her throat was too tight. She had to put it down while she coughed, her eyes watering, and she was sort of glad because she might cry. The choking gave her plausible deniability.

"I don't..." She tried to force the words out through her raw throat. "I don't understand. How can you love me and not be happy?"

"Sam...it's not you. It's about me and what... We've lived a whole life. We're forty, and we've already lived *a whole life*. The kids, the mortgage, over twenty years of marriage. After Ethan left for school last year, I started asking myself what other... *lives* there are."

Other lives. Lives that weren't their boring, normal lives?

Lives where men in their forties went windsurfing and got to have sex with whoever they wanted?

Lives like...

She didn't need to think about anyone else, or make it about anyone else. She started to stand up because she didn't know what else to do, and Will tightened his grip on her.

"I did this wrong," he said. "The most important thing here, and the thing I should have said first, is that I love you. None of this is about *not* being with you. I just... We have lived a life that looks exactly like everyone else in town."

She settled back into her seat. "I don't... It's...the American dream, isn't it? Slightly more kids than average, but we have our own businesses, we have a house, we're a family, we..."

"Yes, but we can keep all those things and also try something new. We can keep those things, but explore different aspects of who we are. I want to try having an open marriage."

"You want..." Her mind went blank for a moment while she tried to make sense of what he was saying.

That was what he'd meant, from the beginning of this conversation. He wanted to have sex with other people. That was what he meant. He wanted…to see her and see other people. He wanted to date other women.

Now that she'd had his children, raised them.

She'd loved him when he'd had a ridiculous mop of curly hair that covered his eyebrows and couldn't last longer than two minutes during sex. She'd taught him how to touch her, and he'd gotten very good at it. He'd gone from dopey teen boy to hot man and she'd been there every step of the way. This version of him, forty, good at conversation, good in bed, was supposed to be her reward for loving him all this time. Now he wanted to give this to someone else?

Now that he'd aged into himself like the finest of wines, he wanted to be with *other* women.

She had trained him. Honed his skills.

She'd had his babies, cleaned his house, done his laundry, and not like he hadn't done his share of household chores. Not that he wasn't a wonderful father. It was just that they'd done the hard part. They'd done the things that broke people up.

Financial stress and buying houses and starting new careers and finding out your middle child was failing math and smoking weed.

They'd done all that and been just fine.

All through the years, they'd chosen each other. That's what a happy marriage was. It wasn't that there were never struggles, but she…she chose him every time, even when it felt hard.

They'd gone from teenagers to mature adults together, and now that they were…like the very best versions of themselves, he wanted to share that? The version of him she'd helped create? That she'd *earned*?

"Why…are you telling me this in public?"

He pursed his lips, cleared his throat—which always meant he was about to say something she didn't like, but that was probably also true. "I wanted to actually talk to you and not the bedroom door."

"I don't think I would have walked away from this conversation. Frankly, I'm riveted."

"You would have."

She would have.

"You don't like conflict," he continued.

"Well, if you knew this would make conflict, why bring it up?"

"Because. Because sometimes I wonder if we make certain choices because the path is well-worn. Because there are examples of this exact life all around us."

"Except we're different," she said. "Because we're friends. We like each other. We…"

"Exactly. We *are* different. I already know I don't want to be without you. When I started thinking about this, I considered all the options."

He'd been considering options. While she'd been grocery shopping, writing articles and having coffee with her friends. While she'd been showing him the new dress she'd bought at Target and then the new underwear that matched, he'd been considering options. She'd been having her normal, everyday life and he'd been…

"We got together so young," he said. "I started thinking about our lives and how it's built on a foundation of doing what the people around us said was right. Our beliefs have shifted a lot over the years, and we're still living a life we chose before. I don't want to burn all this down, but I'm just questioning why we're doing it…this way when there are other options out there."

"Are you cheating on me?" she asked, a sudden anger, a sudden terror rising up in her chest and overtaking everything.

She had missed this entire upheaval inside of him. What else was she missing?

"Hot plates," said their waitress, approaching the table and setting down her steak and his hamburger.

Sam looked up and stared at the woman. The woman smiled.

Sam frowned and looked back at Will as the waitress walked away.

Sam just stared.

"I'm *not* cheating on you," he said. "I never have. I would never."

"You are literally asking my permission to cheat on me."

"I'm not. I am asking if you're open to nonmonogamy, and that isn't cheating. I haven't talked to anyone else about this, I haven't lied to you, I haven't hidden anything from you except the reading I've been doing about open relationships and how to navigate them." She could see his discomfort. He was playing with the fork, his breathing was choppy. It was…a big deal to him. He cared about this, and he was afraid to talk to her about it.

That was the terrible, stupid thing about knowing him and loving him. He'd made the stupid decision to tell her this at a restaurant because he didn't know how to handle it. Because it was hard and not because he was trying to be flippant or hurtful.

But it hurt.

Her heart was thundering so hard, and she was having trouble keeping a thought straight, and she was not going to eat her steak, because at this point if she tried to take a bite of anything she was going to throw it right back up.

"I *haven't* broken your trust," he said. "I wouldn't do that. That's why I'm talking to you. I had to get some things straight in my own head first. I didn't want to say anything before I was sure it was more than an impulse. I didn't break your trust."

And no, she supposed he hadn't.

Except he had.

Because she had trusted him to be the man she'd known, inside and out, for thirty years, the man she'd been married to for over twenty, and he wasn't.

"Trust is a very important part of this," he said. "Like I said,

I've been reading a lot. Communication and trust…you have to have that if you're going to keep a relationship and give your partner autonomy…"

"You have autonomy. Except, the thing is, we had *forsaking all others* in our marriage vows. You don't have autonomy to do things we said we wouldn't do in literal vows."

"That's why we're having this conversation. I don't want to end what we have, I want to expand the idea of what it can be."

She was never cruel. She was occasionally a little mean in the name of humor, but only to be amusing and never to actually hurt anyone, especially not Will. Never Will.

They were never that couple that bad-mouthed each other, not ever. They were united. A team. She'd walked through life feeling that for years now. That she always had him to back her up, that they were always each other's biggest support, and suddenly now she felt so singularly, utterly alone.

This marriage was a badge of honor for her in so many ways. Her best friend Elysia's husband had cheated. It had been such a horrendous thing to watch her go through, and she could remember how clearly she'd known Will would never. They were each other's one and only. They both loved that.

She had been *sure* they did.

Except Will was a man. And apparently what she'd always believed they both found wonderful and romantic, the fidelity she prized, felt like…a lack of autonomy to him.

She thought they'd chosen it.

She thought they'd chosen each other. Only each other.

She had.

She searched around wildly for someone to blame. Someone who wasn't her or Will.

The villain presented himself easily enough.

"Is it… Are you jealous of Logan?" She'd already stopped herself from thinking about him, but now she couldn't help it. It was easy for her to blame her husband's best friend.

Which maybe wasn't fair. Logan was...well. He was the kind of guy most men envied. He was the kind of guy most women wanted.

He was single and had been for years, and God knew he had his share of bar hookups and whatever else.

Maybe *that* was it, it was watching his friend with other women, watching his friend live a single, unattached life that made this seem like something he wanted.

"This is about us, not anyone else," he said. "Don't make it about him just because you don't like him. I'm not jealous of the guy whose wife died, Sam. I don't want to lose my wife. I don't want to lose you."

She looked down at her plate. "What if I say no?"

There was a long pause. "I'll probably keep...trying to talk to you about it. But I won't leave you. This isn't an ultimatum."

That was both better and worse.

If he would be unreasonable then she could be too. She could take her hurt and embrace it, let it be anger. She could just... storm out. Of the restaurant and the marriage. But he was coming to her with...sincere feelings and regrets and desires, and he wasn't forcing anything on her except...

Except the knowledge that their marriage wasn't enough.

She didn't know what to do with this.

She really did want to run away. To take a break from this, because he was right, she hated confrontation.

But especially with him, because it was just so rare, and she'd never really had a great idea about how to navigate it. She preferred to hide from it and let it blow over.

And he'd brought her here, to the neon beer signs and blaring country music, so she couldn't do just that.

"We think life *has* to look like this. We think it's the only way to live, the only way to be in a marriage, because it's what we were told. Why can't we question that? Can we at least *start* at questioning it?"

She didn't have an answer to that. Neither of them took a bite of their food.

"Let's just box it up," she said, feeling tired, and very much like she needed to be able to go into a room—any room—and lock the door and just sit in silence for a minute.

"If that's what you want."

"Yeah, it's what I want."

He signaled the waitress, who came back and looked at them like they were insane for asking for boxes for untouched food.

"Can we get an extra box of rolls?" he asked. "Also to go."

Damn him. For knowing she still wanted the rolls. For transforming just enough to make her feel like the wind was knocked out of her and her whole life was turned on its side, but not enough to be a total, monstrous stranger.

They walked outside and she stopped in the middle of the parking lot, looking at the row of cars, which contained three black SUVs that looked just like theirs and seemed to somehow underline the things he was saying to her.

She'd always loved their life because it was theirs.

She hadn't thought about how much like their neighbors they were.

He seemed to think they had all these things because they were held hostage by some kind of need to be the same, but she'd just felt like she was a middle-of-the-road person.

There was a reason things were mainstream, after all.

That she liked rosé, *Bridgerton* and iPhones had nothing to do with the influence of others. It was just that she liked what a lot of people did. Same as she had the sort of normal life most other people did.

She'd done her best to be…good.

She and Will had done one thing that everyone had known about and viewed as bad. As sinful and out of order, and she'd been running from that shame ever since. But the running path was very nice. It was a good life with a good husband and beautiful kids.

She'd never questioned it.

Not even once.

They got into the car, and the leather suddenly felt sticky rather than welcoming and soft, and she didn't know if that was a real thing or a her thing.

"How do you see our life?" she asked, the question sounding muted.

"What do you mean?"

"I see our life as being…special. Because we have a great relationship. We've been married for twenty-two years, and I'm still so…" Her breath suddenly felt sharp. "I'm still so happy to live in our house and be in our life. I don't care what other people do or what they have. I didn't marry you to be normal. I just am…normal."

He put the car in Reverse, his eyes on the backup camera as he eased out of the spot. When they were on the highway that led back to their neighborhood, he finally spoke again.

"I like our life too. But I see our life as limited. We have barriers and walls built up around what we do, and maybe it isn't even because it's what we want. It's because we learned a set of rules a long time ago, and we're following them without questioning them. Are we…normal because it's what we want or because it's what we were taught to do?"

"I don't get it."

"Monogamy isn't the only way to do marriage."

Suddenly she was just…mad. Because she had seen this summer stretching before them like so many other summers. She'd thought they might go to the beach or maybe go camping. Go to dinner, sit on the back deck and drink wine at night.

Instead he'd detonated this bomb between them, and yes, he was being honest. Yes, he'd done this instead of sneaking around. But she hadn't been ready for it, and it felt brutal.

"You want to fuck other women," she said, the language she so rarely used hard and echoing in the car, like she'd slapped him.

"Sam…"

"No, like, let's be really clear about this. You want to have sex with other women." She realized there was another aspect she'd never considered. Because he had been talking so much about the things you did just because they were the accepted things to do. Maybe there was more to it. "Or is it men? Are you like… Have I been holding you back from…"

"No. Not men."

"So just…you want to sleep with other women."

That was worse. At least if it was men, she'd know what they had that she didn't. She'd still feel upset she wasn't enough for her husband, but she wouldn't have to wonder if it was just about her stretch marks and her forehead wrinkles.

"Yes."

She looked at him and watched his face as they passed Target, then Starbucks, the light from the signs illuminating his face and letting her see a muscle there as it twitched.

It was jarring. The normality of it. Of being out with him, going by stores they shopped at, having this conversation that was anything but normal. Anything but okay.

"Well." She rolled the window down a little bit, trying to get some air. "I'm glad you're being honest about that."

"It's *part* of what I want, yes."

"Am I not hot enough for you? Is it the stretch marks? Is it the fact that my boobs are solidly an inch lower than they used to be?" She rolled the window down a little more.

"No."

"Should I get Botox? Implants? Fillers?"

"It's not about changing you."

"It is, though," she said. "Because I have to change to be okay with this. My idea of what marriage is has to change."

He sighed. "It's not about you not fulfilling me. It's about wanting to experience things I haven't. Some of that is sex. Some of it is just…going out and feeling like…something *could* happen even if it doesn't."

Something about that last sentence made her feel a surge of…

Shame. And her own deeply buried feelings that she'd done such a good job of suppressing, she would never have even thought of them again if not for this.

"You want to do all this while keeping me at home?"

"No, you would be free to do it too, and we would set our boundaries and talk about what we were okay with and…"

"Nothing! I'm not okay with any of it. We are… We would be the people I would make fun of with Elysia and Whitney. I would be texting them right now like, 'OMG you won't believe what Sam's husband just said,' except I am Sam and you are Sam's husband and it isn't funny at all."

He sighed. "So this is about what other people think?"

That struck her as astonishingly unfair. "No, it's about the fact that it's *breaking my heart*."

They said nothing for a long time, and then they pulled up to the front of their house. He pulled the car into the garage, and she wanted to yell at him and tell him not to do that, because for some reason the idea of bringing this all home, into their home, felt wrong.

He shut the engine off and closed the garage door behind them. He put his arms on top of the steering wheel and stared straight ahead, and what shocked her most of all was how sad *he* looked.

"I'm sorry," he said. "But I needed to tell you I… I've never felt trapped by you. But sometimes I feel trapped by *this*."

"I can't separate the two things. *This*," she said, waving her hand around the space, "is *us*."

"I've always loved our relationship. I just want more. I never wanted to hurt you. But I felt like I needed to be honest with you."

I want you to lie.

But she couldn't say that.

You couldn't say that. You couldn't wish that your husband would keep on lying and keep pretending to be happy so that you could keep things just the way you wanted them, could you?

You were supposed to value and prize honesty.

But his honesty was making her frantically scroll through her every memory of them. Every moment. Every time she'd thought they were on the same page when they were clearly reading different books.

She wanted to jump out of the car and run away and...

That was the problem.

"How long have you wanted to tell me this? How long have you felt this way?"

He turned his head and looked at her. "A while. But there's not an easy way to do it, because hearing you say that...that I want to fuck other women makes it sound like something I didn't think of it as. It feels like something bigger to me. Like letting each other have freedom we haven't had while we were giving our kids structure. While we were trying to be responsible and...to not be judged by everyone in town. What if we hadn't felt like we had to get married? Maybe you could have gone to school like you wanted to."

"But I've always been happy I married you."

"Let's go inside," he said.

They did, and they sat on their couch—was their couch too much like the neighbors' couch?—and talked. And talked until their voices were hoarse.

He tried to explain it was about having the opportunity to experience new things without limitations.

She yelled about him seeing her as a limitation.

"Is this just about sex? Is it more blow jobs? Did you need

me to get on my knees and show you that I love you? That I want you and this?" She was embarrassed that she was asking that of her husband, bargaining with her body, but shit, what did he want from her?

"Is there something you want to try? Is there..."

"No." He put his head in his hands. "Because it's about me. It isn't just about sex. It's about... I want to feel like a whole person on my own. Someone who can go out and see where the evening goes sometimes."

"And still come home to your wife who made you dinner?"

"No. I want to come home to you because I love you, and you're my partner. But there's a way we look at marriage in society that's...like we're one."

"Again," she said, "I seem to recall that actually came up in our marriage ceremony."

"I don't believe in some of it. Not anymore." He sat up straighter. "A lot of what we did was to make this...traditional family for the kids. Now we don't have to consider them first. We can consider ourselves first."

I considered us first.

But she wouldn't say that out loud because it was even sadder than offering a blow job right now.

She kept making accusations. He kept telling her it was about *him*.

No matter how mean she got, he took it, and he never yelled. Which made her angrier, because he was making her feel like she was the one who was unhinged, and she wasn't the one who had changed everything. By the time she was done, she felt exhausted and horrible and like she was a stranger too.

"We don't have to do this," he said. "We can go on the road trip you wanted. We can put a pin in this."

Except now she knew. That his smiles weren't all the way real. That when he kissed her good-night, he was going to sleep in a bed, in a life, that didn't satisfy him, and it made her want to light herself on fire to escape the burn of that humiliation.

She'd thought she was living in a happy marriage, and her husband wasn't happy.

He was her everything.

And she wasn't enough.

It killed her to know that being with her in a way that satisfied her was destroying something in him.

"I can't ever forget that this is what you want," she said slowly. "I can't forget and go back to what we had, knowing that the life I love is making you feel suffocated. Knowing that you were keeping up with the Joneses while I was *happy*."

"I'm sorry." He looked so sorry. *So* really and truly sorry and like this was tearing him up from the inside, and she didn't understand why he couldn't do her a favor and scream at her. Call her ugly or say she was boring in bed or something so her anger had something to grab hold of. "I love you, and that's why I wanted to figure out how to navigate this together."

She looked past him, out the window over the kitchen sink. How many times had she stood there washing dishes and looking out at the driveway, waiting for his car to pull in...

"Maybe we should...maybe we...should do this separate for a while."

"I don't want a divorce, Sam."

"Neither do I."

The house looked like a sitcom set all of a sudden. Like it wasn't real. The house she carefully organized every week, that she worked so hard to make theirs. It was her haven, and his prison.

They'd raised three boys here. Ethan had taken his first steps here. They'd measured their heights on the wall by the kitchen. They'd bought the house when Will had started being successful in real estate and her freelance writing jobs had picked up.

They'd celebrated their kids' high school graduations here. Mourned the loss of her mother here. Laughed, cried, made love.

It didn't seem real now.

She was angry, and she was sad, and they'd had such a smooth marriage up until this point that she didn't know how to have conflict like this.

"I need to go to bed," she said.

"Sam…"

"Alone."

They had *never* done this. Never had the kind of schism that made her feel like they couldn't go to sleep beside each other. Sometimes they *did* go to bed mad, because he was right about her.

She didn't like fighting, and sometimes she just shut down. Shut the door for a while and marinated by herself. Then they'd go to sleep silently beside each other, and in the morning it would be a much more amiable disagreement, rather than a fight that had built anger on top of anger.

She hoped that was true now.

In the morning maybe she'd wake up and this would be a weird dream. Or Will would forget he'd ever said anything.

The problem was, though, she would never be able to forget he'd said it.

So she had to figure out what she was going to do.

two

I can't begin to explain this via text. We need to get coffee.

She fired off the message to her group text with Whitney and Elysia before the sun was up, and before Will, who had slept in one of the boys' old rooms, she assumed, was up.

She hated running with an all-consuming passion, though she often made herself do it anyway, but this morning it wasn't for her health. It functioned as an escape.

She put earbuds in, music on. She hated to hear herself gasping for breath when she ran. It was just demoralizing.

Her thoughts followed the rhythm of her feet as she ran down the sidewalk, toward the coffeehouse she always met her friends at. She supposed she'd find out once she got there if they had time to meet.

She had to leave her house either way.

What will we tell the kids?

What if we tried it?

What if he's got a twenty-year-old girlfriend?

He said he didn't.

But he might be a liar.

He's a stranger.

He's a stranger.

He's a stranger.

She let that one play over and over again, because it was upsetting and satisfying all at once.

She stopped in front of the coffeehouse and took one of her earbuds out, and then she could hear her breathing, which sounded less winded from working out and more shattered. When she touched her cheek, she realized there was a tear on it. She wiped it away quickly, then leaned against the brick facade of the coffeehouse, pulling her phone out of the pocket of her leggings.

Pony after drop-off? From Elysia.

Yep. From Whitney.

She looked up at the black-and-gold sign for Pony Espresso, their standard meeting place because they had coffee, avocado toast, and cake, so all moods could be served.

Here.

She walked inside, and grimaced when she saw most of the tables were full. It was loud, though. The sounds of the coffee grinder and the clatter of forks and knives combined with the chatter were a relief in some ways.

She'd been mad at Will for dropping his bombshell on her in public, but thinking about trying to explain what had happened last night in the relative silence of one of her friend's kitchens felt impossible.

It would be better if all her words could be dampened here by the normal town gossip, which usually included such scandalous tidbits as the pastor of the local megachurch using tithes to finance his new hilltop house and the owner of Bella Notte stealing lettuce from the neighboring deli's produce deliveries.

She ordered a piece of cake and a coffee. She wasn't going

to pretend she was out for her health today. This was all about coping strategies.

Not that she knew which coping strategies you were supposed to employ when your husband asked for an open marriage.

An open marriage.

She took her carrot cake and coffee to a four-person table in the back corner of the dining room and sighed with relief when Elysia walked in, her red hair piled on her head in an epic messy bun that looked like it had taken real effort when Sam knew that it hadn't.

Elysia had been styling her wild curls that way since high school. In contrast, Sam had tried many things with her extremely straight brown hair over the years. From making it burgundy to making it blond and trying to style it with a little bit of wave. Right now she had bangs. A mistake she made every five years or so.

Elysia's hair wasn't the only thing that hadn't changed much since high school. She was committed to low-rise jeans and hoop earrings. She was a flurry of movement. Hair and jewelry and the fluttering caftan she had on over her white tank top.

She held up a hand and gestured toward the counter, indicating she was going to order, and Sam waved back.

Whitney came in a few minutes later, her short dark hair perfectly styled, her makeup more suited to an evening out than morning coffee in a small town. Her steps were short and decisive as she crossed to the table, her wedge heels loud on the wooden floor. Whitney was the shortest in the friend group, by a lot, and always wore shoes that gave her a little bit of a lift.

She stopped and turned to the line, where Elysia had just made it to the front. She grandly mouthed *coffee*, then nodded and continued to the table and sat down directly across from Sam.

"What's going on?"

"I can't say it twice," said Sam, looking down at her cake. "Yikes."

"Yeah. Really yikes."

"I'm glad you texted early. I don't have any clients until ten." Whitney did nails at a salon down the street.

"Well, that's good. We might need the whole three house."

Elysia appeared a minute later in a flutter, with coffees and two avocado toasts.

"Oh, thanks," said Whitney, pulling a coffee cup and a slice of toast toward her.

"Welcome. Okay, what's going on?"

She took a deep breath. She'd known these girls since middle school. Known them since before her first kiss with Will. She didn't know if that made this easier or harder.

"Will... Um. He..." She took a bite of her cake and couldn't even enjoy the rich cream cheese frosting. For God's sake, the man had broken her. She put her fork down and pushed the plate away. "He asked for an open marriage."

Elysia and Whitney just stared. Then looked at each other. Then back at Sam. "He..." Elysia said at the same time Whitney said, "What..."

"Will," Whitney said. "*Will* asked you for an open marriage. Straight-arrow, khaki-pants, never-drinks-more-than-one-glass-of-wine Will?"

That almost made Sam laugh, but only almost, because actually, it brought up a very good point. All the ways in which Will lived his life—cautiously and expectedly—had always seemed like his own impulses, and certainly not something to be pushed off onto her or the institution of marriage.

He was a reasonable man. Down to his socks, which always matched.

That made her feel a little more validated in her reaction. He'd never done anything to suggest he wanted something like this. She'd had no reason to suspect he wasn't as content with things as she was.

"Yeah, the very one," she said. "I… I don't know what to do." She could feel tears threatening again, tears she didn't want to cry here, or ever, actually, because tears felt helpless, and what she hated most about this was feeling helpless.

"I don't know what to *say*," said Whitney. "He just doesn't even remotely seem like the type."

"Oh," Sam said, laughing now instead of crying. "I know. You can imagine my shock when he said this to me while we were out on a date."

"This happened *last night*?" Elysia asked.

"Yes."

"What did he say he wants, exactly?"

She felt exasperated because she couldn't say she really understood what he wanted, even after the discussion last night. "To have sex with other women. I mean, he said it was more than that, but that's…you know that is the real sticking point for me. We've never… He's the only man I've been with. I'm the only woman he's been with. It's… I can't even process it."

Her friends were quiet for a moment. "What do you want?" Whitney asked slowly.

"Uh…to not have to think about this? To have not ever heard my husband say that? To go back to my wildly happy, perfect life? Because that's what I had. That's what I've always had. You know that. He and I…we're *us*. You know what I mean. It's been us since we were sixteen. We're the forever ones." She shook her head. "I just can't… I can't believe him. I can't…" Hysteria suddenly had her in its grip. Panic was making her heart beat faster, making her breath short. "I was this man's first kiss. His only. He's jeopardizing our life, *us*, because he wants to have sex with other people."

"I mean…at least he told you, assuming he hasn't already done it." Elysia's words were soft, firm, and felt a little unfair.

Though it was Elysia's husband's affair that had driven home some very deep truths about her own possessiveness.

You have to leave him, she'd told Elysia then. *How can you stand knowing he touched someone else?*

"He *says* he hasn't. But I don't know how that makes it better. He's turned it into some kind of thing where he expects me to, like, sign a permission slip, and if I don't do it, I'm holding him back, and if I do…"

"No, it is better," said Elysia, looking at her directly now. "I'm not saying it's easy or nice to hear. I just know what it's like when your husband does something behind your back and makes you feel like a fool. I know what it feels like to have him already make those decisions about your relationship without bothering to tell you."

Sam closed her eyes. The thing was, she did feel like a fool.

Will's *I'm not happy* was haunting her.

She felt like a fool for *happily* living her *happy* life while her husband was decidedly *unhappy* in it.

"But I have to do something. *Decide* something. I love him. I want to be with him."

Elysia nodded slowly. "You know, when Jake cheated on me, I didn't want to leave him. Because I loved him, and finding out he…did that didn't immediately destroy that love. But I couldn't get past what he did, either. He didn't ask me to. He *blamed* me. That made it easier to leave."

Will wasn't blaming her. Maybe that was why she was starting to feel like this was worse. He was talking to her. Sharing with her. He was doing all the things you were supposed to want people you loved to do. But she hated what he was sharing. She didn't know how to get around that.

"I… I take your point," she said. "But like, what am I supposed to do? Do I do it? And then what? Is this how you end up at suburban sex parties? Am I destined for a life of upside-down pineapples?"

She *knew* everyone in her suburb. The idea of having a sex party with any of them was…ugh.

"I think swinging and open relationships are different," Whitney pointed out.

Sam made a noise that was somewhere between a groan and a whine and put her face in her hands. "I think I do know that. I don't… I have to ask *him*. I have to ask him what all he means. I'm…" She looked up. "I actually like to think I'm more open-minded than any of us were raised to be. I read so many long-form articles, because writing about life is what I do. I like reading about other peoples' lives. I read articles about…polyamory and think, 'Good for them. Sounds like a lot of work, but good for them.' But I've never, ever thought about what I would do in those situations, because I was *so sure* about what my situation was."

Whitney lifted a shoulder. "Have you considered that…it might be fun? I mean, if he gets to have sex with other people, so do you. Everything he said about his life applies to you. You've only been with him. Don't you think it might be fun to…play around a little bit?"

She looked around the room and tried to imagine…any of that. There was a perfectly handsome, age-appropriate man sitting by the door. She could talk to him, find out if he wanted to go out…

She could get rejected.

It would be like being a teenager all over again, wondering if Will *liked her* liked her. But she'd be doing it at forty.

"I don't… It doesn't sound fun to me. Does it really sound fun to you?"

Whitney shrugged. "I don't know. A lot of things sound more fun in theory than in practice. But I haven't been with anyone other than Mark in fifteen years, so on some level…"

"Dating is terrible," said Elysia. "*Especially* when you don't want to do it."

"Why does it have to be *dating*, though?" Whitney asked. "Why can't it just be sex? If you still have the husband, you don't need…"

"This is *not* a hypothetical," Sam said. "This is my life."

Whitney looked immediately contrite. "I know. I'm sorry. I just… You have two choices, right? You tell him no, or you try to give him what he wants. You've clearly never thought about this before, so I'm just trying to get you to think about it."

She looked at her cake. "No. I've never thought about it. I've never thought about being with anyone else." She said it firmly, decisively.

She decided it was time to take another bite of cake. This time it tasted better, and she thought maybe the sugar would serve as a decent Band-Aid for this endless horror.

"Did you just want me to be outraged? Because I can do that too," said Whitney.

She shook her head. "No, that isn't what I want. That's what I'd want if I wanted to divorce him, and I don't. I just want to go back to before he said this. I don't want to think about all these changes. I thought we were only into good changes, exciting changes. Yeah, it's bittersweet to have the kids move out, to have Ethan not even come back for the summer. But I was all about it being a season of us. *For* us."

"We don't have to be fair," Whitney pointed out. "We can do pistols at dawn. Pitchforks at midnight. Whatever you need, you know that's what we'll give you."

She put her knuckles against her temples. "I do. I do know that. It's just… I don't know what I want. I don't know what to ask for, and I was going on and on and around and around in my own head and I was sick of myself, so I need to come here and say some of it out loud. But I don't know. And I'm so resentful that I have to choose anything."

"You know, this is the problem," Elysia said. "Honest or not, if your husband wants to make a life change, you have to react. You don't want to, which I get. I wanted to just...ignore that my husband had an affair, because I didn't want to get divorced. I didn't ask for things to change."

"That's how I feel."

"You have to figure out what you want and put him in the position of having to respond to that. I think he needs to really tell you, like on a granular level, why he feels this way and what he wants from it." Her eyes got glossy then. "If I could have made Jake do one thing, it would have been to tell me when it started. I don't mean the first time he actually slept with another woman, I mean the first moment he knew he wasn't satisfied. What triggered it. What broke between the two of us that it seemed...reasonable to lie to me about where he was, what he was doing. I want the story, the whole story."

Sam nodded. "Yes. Yes, because this is what I can't get past. I thought he and I wanted the same things and felt the same way. I thought we were the same kind of happy and...were we ever? Has he always been living in some quiet suburban desperation?"

"Until you know all that, I don't know how you're supposed to have any idea what you want," Elysia said.

"After he gives you all that," Whitney said, "pistols, pitchforks, a good lawyer or...upside-down pineapples. We'll help with any and all."

She looked down at her wedding ring. It seemed wildly unfamiliar right then. "Okay. He had a house showing this morning at..." She looked at her phone. "Well, now. Maybe I can go home and sit in the quiet and prepare. Or try the setting-all-his-shit-on-fire-on-the-lawn thing. That doesn't sound unappealing." She laughed. "Seriously though, he wants an open marriage, I want him to get rid of his excessive collection of T-shirts he's owned since high school. Like since we're putting cards on the table." That made her want to laugh. Helplessly. All the little things she'd sat on in the name of harmony for years.

And her husband had come out with *let's see other people.*

She really should have complained more.

"If you end up needing somewhere to stay, you know you're welcome to stay with me," said Elysia.

"Or me," said Whitney, "but then, she doesn't have a man hanging out, cluttering the place up."

Sam tried to laugh. "Thanks. I appreciate it."

She walked back home, and she knew she had a little bit of time before Will would arrive. She showered and changed into something nice and told herself it wasn't because she was trying to make him see that she was still pretty.

Except the whole time she dried her hair, put on moisturizer and eyeliner, and tweezed a couple errant eyebrow hairs, she was alternatively hyping herself up and nitpicking the decline of her beauty.

But when she was done, she thought she looked good. And like maybe if she wanted to agree to this thing, she could probably have some of the openness for herself.

She stared at herself in the mirror, and those features she'd just been examining seemed wholly unfamiliar all of a sudden. So did her whole body. So did every thought.

Whose life was this?

It wasn't Samantha Parker's.

Samantha Parker had a perfect life, and everyone knew it. She'd *done things a little out of order*, as people liked to whisper, but then they'd *done the right thing*. They'd gotten married. She and Will hadn't gone to church for years, but that didn't mean they'd let go of everything that had been instilled in them there. More to the point, the culture of the town was…church-driven.

Whether it was Baptist, Catholic, nondenominational, Latter Day Saints or Jehovah's Witnesses…people here often either came from a religious and traditional background, or were still part of one. Was Will right? Was she just…doing things because she'd been conditioned to do them that way?

Was she…indoctrinated?

Was her shame hers or was it…something someone had given to her?

Did she not actually want any of the things she had?

"I'm pretty sure I do," she said back to the stranger in the mirror.

But still, she was starting to wonder if she was making a bigger deal out of this than she needed to. A whole Everest out of what could just be an annoying molehill.

He didn't want to leave her. He wasn't a liar. He didn't have secret horrible porn on his computer.

She didn't *think*.

The doorbell rang and she startled, then walked quickly to the kitchen and peered cautiously out the window by the sink, where she could always get a good look at who was there without them actually seeing her.

It was *Logan*.

Her husband's best friend and the first person she'd blamed for his desire to experience bar hookups, considering Logan was a pro at those.

The problem with Logan, though, was that he was…interesting. He did highly specialized restoration on classic cars for a living and drove them to their owners several times year, which Sam had always thought would make for an interesting article series because it was just…cool. She'd even joked about wanting to pull up stakes and go on a trip with him. Which of course she hadn't actually done, because she knew that she couldn't actually live his life.

Which Will didn't seem to realize.

They'd known Logan since high school. But he was two years older than them, so it had been more casual awareness and interaction than anything else.

Logan had been *that* guy. Hot and kind of brooding, and all the girls had whispered when he'd walked through the halls.

He had a dad who drank too much, an old, loud muscle car

and a chip on his shoulder. He'd seemed mythical and unapproachable.

Her friend group hadn't really known his future wife, Becca, either, though not for the same reasons. She'd been in their grade, and Sam had shared two honors classes with her, but she hadn't started going to school with them until ninth grade, so Sam's friend group had been set already.

It was after high school, after Becca and Logan had gotten married, that she and Will had gotten to know them. Back then, Logan had been working for a local garage, and Will had taken their car in for an oil change, and they'd gotten to reminiscing about high school.

A lot of people they'd gone to school with had left the area. Jacksonville was a small, quaint town, with the larger "city" of Medford the place with most of the big-box stores, medical facilities and schools. There were limited opportunities, and many people went elsewhere—Portland, Eugene, or down south to California—for work and opportunities.

A lot of people had come back in the years since, but right in that space in their early twenties, there weren't a lot of people around that they'd known in school, with most of Will's friends having moved away.

She hadn't understood the connection between him and Will. Except Will just seemed to still find him extremely cool, and was excited that the school's rebel-with-no-particular-cause had thought he was cool enough to hang out with.

They'd have barbecues at the house, and Logan would just man the grill, not especially friendly. But Becca was sweet, and when she'd had Chloe, she and Sam had spent time sitting together, both with little babies and sleep deprivation.

Then Becca had gotten sick.

Sam could only admire the way Logan had been with her during her illness. The care that he'd shown her, the tenderness. She'd seen it then. What Becca saw in him.

Chloe had spent a lot of time at their house when Becca was sick, and a lot of time after. Sam had been happy to be a cool-aunt figure to her, especially since she and Will only had the boys.

That was how they'd ended up combining family vacations and game nights and holidays.

They were friends. Except it always felt like they weren't. She felt like she always said and did the wrong thing with Logan, like every interaction was akin to tossing a knife in the air, hoping she caught it by the handle instead of the blade.

Finding her footing with this man felt precarious at best.

And this was the worst timing ever.

A Logan Martin special.

Was he here to talk to Will? Had Will *told him*?

She'd told her friends, so…so it stood to reason.

She found herself walking quickly to the front door and pulling it open, feeling immediately engulfed by discomfort. He was too tall. She had to look up too far to see his face. It was weird and she didn't like it.

"What are you doing here?"

"Picking up the power washer your husband borrowed from me?"

She huffed. "Was I supposed to know about that?"

"He said it was in the garage. I just wanted to let you know before I went digging in your garage so I didn't scare you."

That was downright reasonable. Nearly kind.

"Oh. Well. Feel free."

"Thanks. Are you…"

Her irritation unraveled. "No. I'm not okay, thank you. Did you talk to Will?"

"About the power washer," he said, his tone maddeningly calm.

"Is that all?"

"We may have discussed a sports team or two. Ethan's summer plans and Chloe's move to Santa Clara. Is that…a problem?"

She tried to read his face, to see if he was holding something back or not. But she couldn't tell.

"No," she said.

She decided to take him at face value because she wasn't going to tell him what was happening. Even if he did know, she wasn't going to have the conversation with him. It was hard enough to look her two best friends in the eye and explain it.

The idea that this man might know more about the state of her marriage than she did made her want to break things.

"I'm going to grab the power washer," he said.

"Okay."

She looked at him, long and hard and until it was difficult to breathe, and he didn't say anything.

"Is there something you need, Sam?" His voice was rough, and it made her uncomfortable in the way only Logan ever did.

"No."

"Okay then." He turned and walked toward the garage. She closed the door, rubbing her chest, trying to ease the tightness there, except she knew it wasn't physical.

She watched Logan from her secret position by the kitchen window. Watched him open the garage—which he knew the code for—and take out the power washer, loading it into the back of his truck. A truck she hadn't seen before, but it wasn't unusual for Logan to be in a different vehicle every third time she saw him.

Logan was unpredictable like that.

She didn't like that. She preferred things uninteresting. She preferred it when things just bumped along. Expected. Predictable. Organized.

That was when Will got home. He pulled in next to Logan's truck and stopped and talked to Logan before coming in, which just about sent her. She was waiting to talk to him. She was his wife, the one he'd just dropped a bomb on, and he was ignoring the smoldering wreckage that was her, so that he could have a chat with Logan.

She watched their faces. Tried to discern if they were actually talking about anything serious or if it was just the sort of thing Logan had said they'd talked about recently.

Kids and sports.

Finally, they said goodbye, and Logan got into his truck. Then Will pulled the rest of the way into the garage, and Sam took that as her cue to find somewhere to wait for him where it wouldn't look like she'd been peering out the kitchen window the whole time.

She went with sitting at the kitchen table with a cup of coffee, because that was at least normal for her, and it only took thirty seconds to make one of those single-brew cups.

By the time Will came in, she was sitting, looking contemplative and yet also beautiful, she hoped.

"Hi," he said. "I wasn't sure if you'd be here."

He sounded uncomfortable. Nervous. This man who had been married to her for more than half of their lives. She had to hand it to him. He'd certainly managed to inject uncertainty into things. Maybe he found uncertainty exciting.

"We need to talk," she said.

"Yes," he said, sitting down in the chair at the opposite end of the table from her.

"I want… I want you to explain it to me," she said. "All of it. Like what exactly this means to you and why you want it and…when. When you started wanting it."

"Okay. Where do you want me to start?"

"Okay." She took a deep breath. "Is this like key parties and upside-down pineapples and stuff? Like do you want to do this with me?"

He shook his head. "No, that's not… No."

"Yeah, Whitney said swinging was different, but I had to make sure that was true in whatever online forums you're reading."

"You told Whitney?"

"I told Whitney and Elysia. First thing this morning."

He made a weird, indignant sound. "I haven't told anyone."

No wonder Logan had been looking at her like she was on bath salts. She felt extremely relieved to hear that. But also defensive. "You've had all the time in the world to think about this. You got to choose the moment. I was blindsided. I needed to talk to my friends about it, and I'm not going to apologize for that."

He nodded slowly. "That's fair."

"Gee, thanks, Will. Glad you find me fair." She growled and lowered her head. "Sorry. I'm going to try... I'm going to try to be fair, okay? And not snarky. Angry is fine, but I'm going to try to not...do that."

He let out a long, slow breath, and she resented him taking the oxygen. "This feeling didn't hit me overnight. I guess... I hoped you were unhappy too."

She laughed. She couldn't help it. "You hoped I was unhappy?"

"Yes. We're always so in sync. I started feeling... I guess unsatisfied a few years ago. Started wondering what else was out there, and I hoped you were feeling that too. That you would say, '*Great*, Will, I have some things I need too.' I just thought maybe I was the first one who was willing to admit that I wasn't happy with things as they were."

"Well, no. Sorry. I was happy. I was happy with everything. We did the hard stuff, and now we're supposed to just get to enjoy it."

She realized, as soon as she said it, that it couldn't be true if he didn't like their life. It couldn't be true if *he* wasn't happy.

"I love you," he said. He'd said it a lot since last night. "Through all of this, all my questioning, I've known that much. It's about me, it really is. But I understand that because we're married, that makes it about you too. But it isn't because of you. It isn't anything you did or didn't do."

Sam didn't know if that was better or worse. To know she couldn't stop it, fix it, learn how to be bolder, kinkier, whatever he might want. To know that this was something happening in him she couldn't change or fix.

Maybe it was good to know it wasn't her fault, but that meant she couldn't do anything. She hated that. She didn't know what she was supposed to do with that.

"We got married so young, and I wanted to do right by you. By the boys. I became a middle-aged man at eighteen. We never got to do the things other people our age did. We didn't go party, we didn't drink, we didn't do casual hookups. I guess this is what a midlife crisis is. I guess this is what it looks like. When you realize this is your life. For me, for us, this is the only life we've gotten to live. Our youngest son is going to Europe all summer, and we never did anything like that. You know other people were spending their summers traveling and having flings. We dated all through high school. We were married before we graduated. We didn't have even a couple of years to find ourselves, to figure out who we were, to make mistakes…"

"Many people would argue," she said, her throat feeling scratchy, "that we did in fact make a mistake. The one that ensured we had to get married."

"That's a good point. We made one choice very young that put us on a path, and now…we don't have to be on that path anymore. Or we can widen it." He let out a ragged breath. "I don't want to blow our lives up. That's what led me to kind of researching all of this. I want an open relationship because it means freedom and honesty. Because to an extent it keeps our relationships ours, but lets us have other things too."

"When?" she asked. "When did you start… What was the moment?"

The breath he let out was heavy with regret, his teeth clenched. He looked away from her, the muscles in his face going tense.

She wasn't going to like his answer. That was clear.

"There was a feeling. You know, just…these weird moments when I'd think…is this it? Is this all life is?"

Those words were like a knife, and she did her best not to look stabbed. She nodded, to show she was listening. If she made a sound, it would be a little bit too much like dying.

"But the actual moment I started realizing what I wanted… it was…Logan."

"Oh, of course it was. You lied about this last night."

"It's not as simple as what… I don't know, I guess it is. It was just watching him. We went to some bar and this woman was flirting with him and he got her number." He covered his face with his hands. "It feels shitty. To admit that I envy anything about his life, because I know he didn't choose to lose Becca, and I don't want to lose you. It's just what I thought then was… he got to live both lives. He got married young, he has a daughter, but he…he gets to flirt when he goes out. He gets to drink too much if he wants. He can travel when he feels like it, and he isn't stuck doing a nine-to-five. I jumped into this when I was a teenager, and I didn't get to make choices. I want to live the life I didn't get to have, see what choices I could make, and I want to do it without destroying what I've got."

She tried to imagine it. Because they were always on the same page, except it was clear now they weren't. That it was a story she told herself, because Will was exceptionally good at seeming fine when he wasn't.

Apparently.

She was very good at seeing what she wanted to.

Apparently.

"I keep trying," she said. "I keep trying to imagine it. I keep trying to picture myself…going out and finding someone and seeing where it goes, and I… I don't want it."

She wanted this life.

Their life.

But she could see that he was always going to question if he could have been happier with something else if he didn't get to try it.

So she tried to imagine that. Being home while he was out. Accepting him being with other women.

Touching him after he'd touched someone else.

She stared past him, through the kitchen into the living room, where she could see the edge of one of their framed family photos. She could see the space they put their Christmas tree in every year.

The edge of the coffee table where they often sat on the floor and played board games.

The arm of the couch, a couch they sometimes sat on, each on their own electronic devices, not talking. But always with their feet touching.

Comfortable, happy memories.

For her.

"I want you to be happy," she said slowly. "I want you to have the life I thought we had. The happiness I thought we had. I want to have it too, but I can't... I can't be happy if you aren't. As much as I want to just pretend this didn't happen, I realize I can't."

You have two choices...

Say no.

Say yes.

She didn't want to say yes. She didn't want to say no. She didn't want to talk about it anymore.

She wanted to close the door on it, and she knew they couldn't. Because whatever she might say about their life, their happiness, from the past few years it was clear she had somehow closed a door on him.

She had never asked if he was happy, she'd just assumed.

In the way he'd assumed—hoped—she wasn't happy.

She had two choices.

Unless she could figure out what the third one was. Somewhere between solving the problem and closing a door.

She looked at him and felt something calm wash through her. She'd been with him for twenty-four years. Married for twenty-two. They were bigger than this. Than his feelings, his doubts, than this conversation.

It was why she couldn't just flip the table and say forget it all.

But this moment was also too big to solve in a conversation, and maybe if part of her even secretly wanted it, it would have been different. Exciting, like Whitney had said it could be.

She didn't want to share her husband. She didn't want her life to change.

What do you want besides that?

She'd wanted to travel. In that way, she had wanted freedom. He wanted to have what he wanted, without her stopping him.

She wanted to have what she wanted.

Option three was starting to look obvious. But that didn't make it easy.

They weren't who she thought they were.

"I care so much about your happiness," she said. "We don't have a happy marriage if you aren't happy, and as much as I don't want to accept that...you aren't happy. I know you wouldn't have told me all this if you were."

"Sam..."

"But I can't watch you do this. I can't talk to you about your... sexual experiences with other women. I can't go to bed with you at night knowing you've been with someone else, I can't. I also can't go back to what we were, because now I know you don't love this life." A sob rose in her chest. "I do. I love this life, so much."

He reached across the table, but stopped an inch short of touching her hand, and she was glad he didn't touch her. For the first time, she was glad he didn't touch her. "I love parts of it. I just want to rearrange some things."

Just the things that felt immovable to her. The things that had felt like foundational supports.

"We got this…we got this summer we didn't expect. Ethan was supposed to come back and now he's not, and…what if… we have a summer vacation?" she said, and just thinking about it hurt. It hurt. She hadn't been away from Will for more than a week, and now she was talking about separating for more than three months. "What if we…put our marriage on pause for the summer?"

He wanted to test out what he thought he'd missed. She didn't think any of that—bars and dating and random sex— was better than what they had. But why not? Why not let him see that? *Know* that?

Let him do it and have her not…watch.

She didn't need anyone else. She didn't need another life. She needed their life. This life.

"I wanted to do this *with* you," Will said.

"I know, but… Will, if you want to try another life, try another life. Then if you decide that you like it better than ours, we'll talk then. About what the options are. But I can't pretend nothing is different."

"That isn't what I want…"

"It kind of is. You want to do this…different thing but you want to have the same thing too, and I'm not sure that's going to work. I can't watch you. I can't let you stay and be unhappy. But I can let you go for a while." She didn't know where that came from, the strength to say it, the strength to believe it.

"I didn't want to let you go."

She nodded. "I know. But I'm not sure there's a way to have everything. Maybe there is. Maybe in a few months I'll have changed the way I feel." She didn't think so. She took a sharp breath. "Just for the summer. We don't talk. We don't see each other. We don't stay here. We go on vacation, in every sense of the word. You can travel, I can travel. You can…do whatever you need to do. Then we'll meet back here and we'll… talk about it."

"So…neither of us lives here."

"No." She felt definitive on that. "If we're doing different lives, we're doing different lives."

"What are the kids going to think when they find out we're going to be gone all summer but not together?"

What are the kids going to think when they find out you want to have sex with other women?

"We'll figure out how to talk to them about it," she said. "We'll make it clear we aren't getting divorced. It's just…"

That word lingered there. *Divorce.* Because if at the end they didn't agree, she knew that was a possibility.

But it wouldn't happen.

In the end he would decide he wanted their life.

It was just one summer. It wasn't going to wipe out twenty-two years.

He was searching. He was curious. She could give him that, even if it hurt. Because Elysia was right, he wasn't going off and cheating. He wasn't betraying her. He'd flipped the script, yes, and that hurt. It was understandable that it hurt.

But maybe they could do this and come back stronger.

She wanted to believe that was true.

"Okay," he said. "If that's what you want."

She didn't want any of it, but she was determined to find some way to fix it. Some way to make it salvageable.

"I don't want it, but… I've loved you for more than half of my life, and I can't love you being unhappy, even if I wish I could magically make this happy for you. I can't live knowing that I'm the only one who feels satisfied with that we have. So yes, it's what I want. On a spectrum of things I really don't want. But that is marriage, isn't it?" She took a jagged breath. "Sometimes you have to compromise in a way that hurts."

Will took her into his arms, and she let him. She buried her face in his neck and tried to hold back her tears.

She needed to believe that if he had this one sparkling summer, like the kind he'd never had in high school because he was with her, and the kind he'd never had after because he was working and helping raise their kids, well...they would get back to who they were.

They'd always had the perfect life.

She needed to believe they'd find their way back to it.

three

In high school, she could remember the promise of summer feeling like the promise of endless possibilities. The beginning of something amazing.

The beginning of this philosophical summer did not feel that way.

It felt like a death march.

The past week had been the thorniest and worst of her whole life.

They'd talked about the logistics of leaving the house empty for three months—it wasn't ideal. Elysia offered to get the mail once a week if Sam and Will were both out of town, and Will had made it very clear he intended to spend the time traveling.

He'd booked a month in Hawaii, and had asked Sam all kinds of questions about the places they had gone last time they'd been there on a family vacation, and it had been all she could do to not smother him with a couch cushion, because did he really expect her to plan his vacation during their separation?

She'd finally groused at him, and he hadn't asked again.

Sam figured she should make some plans. She just felt…listless about it. She'd only gone as far as to book the next week in a vacation rental in town so she could make her plans without Will looming around her.

She was usually so good at planning.

Will had spent years building his real estate business, but he'd started out working for a larger group. Sam had done freelance writing for different online platforms, usually focusing on meal plans, budgets, organization, parenting, vacationing with children. That was her entire life, after all.

She felt like she needed to pull up one of her own articles on the subject to remind herself that she did know how to get a vacation together.

She and Will had planned the scaffolding of this "summer," and it had felt so absurd to open up their phone calendars and synchronize a marital separation. They'd landed on the third week of May, all the way to the second week of September, when Ethan would be back for a week before classes started up again.

She could have laughed. It was so much the same and so much different all at the same time. Planning summer holidays around the kids.

Right now she was circling her bedroom—their bedroom that they wouldn't share for nearly the next four months—like she didn't remember how to do anything.

What clothes did you take with you into an extended vacation from your marriage?

She was glad they'd decided to make the house neutral ground. She couldn't have Will using it as a home base for... dates.

She might be willing to let him have his freedom for the summer, but by God, it would not be on her mattress. She wouldn't be able to get past that.

She'd discovered a lot of interesting things about herself in the last forty-eight hours.

That was one of them. That it made her want to gag to imagine sleeping in a bed her husband had made love to someone else in.

Bleh.

Add the thought of her husband *making love* to anyone else to that list.

She had to think of it as a new…hobby for him. Like the time he played pickleball for a few months and then stopped. Nothing emotional, all just physical. Something he'd get over.

Reduce it to body parts, but not involve emotions.

She didn't *like* it. But she could cope.

She took another circle around the room. Will had taken his clothes out already.

He was finalizing a sale and then preparing to just…not take new clients on for the next few months. What a great life they had that he could even do that. That they could both afford this.

It was ironic, she thought. They'd built this beautiful, stable life, and she'd thought it was so they could enjoy it together, but it was actually the very thing that was allowing them to do this separation.

With Will out of the house, she decided to play the kind of very loud pop punk she had loved since high school that he thought was annoying. She'd keep it on when he got back too. Because they'd done the together part of this, and now they were separate. Not a couple. Two different people.

Not the same page. They might as well be in two totally different books.

She hated it.

So she started singing as loudly and tunelessly as possible, trying to drown out all the confusion inside of her. She opened up the kitchen trash and jerked the bag up, so hard and fast it strained her muscles, and she welcomed it because she kind of wanted to hurt herself right now.

She walked to the front door and opened it, and nearly ran into a human being.

She screeched and dropped the bag, stepping back from the doorway, the wall of musical sound still behind her and *Logan* right in front of her.

Of course it was Logan.

"What are you doing here?"

"I'm here to see you."

Oh.

"I'll get this." He bent down and picked the trash bag up. Before she could say anything, he walked down to the edge of the driveway, putting it in the bin there before walking back to the house.

"Thanks," she said.

"Yeah. Can I come in?"

He looked so…severe. Which wasn't necessarily uncommon for him. "Will isn't here."

"I'm not looking for Will."

Anxiety made her stomach tight. God. Why would he come to see her?

"Well. Come in."

She stepped away from the door, and he moved past her, too tall and broad even for their rather spacious entryway.

They'd spent a ton of time with Logan. Here, on family vacations, and yet she could never escape that feeling that he was too much for any space he was in.

"Will and I went out for beer last night, and he told me that you're separating." Direct as ever.

She'd already talked to her friends about this. In theory, Logan was her friend. Kind of. So it shouldn't be weird to talk to him about it, but it was. It was.

"Yeah, I…"

"He also told me about his open marriage bullshit."

That shocked her. The directness. The disdain. Her friends had been upset, but even they'd been…well, they'd asked her to consider it.

Logan was just flat-out calling it bullshit.

"Oh."

"I told him he's lost his mind."

She looked around. Were there hidden cameras? What was happening?

"You did?"

"Why does that surprise you?"

"Well, because he said you inspired him."

The hard breath he let out sounded like it had teeth. "Good thing he didn't say that to me. I'd have punched the shit out of him."

She didn't have to ask why, and she felt overcome by guilt. It really was a cruel thing to say. That he envied Logan's freedom. Logan hadn't chosen his "freedom."

Becca had *died*.

She'd left a motherless little girl, and Sam would never, ever forget the way Logan had looked that day. Like a monster had savaged his soul and left nothing behind.

"This may come as a shock to you," Sam said. "But I don't think he's thinking clearly."

Logan laughed then, but it sounded hard. "Yeah. Obviously."

"I said *immediately, no*," she told him. "Okay, that isn't true. I said no like twelve hours later, because I...you have to think about it, right?"

"I didn't require any thinking time to come to the conclusion he's being a dick."

It was cathartic to hear someone else say that, because as much as she was on a whole emotional roller coaster—where she was sad, mad and wistful or some combination of all of it with every new breath—she felt like she had to be fair.

Because he had shared with her. Because he loved her. Because she loved him.

"It's just, I felt like... I had to actually try and see if I felt anything more than that. Or if I could give him what he wanted. But I can't. I mean, I can't hate him for being honest with me."

"So he asked you for an open marriage, because he wants to sleep around but he doesn't want to risk losing you. He wants things to change, but he also wants to keep things the same. That's what I got out of talking to him."

"Well… I guess."

"I can't respect it," Logan said. "If you want to do something big, do it, but to put it on your wife like he did to you…that I can't respect. If you said no, you were denying him. If you said yes, you were denying yourself."

Was Logan actually…taking her side? "I did say yes. Well. Kind of." She cleared her throat, but it still felt tight. "The thing is, I don't want to lose him. I don't want things to change, either. What I want is for him to get this *stupid fucking lunacy* out of his system where I can't see it. Then I want to come back here, and I want to go on with our lives like this summer didn't happen. I know he'll want this back," she said. "We have a good marriage."

"Do you?" he asked.

She hated him for saying it like that. It wasn't fair. "Yes. I'm committed to him. To us."

"I know."

Silence fell between them. "He told me he's planning to travel," Logan continued.

"Yes."

"He said you didn't have your plans made yet."

"No. Not all of them. Though I know… I'm not going to be sleeping with anyone else. Because I took marriage vows." She felt instantly hot over having said that in front of him. Really, it was only then she realized how *personal* all this was.

She'd been cushioned by her rage, and in part by her certainty that he actually knew something about what Will was thinking.

That he seemed as blindsided as she'd been was comforting at first, but now she was just standing in her living room raving at her husband's best friend about their sex life. So there was that.

"'Kay," he said, short and tight, his mouth set into a firm line.

"If I wanted to mess around, he and I could just do it together, mutually, high-five on our way to the bedroom with our new partners. But I *don't*. I just want my life to go back to the way it was before. So I'm just... I want to wait it out away from him. I didn't ask for this. I just want... I want to be happy again. Like I was."

He nodded slowly. "Yeah. Well. That I can understand."

She knew he could. He hadn't asked to lose Becca. The love of his life. The mother of his child. Not that this was the same, really. Will was still alive. She had hope of being with him again.

Logan cleared his throat. "So other than being a beacon of purity, you have no plans for the summer?" he asked.

"I want to travel," she said. "We were supposed to... But you know, I was pregnant. Before all that, we'd planned to take this big cross-country road trip. Do all the cheesy things. Then we couldn't. Then we had more kids..."

"But you don't have plans yet."

"No. I just...feel defeated whenever I try to make them."

"That's actually why I'm here. You said you wanted to go with me on one of my car delivery trips."

She blinked. "I did?"

She was sure she had said that once, but she hadn't been serious. Especially now...well, she was just shocked he'd asked her.

"Yeah. Like five years ago you mentioned it."

He remembered that?

"Well, you always make it seem really interesting."

"It is. I have four jobs scheduled for the next four months. Three major restorations, and I have to drive the cars to their respective buyers when all is said and done. It was all easy to do it myself when I was in my twenties. The last few times, Chloe helped. But now she's in Santa Clara, and she has a job so she isn't coming back for the summer. If you want to travel, you can travel with me. Not only will it pay your way, I'll pay you."

"Are you serious?"

"Yes. The first car is a 1957 Chevy Bel Air. I'm taking it out on Route 66 next week, and heading to Chicago. The trip will probably take two weeks. I get paid a lot to drive them over, and I don't bother to rush through it. It's one of the perks of the job. I get to enjoy the car, and I get to enjoy being on the road."

Will told her that Logan made a ton of money on these kinds of cars. Rare vehicles that could sell for millions at auction. A restored car would never be worth what a mint car would be, but it made those sorts of cars more accessible to collectors.

People that certainly had more disposable income than Will and Sam did, but less than, say, Bruce Wayne.

She had a feeling that those were the kinds of circles that were actually quite small, so if you didn't have a pristine reputation, you wouldn't be getting business.

It didn't surprise her to hear that Logan took that seriously.

"How much time between jobs?"

"A couple of weeks at most. It's going to be a really intense schedule. Delivery, come back, finishing touches on the next car, and then out again."

She could imagine this. Riding in classic cars with the top down. Seeing new places.

She could ignore that it was going to be with Logan. That she had no idea what they would say to each other. That she had no idea...

Well, she would just make that future Sam's problem. Because present Sam had enough problems.

She'd been having such a hard time looking ahead past the next week. She hadn't managed to make any plans or herself.

Logan was offering her a lifeline. The chance to do something she'd been wanting to do anyway. "You're an extremely unlikely ally," she said.

"Am I?"

"Well. Yes. It's not like we're historically... I didn't expect you to take my side."

"Sam, you were there for me and for Chloe when we needed you most. If I can help you out now... I... Fuck him."

For the first time, life past the next week seemed possible.

For the first time, the summer felt like it could be bearable. The chance to stay moving, stay busy and not think about Will?

Yes.

She was going to take it.

"Yes. Thank you, I... Yes, let's do it."

He almost smiled, and she felt her heart get tight. "It'll be like all those family vacations we took back in the day."

Oh, all those vacations. Some of which she chose never to think about now.

But life was different.

This summer, she was... Sam. Not Samantha and Will. Just Sam.

"Yeah," she said. "Just like that."

four

"Ethan! Chloe! Don't go too far!" Sam shouted at the bobbing heads of the two nine-year-olds who had started running down the trail without waiting for a parent or an older sibling, and of course she was halfway into the back of the SUV trying to get lawn chairs and a cooler out of the mountain of weird stuff her kids had jammed into the car for their trip to the beach house for the week.

The house, which they'd parked right next to, had beach access down a winding trail and a steep staircase, and of course the kids didn't want to wait to get into the sand. To get sand into *everything*.

"I've got them." Will jogged ahead, running after the kids, with Aiden and Jude on his heels, which left her with all of the stuff.

And Logan.

This was the first time they'd gone on a vacation since Becca's death four months earlier. Will had thought it would be a good idea to invite Logan and Chloe. Sam was all for it. It was just she was used to having Becca as a buffer.

She loved Becca.

She had loved so much how Logan cared for Becca.

But she and Logan...

She didn't know how to talk to him. Maybe, horribly, even more so, she didn't know how to talk to someone who had just lost the love of their life. She didn't know how to handle it. She wanted to say something comforting every time she saw him and knew the impulse was probably annoying. She also didn't know what could possibly be comforting.

It had been six months of shocking, awful hell. How could a thirty-year-old woman have cancer like that?

Cancer that moved so fast.

Cancer that responded to nothing.

When she looked at Logan, she felt that pain fresh every time.

When she looked at Chloe, it doubled.

Chloe had stayed with them for a week after Becca's death. The little redheaded girl hadn't cried until the fifth day.

Then she hadn't stopped.

Sam felt like a part of herself had broken during that torrential outpouring of grief, and it had never quite healed itself.

"Let me get that." Logan reached over her and easily got the cooler out of the mass of detritus it was wedged into.

"I'm fine," she said, as he also took the lawn chairs right from her hand.

"Samantha." There was a faint note of scolding in his voice, and she didn't know what to do with that, except she relinquished the lawn chairs.

She stood awkwardly for a moment, suddenly empty-handed—a phenomenon she had no idea how to handle—and then slowly folded her arms. "Thank you," she said.

"No problem."

He started walking ahead of her down the trail.

"How is Chloe?" she asked, because she wanted to also ask how he was, but she just had a feeling it wouldn't be well received.

"I don't know how to answer that."

"Sorry, I…"

"Fine. She's going to school. She can make it through a day."

"Yeah. Listen… Logan, if you want to have her come to our house after school some days so you don't have to finish at the garage so early, or just…for any reason really, we'd love to have her."

He stopped walking, and turned to look at her. The sadness in his blue eyes seemed to be buried under a glint of something hard she couldn't read, and it made her stomach hurt. "Thanks, Sam."

five

"Be safe," Elysia said as Sam hefted her travel bag—traveling light as instructed by her very very bossy boss—over her shoulder.

Logan was her boss.

Lord.

Elysia had met Sam at her vacation rental at checkout time—to send her off and to get a key to Sam's house.

"We'll be safe," she said, her stomach getting tight, and she didn't know why, but she sort of loved it.

She felt excited.

This was unknown.

This was adventure.

She was still angry and hurt and uncertain and a whole lot of other things, but she was going on a damned adventure.

"I still can't believe you're doing this."

"I have nothing else to do," she said.

"I mean, you could write a piece about…"

She put her hand up. "I'm not writing about this. Not now. Not ever, because I am never letting anyone know this happened to me."

"You don't think people have figured it out?"

"No. I haven't said anything."

"You kind of did when you changed your social media profile pic to a selfie and put up a quote about strength."

Sam made an exasperated sound. "That doesn't mean anything."

"It does, and trust me, people have guessed. Don't you ever divorce-stalk people?"

She blinked. "Well. Sure. But when I do it, it's different, and *we* are not getting divorced."

"I know. You're separated. It's different. What did you tell your kids, because they're bound to hear gossip?"

"They're boys, El. They aren't going to get small-town gossip."

"But if they do?"

"We're just spending a summer apart! It doesn't have to be a big deal, and God knows the boys don't need to know their dad is… Anyway, Will should have to do it since he's the one who started it."

"Sure, but who's going to get it in the neck if the kids find out in a weird way?"

She growled. "Me. Because I'm their mom."

"Yes, ma'am, as I think you know." Elysia sighed. "Sam, I am familiar with kids blaming their mom. I'm *mean to Daddy.* Sadly, my kids are little, so I can't shout back about how Daddy is an asshole who likes to put his penis in other women."

"I've never understood how you did it." She shook her head. "How you didn't…tell them he cheated on you. He's the one who ended your marriage."

She nodded. "Sure. He is. But what happened between him and me is exactly that. It's between us. It has never had anything to with what kind of father he is to the girls and…the way I idolized that man. I thought he was just the greatest, best, most perfect husband." The sadness in Elysia's eyes made Sam feel like sitting down and crying. Worse, she knew exactly what her friend felt. As far as thinking you knew someone, she understood. "I couldn't bear to be the one who took that feeling of admiration from my girls, because even though he's not still that husband for me, he's still that dad for them."

"I'll think about how to handle it," Sam said. "Because the problem is, my kids are adults, and as much as I don't want to throw Will under the bus entirely..."

"I think they're old enough that you can find a way to talk about it that's honest," Elysia said.

She looked out the window and saw an aqua-colored car with a white convertible top, up for now, and dramatic fins on the back, pull into the driveway. Logan was in the driver's seat, his forearm resting on the steering wheel, sunglasses firmly in place.

The...car was beautiful.

She looked back at Elysia.

"I'm going on an adventure. To think, a couple weeks ago I was just going to Texas Roadhouse."

Elysia smiled. "Life is weird like that."

"I wanted rolls. I got a trial separation and a road trip with a man I struggle to exchange ten words an hour with."

"Play music," Elysia said. "It'll be fine. And text when you get to the hotel for tonight."

"I'm sure I'll text before then."

She walked out the front door into the warm morning, and pulled her phone out of her pocket. She scrolled through her contacts until she found Will My Love, a name she'd been using for his contact since she was literally twenty.

She opened it up and hit Backspace until it was just: Will.

She let out a hard breath and stuffed her phone back into her pocket, just as Logan got out of the car.

"This is beautiful," she said.

"I didn't know you were into cars."

"I'm not especially. But even a car philistine such as myself can recognize the beauty in this one."

He opened up the passenger's side door and went around to the back of the car, popping the trunk, and reached out for her bag. He was always doing things like that. Like it was muscle memory, and she didn't know if it was an intense streak of chivalry he'd carried with him since childhood, or just a lingering habit from being a single dad for the last ten years. Taking everything, holding everything.

There was a box in the back that took up half the space, and a very small duffel bag shoved all the way to one side.

"I need to drop a care package by Chloe's. Since we'll be driving by."

"Oh. Of course." She frowned. She didn't know how she was going to explain her presence to Chloe.

"I already told her you'd be with me," he said. "She's excited to see you."

"She didn't ask why I was with you?"

"I told her I hired you to be my relief driver. You know, nineteen-year-olds are very self-absorbed, even the good ones. It's part of their charm. She didn't question it deeply."

"Sorry. Of course you want to visit her. I'd like to see her too. I'll try not to make everything about my current trauma."

She got into the car, and then he did the same. The interior was beautiful. The dashboard the same high-gloss aqua as the exterior, with a chrome streak running through the front where the radio was. The seats were cream-and-aqua leather. The whole car reminded her of saltwater taffy.

She rolled down the window, the crank a strange throwback to childhood she hadn't thought about in decades, and waved into the house at Elysia as they reversed and pulled out of the driveway. "She said we had to be safe," she told him, and then felt slightly silly.

He reinforced that by giving her a sideways glance that definitely suggested he thought she was silly.

"You know, when someone says something like that to you, you...have to make sure you say okay. You're driving first, so I had to say it to you. Like when you say you'll pray for someone, so you have to immediately say, in your head of course, 'God, help them out.' So you don't forget, because you can't lie about praying for someone."

"I...don't know any of that, Sam."

"It's...the rules, Logan."

"Who says?"

"To...to being a good person."

She heard herself. It made her think of the conversations she'd been having with Will. About why they got married and the expectations of other people.

It was okay to want to please other people. They lived in a society, after all. Sure, her mom and dad had always had a really clear idea of what a good person was, but mostly Sam agreed.

It was okay to care about that.

They drove through the familiar streets, and it was a wholly unfamiliar vantage point. Not just because she was used to either driving in or riding in an SUV, but because she couldn't remember the last time she'd ridden in the passenger seat when a man who wasn't her husband or her father was driving.

She looked down at her hand. At her wedding ring.

She'd changed her husband's name in her phone, but had left her wedding ring on.

You are still married to him. It does make sense.

"Music?" she asked.

"Sure."

"Can I plug my phone in?"

"This is a 1957 Chevy Bel Air. It doesn't have a USB so you can plug in your iPhone."

"But you...restored it."

"Yes, I restored it. I didn't change it into some godless Frankenstein's monster of a car."

"How do you listen to music?" she asked.

He tapped the radio, which was a small, analog-looking unit right next to a gold cursive *Bel Air*.

"It's an AM radio," she said, looking at it and feeling like she might as well be turning the knob on an egg timer.

"It is. They didn't start putting FM in cars until—"

"How do you live like this?"

"Talk radio can introduce you to new perspectives."

"I've been in my dad's garage, thank you. I've heard it all."

She started to press the channel buttons and mostly got static. Then finally found a station playing tinny-sounding '80s rock. But nothing so popular she recognized it.

She laid her head back on the seat and resigned herself to her fate. Because it was music or trying to make conversation with Logan, and she had no idea what to talk to him about.

Well, she did.

Kids.

But she mostly knew what was going on with Chloe. Chloe often texted Sam herself. So it would be a short conversation.

She did know how to talk about things other than her kids. She did it with Elysia and Whitney all the time. Whitney didn't have children and would often remind her and Elysia of that. She did not have to speak the language of petty school board squabbles and homework drama when they got in too deep. It was grounding to have a friend who steered the conversation out of that rut.

But that was what Sam had in common with Logan.

The only thing.

She had to save it. Because they were staying in Bakersfield tonight and it was a nine-and-a-half-hour drive, and that was without the stop in Santa Clara.

She looked over at him. He had his forearm resting on the

top of the steering wheel, and he seemed to be enjoying the music. Deep was his lack of concern over the quality and content of the music, so it seemed.

He was wearing a white T-shirt, his dark hair pushed back off his forehead. In the era-appropriate car, it was all very *Rebel without a Cause.*

The truth was—and since the '80s music wasn't loud enough to drown the thought out, she had it, fully fleshed out and everything—Logan was a hot guy. Very much not in a handsome-dad-down-the-block way. But in a brooding, sort of dangerous, it-seems-unlikely-he-would-live-on-your-street way.

He did not give cul-de-sac vibes.

He was too rugged for that.

If he said he lived above his garage and existed only on cigarettes and whiskey to keep his stomach hard and flat and his attitude mean, you'd believe it.

That he lived in quite a nice house—though not on a cul-de-sac, on a little ranchette down at the end of town, with about three acres—and had raised his daughter in a perfectly stable environment, all things considered, didn't really mesh with his appearance.

When he'd pulled up, maybe it hadn't even really been the car she'd admired.

Maybe.

She was done with Logan's looks now.

The music wasn't *that* bad.

Then suddenly the music was Fall Out Boy.

She had two thoughts: Was she so old the music of her youth was in this random AM radio station? And also, well, yay.

Because at least she knew it.

He was merged onto the freeway as the song started to pick up, and she looked out the window at the view, which was a familiar enough view but felt wholly different now because of where they were headed. Also, who she was with.

Without thinking she started to sing along. Badly.

"I can't do it," he said. "Reach behind the seat. There's a portable charger and a Bluetooth speaker."

"You are a liar!" she said, turning and reaching over the back of the seat and finding everything he'd claimed she would.

"Yes, I'm a liar. I thought it was funny. But it was only funny until you started singing."

"How long were you going to let that go on?"

He shrugged. "An hour or so."

"Why?"

He didn't say anything. He just smiled and looked at the road ahead while she fussed around with the cord, the battery, her phone and the speaker, but once she got it going she was able to pull up one of her playlists.

"It's still Fall Out Boy."

"Lord save me."

She grinned. "I can put some good old-fashioned worship music on there, if that's a request."

"It's not."

He let her have control of the music, though. So his irritation seemed a little bit for show.

"What would you choose?" she asked.

"Disturbed. Fuel."

"Naturally." Because of course he would be a fan of the hard rock of the early 2000s.

"I also like Chappell Roan."

"Oh, you do not."

"I have a nineteen-year-old daughter. Chloe gets to choose the music when she rides with me."

She laughed. "I do not let my boys choose the music."

"Why not?"

"Because, it might be perfectly fine for me to listen to music about women's anatomy being juicy or otherwise, and quite enjoy it, thank you, but I don't want to listen to it *with* them.

So best we both pretend that's not the kind of thing we're listening to at all."

He chuckled. "You like denial."

She was going to just laugh and move through the moment, but something stopped her. "I... What?"

"Was the statement unclear?"

"I don't like denial."

"You just told me denial works best for you when it comes to your kids' taste in music."

"That's normal parental levels of denial," she said.

"Is it?"

"Do you want to know everything about Chloe?"

He cleared his throat. "I believe in boundaries. That's different than denial. I need to keep Chloe safe, but much in the same way she doesn't need to know everything about me, I don't need to know everything about her."

"Boundaries. That's your superior way of saying denial?"

"I don't care if it's denial, actually. You're the one acting triggered by the word."

She knew why. Because it felt like he wasn't talking about music, or her kids. It felt like he was talking about Will.

She put her elbow on the window ledge and her chin on her hand. "It's just a normal amount of coping," she said. "Not a high level of denial."

She watched the scenery change from hills to trees. Then as they wound down the mountain into California, the view opened up again, and California Welcomed Them with a blue sign with a cheerful poppy on it.

Then they stopped at the check station, where the person working asked if they had fruit and waved them through before they even had a chance to answer.

She couldn't let go of what he'd said. "You can't say things like that and not explain," she said.

"I think I can."

"No. You can't. It sounded like you meant something deeper, and now I want to know."

"What do you want to know?"

"Did you mean me and Will?"

He let out a hard sigh. "No, Sam. I didn't. I meant exactly what I said."

Her cheeks felt hot. So maybe she was now obsessively digging for the truth behind everything because she must not have done it when she should have with Will.

Maybe his comment felt weighted because it was.

To her.

Even if he hadn't meant it to be.

"It's just…he's your friend, Logan. I have a hard time believing he didn't say anything to you, or give hints about what he was feeling."

"I don't know more about your marriage than you do. Even if he had said something, I would never assume that what he said to me was more true than what he said to you."

"Why is that?"

"Because some guys like to talk shit. It doesn't mean anything. Don't you complain about him to your friends?"

"Sometimes, but…"

"Do you *mean* all of it or are you venting?"

"I mean, sometimes both. I believe all of it, and I love him, and I need to say it them because it might not help to say it to him."

"So that's exactly what I mean. But no, he never told me he had a burning desire to have an open marriage." He laughed when he said it.

"You think that's funny?"

"I don't get it as a concept. What the fuck is the point of marriage, then?"

"Some people find it very…"

"Fine," he said. "But it's not the deal you had."

"No. It's not. But don't make me feel like I have to defend him. Please."

"You don't have to. There's no one here. I'm his best friend, remember? You're his wife. If there was a nicer take to be had on him, one of us would have it."

Logan had taken her side here. Unequivocally.

"He said he envied me?" Logan asked.

"Yes," she said. "Not the reason you're single, but that you have freedom."

"He knows me well enough not to say that bullshit."

For a minute there was nothing but the sound of the engine, other cars, their tires on the road, and the pop punk she still had playing.

She was tired.

She was tired of thinking about Will. Worrying about Will. Wondering about Will.

For twenty-four years she had thought about that man. Every decision, every desire, every need, had been wrapped around him.

She had left because she didn't want to know what he was doing.

But it also meant she was free to just not think about him at all.

"I'm done talking about him," she said. She sat up straight and took her wedding rings off. "This isn't about him. It can't be."

She stuffed the ring and the band into a zipper pocket in her purse, her hand feeling weird, the ratio of her ring finger just wrong.

This wasn't forever. It was for the summer.

"He's in Oregon," she said, leaning her head back against the seat. "I'm going on my road trip. He doesn't get to come with me."

six

They made it to Santa Clara around two thirty. Logan was a ruthless navigator who kept all stops to the bare minimum.

"I want to sightsee when we're actually on Route 66," she said as they pulled onto campus and tried to follow Chloe's directions to her student housing.

"We will. But there's no sightseeing I want to do along I-5, and we have to have time to visit with Chloe and get to Bakersfield before it gets too late."

"Because we'd hate to miss the stunning attractions in Bakersfield?" she asked dryly.

"Because we need to get there at a reasonable time, to get up early, to get on the road," he said, as if he were talking to a child.

Then again, he usually did this with Chloe.

When they pulled into visitor parking, he texted and waited for Chloe to give them the okay before they started to head up to her room.

Before they did, he took the box out of the trunk. "What did you bring her?" she asked.

"Just stuff."

She rolled her eyes as she followed him into the building and tried not to think about how weird it was that she was visiting Chloe in her dorm. She could remember when she was a little girl, and yes, all her boys were grown too, but it was weirder sometimes when it was someone else's child you'd known forever.

She hadn't gone to college, but she'd now moved all three of her sons into dorms and knew they were all like this, even if they looked totally different. Filled with school pride, and also the naked resentment of said school pride, teenage panic and hormones.

She didn't miss being young.

Because being older is so much better?

It *had* been.

Shit, now she was basically a teenager in a forty-year-old body.

Yet again, she questioned Will's sanity.

Why would you sign up for debilitating insecurity *and* unexplainable neck pain?

She was also old enough to know life wasn't made to order. She was still human enough to resent it.

They got into the elevator and took it to the second floor, where Chloe's room was. There was a living area up there with kids lying on the cheap furniture. It didn't remind her of college. It reminded her of being a poor newlywed, with the perfect combination of cheap furniture from box stores and free furniture from family members and elderly people in the neighborhood.

She and Will had had a pair of shocking-looking floral couches that they'd gotten from an older man down the road when his wife had died. They'd tried their best to put slipcovers on them, but the slipcovers were—by necessity—cheap, and they never stayed. In hindsight, the couches had looked like they were sloppily covered in black blankets. The floral couch would have been better, but she'd thought they were old lady, and at the time she was so committed to this life she was making.

The one where she was an adult. She wouldn't have flower garlands and roosters and the things her mother thought were cute that Sam thought were dust catchers. She'd been all about sleek things. Black and red. Then brown and teal.

She'd been nothing if not a victim of early 2000s style.

Her thoughts were pulled away from her poor decor choices when she realized that Logan hadn't paused, but was walking quickly down the hall, so she scampered to keep up.

He knocked firmly on one of the doors, holding the box with only one hand, and it only took a second for it to open. Bright, redheaded Chloe was there, and immediately threw her arms around Logan.

His face changed.

He smiled when Chloe wasn't around, but it was always sort of cynical—at least in Sam's presence. This was a real smile.

"What did you bring me?" she asked as soon as he let her go.

"Let me in to see if you've trashed the place yet and I'll show you."

She moved to the side, and Logan walked past her, and that was when Chloe's eyes met Sam's. "Hey!" Chloe moved out of the doorway and gave Sam a hug, and Sam felt fragile right then. Because Chloe reminded her of afternoons after school when she'd had all the kids home, and she'd made them peanut butter and jelly sandwiches.

She wanted peanut butter and jelly all of a sudden.

"Good to see you, Chloe," she said.

"You too." Chloe was about half a foot out of her room, and there was something hesitant in how she was looking at Sam. "Um. Why are you with my dad?"

Right, so, sadly for Sam, Chloe wasn't the myopic, selfish nineteen-year-old Logan had tried to write her off as, and had simply realized her dad wasn't fertile ground for interrogation.

Sam had always felt close to Chloe. She'd talked to her about periods and first dates and birth control. God, had she ranted at her about birth control. *Even if you don't think you're going to do it, Chloe!*

She didn't have a daughter. Chloe didn't have a mother.

They'd always been close, and of course Chloe was picking up on the weirdness here. Sam also wasn't going to lie to her.

"I'll tell you, but you can't text Ethan about it. He's overseas, and it's just not...not a good idea. I'll tell him when I get a chance to call."

Maybe she wouldn't. Maybe they could go the whole summer without it coming up.

Chloe's eyes went slightly round. "Um. Okay."

"Will and I are separated. We aren't getting divorced," she added quickly. "We're like...on a break. I needed something to do, and your dad hired me to do the cross-country drives this summer."

Chloe looked oddly perplexed but also...relieved by the explanation.

"It's nothing... It's not personal. Me traveling with your dad," she said, her stomach going tight. "He had a job opening, and I suddenly have a weird amount of time."

"You're not getting a divorce?" Chloe asked.

"No. It's just...you know, we got married really young. We're basically just taking separate vacations."

When you put it like that, it didn't even sound like a big deal. When she ignored the fact that he'd be sleeping with other women, it was like...so not even a thing at all.

"It's going to be fine," Sam said, trying to project a confidence she didn't really feel. "I'd love to see your dorm."

She smiled. "Come on in."

The room was sparse, with beds against both walls, a small stretch of counter with a rice cooker and a hot plate, and brightly colored tapestries covering the walls.

"Looks great in here, and you don't even have all my forks stashed in a cup on your desk," said Logan, continuing to unpack the box he'd brought in.

"I'm not going to your house to get a fork," Chloe said, "so obviously not."

"Well, I still consider it growth. Do you have time to go to late lunch?"

"Sure," she said. "If you have time."

"I have all the time in the world."

"I'm not hungry," Sam said quickly. "You guys should have lunch together. I'm happy to go…shop or something."

"You'd probably like Santana Row," Chloe offered.

"Great. I'm happy to cool my heels there. As you know, shopping options are limited at home."

Chloe laughed. "Yes, I do know."

When they got outside, Sam offered Chloe shotgun, even though Chloe protested. Sam watched the ease between Logan and Chloe from her position in the back seat. She knew Logan was a great dad. She'd seen him with Chloe any number of times, and in many different circumstances. But maybe it was just having been with him alone for all these hours and seeing how different he was now in contrast that made her so aware of it.

He wasn't easy with her. It wasn't all in her head.

"This is where all the shopping is," Chloe said, pointing at a row of very nice-looking stores.

"Great, you can dump me out here."

"There's tons of food just like two blocks up," Chloe said. "We can eat here."

She got out of the car and waved, leaving them to debate that while she headed for the first store. Was she so fragile that she couldn't handle being around someone whose family was in order? They were a smaller family unit. Not one without tragedy. But they were them, like always, and maybe that was part of why she'd suddenly felt uncomfortable.

She started idly taking clothes off the rack and draping them over her arm. Then she took a bikini off one rack.

She never wore bikinis.

She often made an exercise of looking at all the women on beaches who did. She thought they looked good. Whether they had toned abs, visible ribs, or bellies on proud display, she could see how a bikini worked for them. She tried to apply that same love for her own body and had never been able to manage it.

This was pivotal, she realized, because she could fold in on herself here, die inside over the fact that her body wasn't enough for her husband. Her body that had given him three children and years of sex, but was somehow not as exciting as the unknown bodies he might find outside their marriage.

Yeah, she could hate her body for that. Easily.

It would be a short sidestep on the trail of uneasy confidence she already walked.

But she'd left him in Oregon.

Her body had gone with her. It always would.

It was hers.

She stood there, feeling wholly undone by that realization. She'd felt part of a couple for so long. They'd given each other easy access to their bodies. She'd trusted him, so it had been easy.

Plus she'd had three kids. They'd come out of this body. She'd fed them from her body. Been pulled on, tugged on, puked on for years.

Now the kids were grown. The husband was gone.

She had herself.

Her body was hers.

Normally she asked Will if he liked what she chose. She took selfies in the dressing room because she wanted him to like it. He wasn't controlling. It was her. She was so dependent on his approval that she asked him for it when he probably didn't care what she did at all.

She'd been a child who asked her parents. A teenager who asked her friends.

A woman who asked her husband.

She'd gone straight from her parents' house to Will's.

She went into the dressing room and started trying things on and asking herself if she liked them. Which was really hard, and it took a lot of willpower to not at least text things to Elysia and Whitney, but she was trying to marinate in her revelation.

That her body belonged to her, and she had to choose to be nice to it—to herself—and not let herself pick apart every lump and curve that didn't fall right where she wanted it to. Not pick apart the stretch marks and other imperfections that made her a human being and not an ad, airbrushed to impossible smoothness.

She put on the bikini and bent over, watching the shape of her body change. A shape that she would have called unflattering an hour ago but was trying to see differently now.

She decided against the bikini. Her liberation might not be found in showing her whole stomach and half her ass in public. Maybe eventually it would be. Right now it felt like it would just make her self-conscious, and she didn't need to heap difficulty onto her situation.

It felt like a win to choose a skirt and two dresses without asking anyone else's opinion, though. She did the same at the makeup store she went to—she really did love makeup—where she chose the kinds of lipstick colors she normally would have thought were too bold.

When Chloe texted her to say they were finished with lunch, Sam went out to wait for them on the sidewalk, and hurriedly got into the back seat again when they pulled up, dragging her bags in behind her.

"Good thing we off-loaded Chloe's care package. But remember, you have to fly everything you buy back with you."

"I'll manage," she said.

She knew she sounded a little snappish, but honestly. She was used to managing space and travel for four other people. It wasn't like she didn't know how it all worked.

She listened to Logan and Chloe chat all the way back to the college and then shifted her position to the front seat and waited in the car while he walked her to the door and gave her a hug. Sam looked down at her phone.

He got back into the car and put it in Reverse.

"It's hard," she said, not really knowing she was going to say it out loud until she did. "Leaving them."

"I'm proud of her," he said.

"I'm proud of my kids too. It doesn't mean it isn't hard that they moved away. Jude met a girl going to school on the East Coast, and right now they're planning on staying there after graduation. I'm proud of him. But it doesn't mean it isn't hard. They...they're your whole life. Until they go have lives of their own. Which is exactly what you raise them to do, but..."

"Did you write this into one of your parenting articles?"

"Ouch. And yes. I believe I did." She would be more offended if it weren't true. But she was trying to be nice.

"I think I read that one."

She paused. "You...read one of my articles?"

"I read all your articles, Sam. It would be weird not to, wouldn't it?"

"I... No. I don't think anyone else reads all my...or they don't talk to me about them, anyway. They're just...little pieces that go on to whatever different news aggregate or blog. They're not anything major." She blinked. "Why do you think it would be weird not to?"

"We're friends."

Logan thought they were friends.

She had never thought of him as her friend.

He was *their* friend. A family friend. Who was bonded to them in the context of that. Him with Chloe, with all of them.

She looked at his profile as he took them back onto I-5.

"I don't think any of my friends read all of my articles."

"Well, I've found them useful, actually. I've been a single dad for ten years. Your meal planning and organization stuff is good."

He'd used her tips. They'd helped him.

It made her feel...disoriented. Profoundly so.

"I'm... I'm glad." She cleared her throat. "I didn't mean to be trite by...quoting myself. It's just...anything like that I write is me processing my own stuff. It was hard when the boys moved out." She laughed. "I didn't think I'd be moving out."

"Life is a series of surprises. More often than not, kind of terrible ones."

"That should go in a greeting card."

"Or another article."

"I'm not writing about this," she said.

"Why?"

She sighed and rubbed her forehead. "Every life crisis doesn't need to be monetized?"

"Fair enough. Though I wasn't thinking of it in those terms."

She shook her head. "Everyone needs to learn to organize their pantry. Not very many people need to learn to navigate their husband asking for an open marriage."

"A lot of people need to learn to deal with life changes they didn't ask for, though."

"My life didn't change. My life is on pause, so while it's on pause, I decided to step out of the frame and explore."

"Uh-huh."

"You don't believe me?"

"I know you, Sam. I don't know how you're going to go back to him after knowing what he's been doing all summer."

"I'm not going to know. I'm going to take him back, no questions asked."

"Ah. The denial."

And that infuriated her, because she couldn't even argue with him. Maybe it was denial. Maybe a little dose of denial was how everyone got through life.

She liked to think that as a parent, she was a consistent disciplinarian. But she did often pretend she didn't see something so she didn't have to punish her kids. If that was denial, fine. It allowed her to create boundaries, consistency, and to not be permanently installed up her kids' asses. So there.

They ended up stuck behind a tractor on the road going east to Bakersfield, and it made the last twenty minutes take forty. By the time they pulled into the Holiday Inn, she was exhausted. Who knew riding in a car all day even without kids could be so tiring?

You might not be with three little boys, but you are with him.

True. Fair.

They walked up to the attendant at the check-in counter and got their room numbers and key cards.

"I want to get on the road again at six," he said.

"Six?" she parroted. She looked at the sign sitting on the front desk. "Breakfast doesn't start till 6:30 a.m."

"It would be a damn shame to miss your ride over a continental breakfast, Sam. We need to make some headway tomorrow."

"Aren't we going to Flagstaff? That's like eight hours."

"I thought you wanted to sightsee?"

"I do but are you planning on feeding me and giving me coffee at some point?"

"I wouldn't dream of denying you. I like all my digits right where they are." He held up his hand and wiggled his fingers, and then began to walk toward the elevator.

She went after him, just managing to get inside before the doors slid shut. He pressed Two, and then pressed Four.

"I don't understand the implication," she said as the elevator starting going up.

"Maybe you've forgotten," he said, the pitch of his voice lowering. "I've traveled with you before."

Something about the way he said it made time seem slower. She looked at his face, the lines there. His blue eyes. His mouth.

She blinked hard.

The elevator reached its floor, and maybe it was something about the way it swayed when it stopped that made her feel like she was turned a little sideways.

The doors opened, and he stepped out. "I haven't forgotten!" she said.

"See you at six."

The doors slid shut again, and she rode the extra two floors up to the fourth floor. She stumbled down the hall to her room and unlocked it quickly with the key card.

The room was dim and cool, all of the bedding white, and she was ready to stretch out on that bed, order late-night food delivery and just breathe.

Maybe it was being in a hotel room alone. Maybe it was being away. Something giddy built in her chest, and she took three large hops across the room and leaped onto the bed, laughing when she sank into the mattress.

She was so glad she had gotten away.

She was so glad she was here.

Now she was going to order whatever the hell she wanted and eat it in her pajamas.

seven

US Highway 101
SUV caravan
Family vacation—nine years ago

The kids were running around in the light of the bonfire, the waves crashing against the shore. There was a little row of cottages, all lit up, right on the ocean, all part of the beautiful resort they were staying at in Monterey.

Will and Logan had beer, and Sam was enjoying a Diet Coke—she was a cheap date.

Will made a noise, then pulled his vibrating phone out of his pocket. "Oh, dammit."

"Take it," said Sam.

"We're on vacation."

"Is it a client?"

He pulled a face. "A difficult one."

"Better take it," she said.

"And come back with more beer, and another Diet Coke for Sam, or we'll lose limbs," Logan said as Will retreated from the bonfire.

"Why...what?" Sam asked as her husband retreated.

"Coffee in the morning. Diet Coke after noon, and God forbid we deny you."

He wasn't wrong. It made her skin feel too tight. She took a long sip of Diet Coke and turned toward the kids, a little more dramatically than she meant to.

"How is the writing business?" he asked.

She lowered the can quickly. "Oh. Good. Good. I've got a couple of new blogs and sites I'm doing content for right now. Some of it's fun. Some of it's like...testing internet cooking hacks, which mostly so far has made a mess of my kitchen."

She cleared her throat. "And the...the cars? How are the cars?"

He chuckled. "Going."

She nodded, then looked over at the kids, spinning circles in the sand and laughing. "I love seeing her laugh," she said.

"Me too." His voice was rough when he said that.

"How is she?"

"You see her three days a week," he pointed out.

"Yes, but she's distracted when she's playing with the boys. How is she at home?" She could talk about this. About Chloe. She was a common concern they both had.

"I never know how to answer the question," he said. "You aren't the only one who asks, but you do ask a lot."

That put her on the defensive, which made her feel a little bit crappy. You weren't supposed to be defensive if your motives were pure, right?

"It seems rude not to ask. I... I worry. About both of you, actually."

He frowned, the firelight throwing the features on his face into stark relief. He looked carved out of granite then, his cheekbones hard and high, the cut of his jaw sharp, his mouth severe. "About me?"

"I'm sure in a lot of ways it's a really good thing you had

Chloe." She closed her eyes. "But have you had a chance to fall apart?"

"It's been more than a year," he said.

"I know."

"No," he said. "I haven't. Because falling apart doesn't do anyone any good."

"But…but…"

"But what? My wife is dead? I know."

She realized he was being hard to push her away, and he was Will's friend, not hers. Maybe he and Will had had any number of productive conversations about grief and healing, and hell, she didn't know anything about loss.

She'd never been close to her mother's parents. They'd lived too far away for her to develop a relationship with them. They'd died when she was seven and fifteen.

Her paternal grandparents were still alive.

She didn't know anything about this, but she felt bad that all she'd managed to do was give him the same trite questions that everyone else did. Her intent might be good, but it wasn't doing anything for him. It was about salving her own guilt.

I checked in on the widower, and he says he's doing okay. Now I can check that box.

"Yes," she whispered. "Your wife died." Her eyes suddenly filled with tears, and she decided not to hold them back. "I'm sorry. She was just a really great woman, Logan."

He looked up at her, the flames reflected in his eyes. "She was."

"Is it weird I didn't sit around and cry about it last year? Is it weird it makes me want to cry more now?" she asked.

He shook his head. "No. I do. Chloe has grown two inches since Becca died. Sometimes I think…it's two inches she never got to see. She's getting tall. She'll probably be taller than Becca was. She'll grow into a whole woman someday, and her mother will never get to see. That makes me sadder than anything, and the more time that passes...well, I'm watching it happen, that whole sad realization." He paused, his indrawn breath sharp. "The more time passes, the longer it's been since I've seen her. It makes me miss her more."

That all hit her hard. The thought of watching her little boys grow into men was a bittersweet one. But the thought of not watching them grow at all was crushing.

She pressed her forearms to her thighs and leaned forward, looking into the fire.

"That's just shitty," she said.

Then, much to her surprise, he laughed. Not hearty, a little rusty, but a laugh all the same.

"It is. Thanks." She looked up at him as he took another sip of his beer. "That's something no one's said to me before, and it's the truth."

eight

Now

"Your turn to drive, sunshine."

Logan tossed the keys her way, and she watched them hit the ground. Then looked back up at him. "I haven't had my coffee yet."

"I know." He smiled and her, and she wanted to punch it off his face. "Because breakfast doesn't start till 6:30 a.m. This was poorly planned."

She rolled her eyes and bent down to pick the keys up. "I'm driving us through Starbucks."

"I can't stop you."

"No, you can't. I've taken women's self-defense courses, and I am well-versed on how to attack a man's fleshy parts viciously with nothing but a set of car keys."

"I don't want a demonstration."

She slid into the driver's seat and, without thought, ran her hand over the dash. It was a beautiful car. She could honestly say she'd never felt the urge to pet a car before. But this one was...well, it was a hot car.

She put the keys into the ignition—a novelty since her car had a push-button start—and turned the engine over.

She closed her eyes and just savored the moment. This sounded like freedom.

She was a little crabby because it was so early, but in general, she was still riding on the euphoria that had overtaken her last night. The first moment she'd felt…happy since all of this started. She could keep on feeling happy.

This was freedom.

She was going to enjoy it.

"Head out of the parking lot and turn left," he said.

"Map me to coffee," she said.

With a lot of grumbling, he acquiesced. In under five minutes—five minutes; he was a drama queen—they were back on the road.

And he had also gotten a coffee.

She was glad they'd gotten coffee, because it was clear the drive was going to involve quite a few hours of nothing but dust and scrub brush.

The rolling hills soon turned into bigger mountains, the short, scraggly plants giving way to twisted clusters of Joshua trees that looked like they belonged on an alien planet rather than in the eastern part of California.

Desert towns, Sam quickly decided, were like dry coastal towns. A tacky, quirky sensibility seemed like a prerequisite for living there. Sam loved it. The landscape was monochromatic—various shades of tan beneath a sun-bleached sky—but the buildings were bright pink and teal. One had a giant roadrunner painted onto the side of it. They passed caravans selling tacos and a vintage thrift store called Funky and Darn Near New.

She looked down and saw the gas gauge was migrating toward *E*, and she wasn't sure how plentiful gas stations would be the rest of the drive to Flagstaff.

She pulled into one of the smaller stations just off the highway, and Logan opened the passenger door. "I'm going to grab some snacks."

She wrinkled her nose. "Um. Okay, I hate to admit this, but I haven't ever actually pumped my own gas."

He tilted his head to the side. "What?"

"Well, we were never allowed to in Oregon, and I still don't go to the self-serve pumps! I've never not been on a road trip with Will, and he just does it."

"Oh, well, there is a first time for everything, Sam. Consider this an education."

"Do you have to say it like that?" she groused.

"I do."

She got out of the car behind him and stared at the pump.

"The directions are on it," he said.

"Yeah, I know, I know." She turned and looked around for the gas hatch.

"Sorry, this actually isn't fair." He walked further to the back of the car and opened up a hatch she hadn't seen on the fin, made of chrome and blending almost seamlessly with the rest of the trim. Behind that was the gas cap.

"So the car is, like, complicated on top of everything else?"

"Yeah," he said, "sorry. But now you know, and the rest will be straightforward."

"It isn't straightforward!"

"Okay." He moved closer to her, and she was awash in instantaneous regret as his scent overtook her. Soap. Skin. Him.

"Hang on," she said. "I just… I'll swipe my card."

"No, I'll swipe my card." He leaned forward and did exactly that. "Choose the kind of gas you need."

"Which kind?"

"Premium. I don't play with my cars. Now get the nozzle out." He gestured to the unwieldy-looking thing stuck into the gas pump.

"Okay." It had a lever, and she pressed it before pulling it out.

His hand was suddenly over hers. "No. Don't do that."

Suddenly the mid-morning sun felt unbearable. Her skin felt unbearable. Too tight and not her own, as goose bumps broke out over her body in response to the firm press of his hand over hers.

"No trigger," he said, his voice a little softer, no less raspy, as he removed his hand from hers.

"Okay." She released her hold on it and then went to the gas tank, figuring the gas cap out easily enough before slipping the nozzle inside.

"Now you want to lock the trigger down."

She fumbled with it for a second, but he didn't move back to help her. He kept his distance.

"Got it," he said, pointing toward the numbers that were now counting upward. "Going to get snacks."

"Okay," she said, leaning against the side of the car and crossing her arms as she stared across the street at the rocks, twisted trees and rugged mountains.

She felt very suddenly outside her body. But at the same time very conscious of her hand, and the feeling his had left behind. Of the heat and pressure.

She reached over and traced the place he'd touched her.

Logan always made her feel so…

So uneven.

She jumped when the trigger on the gas pump popped, signaling that it was finished. Then she managed to get it put back into position herself, got the cap back on the tank and closed the hatch. She chose to focus on the triumph of having done something—admittedly simple, that most people could do—for the first time.

"I am expansive," she said to the tumbleweed resting right against the front tire.

It did not answer.

She heard gravel crunching behind her and turned and saw him walking toward her across the gritty parking lot.

"Road snacks," he said, holding up the bag.

"I want real food," she said.

"This," he said, getting into the car as she did, dumping the bag out over the seat, "is real food."

"It's Fritos."

"Fritos are food."

"It's not a full spectrum," she said, examining the rest of the haul. Powdered doughnuts, potato chips and Milk Duds.

"Not true." He dug into the bag. "There's jerky."

"How are you…" She waved a hand toward his general physical perfection. "That."

"I work out all the time."

"Really?" she asked as she buckled up, started the car and got them back on the road.

She hadn't expected that answer, because honestly, even if it was the truth, she wouldn't expect him to admit it.

"The better to keep the demons at bay, Sam."

She had no idea if he was serious or not, but the comment swirled around in her head, along with the hard rock music he'd chosen to put on.

"Working out all the time is not how it was suggested to me you spend your time," she said, not sure if she'd regret going down this path or not.

"Oh, meaning you were told I live a life of general debauchery?"

"It was implied, yes."

"I dabble in debauchery. I'm not going to lie about that. You have to do something with the nights or they get long."

She'd never really thought about what all that meant. Not in a detailed sense. She knew Logan went out a lot, and had the sense that he hooked up—*hooked up*, like he was in his early twenties or something. But she'd never really…

Of course he did.

It was far too easy for her to imagine, suddenly, the impact of the man, were he to walk up to you in a bar.

"But it's certainly not my whole life," he said. "It's not...not a goal to aspire to."

She frowned. "If you don't like it, why..."

He turned to look at her. "I like parts of it. I like the part where I'm not thinking about anything. But after...all the thoughts you didn't have for those few hours hit you, and they hit hard. It's deferring pain, not stopping it. Sometimes it's still worth it. For a little bit of oblivion. But it doesn't fix jack shit."

Was it still that hard?

A canyon of terror opened up inside of her. Was this what happened to you when you lost the relationship you wanted? Yes, Becca had died, but if Will ended up leaving Sam...would this be her?

Ten years on and not okay.

Not healed.

Just looking for bandages to put on the hemorrhaging wound that was your soul? It was a horrific thought. A terrible idea.

No. Things will go back to how they were.

This will never be you, because you and Will aren't finished.

Again she deliberately shoved those thoughts to the side. She wasn't supposed to be linking all this back to her. And she really wasn't supposed to be tying everything back into Will.

"That doesn't seem fair," she said. "What...would fix it?"

He opened up the bag of Fritos, the gesture alarmingly casual for the subject matter. "I don't have the slightest idea. But I've come to the conclusion that some things aren't fixable."

"You just have to walk around wounded for the rest of your life?" She didn't like that at all.

"Yep," he said, taking a handful of chips from the bag. "There are certain things you don't control in life. You can't choose to have everything you want. An unpopular conclusion in this modern culture," he said, his tone dry.

"Unpopular because it sounds sad. People want to be happy."

"I didn't say I wasn't happy. I have Chloe. I have a job I love. I'm often happy. I'm just also often sad. Unfulfilled. That's part of life, isn't it?"

"People want to be happy more often than they're sad."

He laughed. "That's generous. People want to be happy all the time. They don't know how to handle hard feelings, or being uncomfortable. I'm not great at it either, or I probably wouldn't go out and get drunk and sleep with a stranger as often as I do."

She winced. She couldn't help it. The words were so hard and blunt.

"I have just accepted that there's a certain level of pain I'll always have to live with," he said. "It's the cost of life. It's the cost of loving anything."

She knew that loss—the kind of loss he'd had—didn't just heal. The finality of it was hard, and it always would be.

She had more of an understanding of that now.

But her mother dying was the natural order of things, even if losing her when she had had seemed way too early. Losing a partner, especially as young as Becca and Logan had been, that was unthinkable.

Maybe accepting that it would always hurt was the healthiest thing he could do. It didn't seem fair, though.

"Yeah, I... I don't have anything to say. I don't have any wisdom for that."

"You don't need to."

She always felt like she did. Like it was her job to smooth over the cracks in things. Though she could remember the night she'd sat around the bonfire with Logan and just told him that loss was shitty. That hadn't been profound, but it had been true.

She stopped herself from pulling on that loose thread. The memories of all the vacations.

He'd started it last night in the elevator, and she was determined...

She never thought of those.

She certainly wasn't going to do it now.

"Frito?" He shoved the bag her direction.

She took her eyes off the road for a moment and met his. "Yeah, okay, I'll have a Frito."

She plunged her hand down into the bag and grabbed some chips, and he turned the radio up.

"Did you make reservations?" she asked as they neared the town.

"Nope. Figured we'd do a walk-in at whatever is roadside."

"Oh, excellent," she said. "I have tacky roadside motels on my bucket list."

"Are you being sarcastic?"

"No. I mean, in the sense that I don't have a bucket list, I guess so, but I genuinely love the idea of it."

"I didn't see you as the kind of person who secretly liked tacky things."

"It fascinates me. The bold lack of sophistication is something we could all learn from." To prove her point, she popped the whole handful of Fritos into her mouth.

"I guess I've mostly seen you in more controlled contexts."

"Parenting while on vacation?"

"Yes." He leaned back and settled into the seat, and she tried not to track his every movement out of the corner of her eye. "You were sort of the cruise director for all those trips."

"I'm very good at that," she said.

"You are." She could feel his smile. So profoundly she had to turn and look at him. The corner of his mouth was kicked up, just a little bit. "How does it feel to let someone else direct the cruise?"

"I… You are…" She laughed and shook her head. "I'm not sure. I'll get back to you once we've been through a few ports."

"I'll be sure to hand out a survey."

"Please do."

nine

Anacortes–Orcas Island route
A ferry
Family vacation—seven years ago

It was a beautiful afternoon, even if the Pacific Northwest wind was determined to make sure the sun didn't warm them too sufficiently.

"Someday, Hawaii," she said resolutely when a gust of wind came up off the ocean.

"Someday," Will agreed, lifting his wineglass.

They were sitting at a big wine and food festival happening at farm on Orcas Island. The kids were all playing games under the supervision of festival employees, though Jude was looking a little bit over cool for all of it at fourteen. Though she could see he secretly wanted to play all the games, and that the excuse of keeping an eye on his siblings so that he had to participate was probably welcome.

Will's focus was abruptly pulled over to the opposite side of the big field, where drinks were being served. There were several bachelorette parties in attendance at the festival—

easily identified by the short skirts, sashes and groups of women with similar aesthetics flocking together. It seemed as if a couple of the bachelorette party attendees were focused on Logan.

"That's a lot," she said, taking a sip of the flavored sparkling water she was drinking.

These damned fancy things and their lack of actual Coke products.

She preferred drinks with actual flavor, not drinks that tasted like the last gasp of a dying lemon had been given in the room next door, so as to only gently infuse the fizzy liquid.

"It's like he got rolled in honey and put on an anthill, and women are the ants," Will said.

"Sound slightly envious there, babe," she said, unconcerned, her gaze fixed on Logan. "Does he... I mean, it's been almost three years, but..."

She couldn't imagine that. Losing Will and starting over. Having even the slightest desire to start over.

"*He's* not dead, Sam."

"No, I get that. I get that."

It was just that for her, sex was...so intimate. The idea of being with someone else was something she really couldn't wrap her head around.

It felt weird to see him, Will's friend who had been with Becca, and then alone, chatting it up with random women.

She wrinkled her nose. "I guess I can't really understand why a hookup would *fulfill* anything."

Her husband stared at her. "You don't get why..."

"I get having *needs*. Obviously. It's just... I don't know what I'm trying to say." She took a breath. "After being in love, being in a committed relationship, it just seems like it would be hollow."

"Not everyone feels that way."

Logan said something to one of the women and walked back over to their table.

"You get a phone number?" Will asked.

She wanted to excuse herself.

She suddenly felt uncomfortable there, witnessing this thing she'd never been part of before. Even more uncomfortable watching her husband's interest.

"Yeah. We're on vacation. I'm not interested."

"We're all in the same vacation rental, and the kids were planning on staying up and sleeping out on the deck with a movie on the projector screen. She won't even notice if you leave," Will said.

Wow. So fucking helpful was Will. If only Will had been so helpful when she'd been packing for this trip last night.

Logan's gaze slid back over to one of the tight-dressed, short-skirted women. Then Logan looked at her.

"Sam?"

For a moment, she was lost in the context of the question, her thoughts tangled up.

"Is it a dick move for me to leave for a while tonight?"

She blinked. "Oh…well. I… We'll be fine."

She realized that wasn't an answer to his question. She felt uncomfortable, but she couldn't explain why. It was a big family vacation, the kind they'd been doing for years, and she knew that it was hard for Logan because his family had changed shape. But still.

"Let us," Will said emphatically. "Shit, man, you deserve it."

She thought way too long that night about why Will thought Logan deserved a random hookup.

But by morning, when Logan met them at the vacation rental so they could all go on a bike ride, she'd let it go.

Because there was no reason to hang on to it.

ten

The roadside motel in Flagstaff had indeed proved to be tacky in all the best ways. A rounded adobe building with "Southwestern Flare!" (their words) festooning every room. Meaning extraordinarily loud geometric shapes in purple, yellow and teal.

It's like a preschool class got into a bar fight with a Taco Bell in the 90s, she'd texted to Elysia and Whitney.

How is the trip? Whitney asked.

Good so far.

Is Logan behaving? Elysia asked.

He never doesn't behave.

You don't like him, though, Elysia pointed out.

I didn't say I didn't like him. I like him. I said he's Will's friend and not mine.

That felt so disingenuous after the last couple of days, but there was no untangling all that over text.

Anyway, she'd never untangled Logan within herself. She wasn't about to do it this way, to two other people.

She and Logan had gotten two singles that were at opposite ends of the building from each other, and while Logan had gone to the room to take a nap, she'd opted to head out and explore the town.

She'd wandered around the historic part of town, enjoying the red brick and cheerful bunting draped over the railings of the old buildings. She'd gotten some very good chips and salsa, a mediocre burrito and a kitschy knitted burro she most certainly didn't need.

Then she'd gone back to the motel room and had chosen a dress for the evening, and had considered texting Logan and asking if he wanted dinner.

Then she'd walked down the walkway between their rooms and knocked on his door, to no answer. She'd decided against figuring out his whereabouts since he'd just mentioned the occasional debauchery.

The car was gone.

It occurred to her, for the very first time, that Logan might... he might have appetites that were such he would be hooking up on this trip.

Now that she'd considered that as a possibility, she couldn't get it out of her head.

For God's sake. Was she doomed to be beset by men and their base urges?

She didn't have the patience for it. Was he like...in some other woman's hotel room? Or out at a bar? Was she going to have to concern herself with traffic control when approaching his motel rooms?

These were questions which annoyed her.

She walked back into the part of town she'd already been

to and found a restaurant with a big outdoor seating area with lights overhead, and pink flowers growing over the trellis. There was a live band playing mariachi, and she was moved to a small outdoor table with two chairs near the music.

She ordered a margarita—which she never did—and watched people dancing and laughing, totally absorbed in the atmosphere until a man's voice broke through her thoughtless haze.

At first she thought it was the waiter and looked up, surprised instead by a man with blond hair and a blue button-up shirt.

"I'm sorry, I noticed you were alone."

"Yes," she said, nodding and wondering if this was the stranger danger she'd been warned about for most of her life.

Cover your drink.

Tell him your husband is in the bathroom.

Tell him you have a concealed carry permit.

She looked at her drink, and kept her eyes fixed on it for a long moment before looking back at him.

"I was wondering if you might like some company. I'm alone too."

She had no idea what to do. She'd never been in this situation before.

She'd been with Will since she was sixteen. Not single from the moment things like this might have actually started happening to her. She never traveled alone. She was always with her husband, a group of friends or her kids.

"I'm not *alone*, alone. Just so you know," she said. "If I don't go back to the motel tonight, my friend will send out a search party." She held her arms out. "He's very big."

He laughed. "Okay, point taken. You can't be too careful, I guess."

"No." She wasn't sure she wanted him to leave, though. "You can sit. For a bit. I just wanted to lay out expectations."

He smiled. "I'm Jonathan."

"Samantha."

Then she reached into her purse and grabbed her phone, sending Logan a very quick text. I'm at Casa De Flores, no need to come by just wanted to give you my location. She tucked the phone quickly away again.

"Nice to meet you, Samantha."

"You too."

He didn't know people usually called her Sam. He didn't know her.

He was a nice-enough-looking man. He had a pleasing symmetry about him. But that's all it was. Pleasing. It didn't make her feel like she was struggling to breathe, or like her skin was too tight or…

She cleared her throat. "Are you…from here?"

"Uh, no. I'm here on business."

She wondered if he had a wife at home. But that didn't matter. Because she had a husband at home. *Nothing* was going to happen.

This was just a novelty. A wild, out of her every experience novelty. Wasn't that the point of all this?

"What kind of business?" she asked.

"It's a real estate agent convention," he said.

She laughed because she really couldn't help herself. "A real estate agent? Wow."

"What?"

"I have a type," she said, taking a sip of her margarita and grimacing. "Or a type has me. I don't know."

"What do you mean by that?"

Well, she'd walked herself into this one. "My uh…my husband is a real estate agent."

He looked down at her hand, which she knew was bare. "You're married?"

Well, this was the moment. She could say yes, and he'd probably leave, and she wouldn't know what it was like to spend the evening being flirted with by a random man, or he'd stay and prove he was maybe a little more of a creep than she could enjoy even just for a conversation.

But why flirt with him at all?

You're Penelope to his Odysseus, remember?

Flirting wasn't sexing it up with sirens, so her inner voice could calm the hell down.

"Separated," she said.

"Sorry. Been there. Not fun."

She laughed. "No."

"What brings you here?"

"Oh, I'm traveling with a friend who restores classic cars. I'm the secondary driver on the trip."

"Wow. What kind of car?"

"A 1957 Bel Air."

"I have no idea what that is," he said, smiling. "I guess that makes me uncultured."

She shook her head. "I wouldn't have known until recently, but I'm now intimately acquainted." She regretted her choice of words slightly. Except he looked like he was genuinely enjoying talking with her.

What a novelty.

A man who hadn't known her since high school. Who didn't just think he knew everything about her, but had to actually ask.

She had to ask about him too.

So they just chatted. Over one drink, then two, then a plate of nachos.

Maybe dating apps were a horror, but this wasn't. This made her feel…attractive. Interesting. More like a woman, and not a wife, a mom, a volunteer. All the things people in her immediate community considered her first and foremost.

He had two kids, and had been married fifteen years before it had dissolved. She didn't ask for his messy details and he didn't ask for hers.

"Want to dance?" he asked.

"I don't think I know how to dance," she said.

She wasn't going to tell this stranger she'd gotten married at a church that hadn't allowed alcohol or dancing at weddings (or anything else for that matter, and that even though they'd shifted their stances on things over the years, they hadn't suddenly become big fans of going out dancing).

"I'm bad at it, so that's just fine."

"Yeah. Okay."

He extended his hand and she accepted it, and she felt that same sort of giddiness she had when she'd realized she was in the hotel room alone.

Freedom.

This was her decision.

Her evening.

He led her to the dance floor, holding the one hand still, his other arm wrapped around her waist. It didn't electrify her, though it was strange to let a man she didn't know hold on to her like this.

But there was no one here who knew them to judge her, and there was a kind of freedom in that too.

She was ashamed to admit—in the glorious music-filled moment—that a lot of her issue with what Will wanted was knowing how people in their town would react.

Even worse, if they didn't get back together.

That's Samantha Parker. She's divorced.

The visceral image of any one of the town's church ladies whispering behind their hands to someone else in the grocery store…

She pushed all that away, and let the rhythm move her, even if she wasn't moving very well. Jonathan didn't seem to mind. He seemed to be having as good of a time as she was. It made her feel lighter. Less cynical. She could only hope he didn't transform into a creep at the end of the evening, because if he just wanted the same thing she did—a minute to feel like maybe she was interesting, desirable even, to a random person—a little while to have some fun…well, that was nice.

"I think it's my turn."

The low, masculine voice that cut through the music and the sound of the crowd, without even needing to be raised, stopped both her and Jonathan.

"Logan…"

Jonathan looked at him, and then at her. "I thought you said you were separated?"

"I did," she said. "This is…my friend."

"And her friend would like this dance," Logan said.

Logan was a good five inches taller than Jonathan, and a lot more muscular, and even if he weren't, she had just met the guy. He was hardly going to get into an altercation over her—a woman who had made it pretty clear she wasn't sleeping with him, that he'd just met.

"Sure thing. Hey, your drinks and nachos were on me," Jonathan said, touching her arm. "Thank you for the evening."

Before she could say anything more, Logan had taken her hand, wrapped his arm around her waist and pulled her against him.

She felt like a cat being forced into a scalding tub of water. She wanted to scratch and scramble against him, her heart beating in a way that was like panic. And why? She'd been in the arms of that stranger and it hadn't been anything like…

You know why.

She didn't struggle. She did push back against that thought, though.

She professionally pushed back at these thoughts.

The song changed, and the way Logan held her shifted subtly, and the way he danced…

It was different.

"Where did you learn to… I didn't…" She stopped talking

when she met his eyes, which might as well have been two chips of ice.

So cold, when his body was so…hot.

"You really want to talk about where I learned to dance?" She shook her head. "No."

"That guy could be an axe murderer," he said, his voice hard.

"I don't think he was."

"So confident?"

"You don't get a lot of Jonathans in khakis committing serial murders." She laughed. "Jonathans in khakis who are also real estate agents."

Suddenly his stern face shifted and he laughed, but just a little. "A real estate agent. Wow, Sam."

"We were just dancing," she said.

"Nobody dances at places like this just to dance."

The air between them seemed to contract, and she looked away. "I do. I did. I never got to do that. I never…"

She was unbearably aware of his hand holding hers. It was rough. Much rougher than she'd imagined—not that she'd imagined how his hands were. His hold around her waist was tight, and suddenly dancing seemed like an absurd thing people did.

With strangers. With friends.

Why did they do it?

She would never hold his hand walking down the street. Would never let him wrap his arm around her. But put them chest to chest and set it to music and it was supposed to be just fine?

"I've never done this," she finished, the words a whisper. "We never went out dancing."

"What a fucking idiot."

She looked up at him. "It's not Will's fault. It's like, we were never into that kind of thing. You know, when we were kids and in youth group and stuff, that was all associated with *par-*

tying. We went to the school dances, but after that…no. Then when we were older, we had kids anyway."

"Did you ever ask him to take you?"

She shook her head. "I was fine without it. I only did it tonight because he asked me, and I wondered why I never did it." She looked up at him. "There are so many things that I just never did, so it never occurred to me that I could start if I felt like it."

She wanted to look away from him. But she couldn't. His eyes were glittering blue in the dim lighting, and she was forced to take in the differences between him and the man she'd been dancing with before.

He was taller. Broader. Harder.

It was like being held against a mountain with fire at its core.

A volcano.

Everyone knew a volcano was dangerous.

Yet here she was. Pressed against the masculine equivalent.

She felt his fingers move where he was holding her, his palm on her lower back. She was acutely aware of the shift. Of the way his calloused skin caught against the silken fabric of her dress.

Her breath caught in her throat in response.

She couldn't not think of him as a man.

Jonathan had been a symbol. Of a moment, a rebellion, an opportunity. An experience.

Logan was a man.

She'd watched the way women acted with him.

She'd…

He gripped her hand just a bit tighter. His thumb moved over her knuckles. That didn't seem like a strictly necessary part of the dance.

The song ended, and she stepped back on an exhale.

"Okay, I'm tired. I didn't get a nap in earlier," she said.

He looked at her long and hard. "All right, we'll head back."

She nodded. "Yeah. I... Yeah."

She looked over at the table she'd shared with Jonathan to find it empty, a check with a long white receipt sticking out of the top.

"Let me just make sure he paid," she said.

She walked over to the table and picked up the little leather bifold and saw that he had indeed paid and signed. She'd found a unicorn. A man who'd actually just been nice for nothing. At least, that was what reading about the dating scene had led her to believe. Not that it had been a date.

"Good to go," she said, straightening and walking through the courtyard with Logan, keeping a few feet of distance between them.

The car was parked at the far end of the lot.

"Why did you...why did you come here? Did you need to order dinner or..."

"I came because you said you were here. I didn't like the idea of you being here alone."

"Why?"

"Reasons like the one I walked in one."

"Me dancing with a perfectly nice man?"

"A stranger."

"Oh, so all the women you hook up with aren't strangers?" She hadn't meant to fire that barb at him, but lord, it had been easy.

As if the years of it had been sitting right there in the back of her mind. The memories of him at a few weddings they'd all been at, him and the bachelorette party girl on Orcas Island. The stories her own husband told.

His admittance of occasional debauchery.

"It's different and you know it."

"Every woman who has sex with you is praying to the gods you aren't a serial killer looking for a new flesh suit, so the fact that you think it's okay for those women to go out and determine their own risk level but it isn't okay for me smacks of penile hypocrisy." She laughed. "And I am sick to death of that."

"It is different," he said, "because you're you. Samantha, you haven't left the damned house in twenty years."

"I have! I've been on plenty of vacations. You've…" She stopped herself. She had to stop herself. "I've left my house, you condescending dick."

"With Will. With the kids. With protection. You haven't been out on your own, and I feel like you need the same damned primer on safety that my nineteen-year-old does."

She took a step back, fury making her inarticulate. "I… I am not nineteen. I am not a kid. I am a grown woman, and I know what happens out here in the big bad world. I am not naive enough to believe a man in a restaurant in Flagstaff, Arizona, is my soulmate because he bought me three margaritas and some chicken nachos."

He let out a short, one-note laugh. "Well, good to know."

They stopped in front of the car, in front of the passenger's door, and he reached out and opened it. "Get in."

She replayed the words that she'd just said out loud back in her head. "Well, and I have a soulmate, so even if he bought me a whole tequila factory, he wouldn't be my soulmate. So we're clear."

He just stared at her for a long moment, the competing light from the full moon, white and ambient, clashing with the pink neon coming from the restaurant, chiseling sharp angles in his already sculpted face.

"Get in the car, Sam."

She could fight him, but why?

He was mad at her, but why?

She was a lot madder at him than she should have been.

So she got in the car and let him drive the two minutes back to the motel without making commentary on anything.

"Knock when you're up," he said, pulling up to the front of her room.

"No set time?"

"No."

She got out of the car. "See you tomorrow."

Then she walked to her room, used the key card to get inside, and closed the door behind her, the relative silence pressing in on her. She could still hear road noise. The sound of the pipes. What she hoped was a TV in the room next door.

She focused on those things, on those sounds, as she got ready for bed.

Anything except focusing on what had happened tonight.

On the truth that was just beneath the surface of it all, waiting for her to unearth it.

Instead, she got into bed and pulled the covers over her head.

eleven

US Highway 101
One SUV, one 1973 Pontiac Firebird
Family vacation—six years ago

She couldn't sleep, so she was up at dawn yet again, putting her tennis shoes on and getting ready to go for a walk. She was glad that they'd gone away for the vacation, but her mom's cancer diagnosis felt heavy today.

It had felt heavy when they'd first found out six months ago, but she'd finished her chemo treatments the previous month, and her blood tests afterward had been good for one month. Following that, the numbers on her CA-125 had started to climb, indicating the ovarian cancer was back.

There was no genetic link. That was supposed to make her feel safe, and it didn't. It made her feel guilty, worrying about herself at all.

But she did.

She worried about her health.

She worried about what she'd do when she didn't have her

mom in her life, and she wasn't ready to face that. She just wasn't ready.

They were close. They always had been. She walked down the street to her childhood home almost every day just to chat for a while. The kids saw their grandma every day. It…

It didn't seem real.

The vacation rental was huge. Big enough that Logan and Chloe were staying in the same house. The massive windows looked over Haystack Rock at Cannon Beach, and they'd had a great couple of days enjoying the little town, the beaches, and the elk herd that slept in the field near the house.

She'd been taking early morning walks in the mist, trying to clear her head so she could put on a brave face for the rest of the day. This was a family vacation. She didn't want to weigh everyone down with her worries.

With the statistics that lived in her head and told her that no matter how much she wanted to believe in miracles, climbing numbers this soon after the end of a top-line treatment were bad.

She opened up the front door and went outside. The air was sharp and cold, heavy with mist. She inhaled it deeply, closing her eyes.

She stuffed her hands in her pockets and had started down the road when she heard footsteps, pounding harder and faster than her own. She looked up and saw a jogger partially obscured by the fog.

Then he stopped. "Sam?"

It was Logan.

"Oh, hi. I didn't know you were up," she said, her shoulders going up to the bottoms of her earlobes.

"I get up and run every morning, and try not to wake anyone up."

"I've been walking. I guess we usually miss each other."

His mouth turned up into a half smile. "Yeah. I guess we do."

"Anyway...just walking."

But he turned and started to walk along with her, as if he'd been invited.

"Any particular reason for the early morning walks?"

"A reason for your run?"

"Yes," he said.

"Oh."

"How's your mom, Sam?"

She breathed out, a short, painful sound exiting with it. "I don't think very good. I don't... I'm just thinking."

"I get it. You know that, right?"

She paused. "Yeah, I do."

"Remember what you told me about loss? It's just shitty. So is stuff like this."

"Thanks," she said. It seemed insufficient, but it felt good to have someone say that. To have someone acknowledge how hard it was. "I'm just trying to be normal. I'm trying to have this vacation and be...happy and everything for the kids."

"You can't always do that," he said.

"I want to protect them."

"I get that. But who's protecting you?"

They took five more steps. She counted the sound of their shoes on the damp ground. "Will."

He cleared his throat. "He is my best friend. Has been since we were in our early twenties. But he isn't good with this kind of thing."

It was true. It was so true, and she felt disloyal agreeing with him. So she didn't. "He just hasn't had practice with it, but he tries."

"He doesn't know how to handle an unhappy ending," Logan said. "Just letting you know. He's one of those people that needs things to be a certain amount of okay, and if they aren't, he can't deal."

"He's my husband," she said. "Not my friend. No offense. And nothing tragic has happened yet."

"I know." He paused for a second. "If you need anything, you know you can ask. You were there for me when Becca... You've been there."

She let that settle over her like the mist. She didn't want to be having this conversation. He was right. Will was an optimist, and she felt like she needed that. Most of the time. But she also felt like she'd been drowning in a sea of worst-case scenarios with no one to take her hand. That wasn't fair. She hadn't asked Will to. She didn't know how to ask. That was her problem. That she didn't know how to ask for what she needed because she didn't have any idea what she needed, and how was that Will's fault?

"Thank you. If I need anything, I'll let you know."

She expected him to go back to the house, but he didn't. He just walked with her. There was a strange sort of restlessness that she felt. An urge to move closer, and to move further away all at the same time.

But she just kept walking in a straight line, and Logan walked along with her.

By the time the walk was over, she felt less alone than she had before.

twelve

Now

He didn't wait for her to knock. He was the one who knocked.

She jerked the door open with her blanket wrapped tightly around her shoulders to preserve her modesty—and halfway over her head to conceal her bed head—and there he was, holding two coffee cups and a paper bag.

"It's early," she said.

"Yes, and we have a stop to make that I think you're going to like, so let's get a move on."

"You said I could come wake you up."

"But then you didn't. And it's time to go."

"You said there was no time!" she protested.

"Yes, I lied." He smiled.

"Feh," she groused, shutting the door in his face and going back into the room. Most everything was packed away, and she had shorts and a tank top picked out for today and her most basic skin essentials out on the bathroom counter.

There was presumably no time to shower. Anyway, the idea

of lingering beneath the hot water, naked, while he was just outside the door was a no for her.

She put her bra on, changed her underwear, stuffed her pj's into her bag and then dressed the rest of the way, putting on some moisturizer and SPF, and putting her hair in the fastest of messy buns. Then she collected her bag and opened the door. She led with her outstretched hand.

"Coffee," she demanded.

"Here you go." He handed her the cup.

"What's in the bag?"

"Breakfast burritos."

"Yum."

He turned and started walking toward the car.

"Hey! I want my burrito."

"We need to get on the road."

She moved faster, then stopped. "Are you…are you baiting me?"

He turned and looked at her over his shoulder. "Maybe."

She didn't know if he was playing with her or not. And after last night…

This was the problem with him. With them. They were uneven. Trying to have a relationship with Logan was like walking on a rocky trail. Smooth for a while, an uphill battle, a deadly pothole that might send her plummeting to her doom…

A nice view.

She coughed.

"You okay?" he asked.

"Just fine."

He got into the driver's seat, and she hopped into the passenger side. "Burrito," she said.

He threw the bag into her lap, and she unrolled the top and peered inside. There were two foil-wrapped burritos in there. "Are they the same?"

"One is sausage, one is vegetarian."

"Which one is mine?"

"Both. I ate one already."

"Oh." She turned them until she saw writing on the foil in black marker, and selected the sausage.

He backed out of the motel parking lot and they started down the road, going over a big, painted-on logo for Route 66. They'd passed a few of them, but she had noted them each time.

She'd always wanted to do this. How weird to be doing it with Logan. And breakfast burritos.

"So, where are we going?" she asked once she'd gotten through half of her coffee.

"You'll see."

She rolled her eyes. "Really?"

"It's a surprise, Sam."

She laughed. "Um. Well, Logan, I used to like surprises, but after the last one, I'm on the fence."

He laughed, and she wondered if maybe today would be an easy section of the trail.

She tried not to think about last night. It had been weird and fraught, and she was sort of embarrassed about…all of it. Jonathan. Dancing with him. Dancing with Logan. Sniping at Logan about any of it.

Thinking too much about the heat and musculature of Logan's body.

She attacked her burrito with relish, mostly because it was an exceptional distraction.

"So you always drive side roads when you take the cars to their buyers?" she asked.

He nodded. "Yes. Honestly, some of these cars aren't up to speed for freeway travel. They're great, but I'm going to be in the slow lane the whole way with some of them. Plus, I prefer it. It keeps it from being a grind and turns it into a job perk. Like I said, I charge enough to build the extra time in."

"It's a great idea."

"It's the point of working for yourself, right?"

"In theory," she said.

That had never really worked for Will, who had seemed at the mercy of his clients and his schedule most of the time. But he was successful, and she wasn't complaining. Even internally.

"Is that how it is for you?" he asked.

She looked out the window. "Oh, I wouldn't go comparing me to what you do. I pitch articles when I need work or have an idea. I'm not running a full-time business."

"Do you think you'll make it one now?" he asked.

She blinked. "I don't...know. I'm not really sure that I have enough to say."

"I think you could write a book about managing a household. God knows I found it useful."

She shifted in her seat. "It's all stuff anyone can google. I don't have any particular insight into anything."

"Even if I believed that, you explain it in a way that's interesting and easy to understand."

"I don't think I bring anything new to the conversation. Household and organization and meal planning stuff...it's pretty saturated."

"Well, not that then. Something else."

She took another sip of coffee. "Nothing about me is interesting."

"Seriously?"

She could feel him looking at her, and she was forced to turn her head and look at him right back. "Present moment excluded," she said. "Even then, it could be argued my husband is out being a lot more interesting than I am."

"He's out there being a cliché. Don't give him that much credit."

"Ha ha," she said rather than laughed. "Sometimes I really do like you, Logan."

"Why don't you think you're interesting, Samantha?"

Okay, now she liked him less. "I just think...doesn't everyone think that they have something interesting to say, and really they're just like everyone else? Talk about being a cliché."

"Why do you think that?"

"I... I don't know, Logan. It's just, not everyone thinks they can just be a classic car...restorationist, or whatever your official title is. A lot of people think they can write. Or think they have great ideas that need to be written about. I just... What separates me from them?"

He didn't say anything for a minute. "Whether or not you do anything about it, I guess."

She had nothing to say to that. All she could do was sit with it.

Talking to him was always sharp. She just never knew which way it would cut. She didn't have any other relationships like this. Not that she really considered what they had a relationship. It was a *happenstance*. Because she'd known him since high school, and he and her husband had been best friends since they were in their twenties.

But either way, she had nothing else like this in her life and never had.

She didn't dislike parts of it. He challenged her, and she felt free to challenge him back in a way she never did with anyone else.

She'd been taught that it was better to make things smoother. Her mom had always told her that. Her mother had just been naturally kind. Sure in her opinions on how things were supposed to work, yes, but naturally kind.

You have a strong personality, Samantha. You have to make sure you don't run your husband over. No man likes that.

Well, she never ran her husband over, thank you. She'd learned very young that she couldn't have confrontations without wanting to get out the matchbook and set things on fire, so she'd learned to not have them.

But Logan made her feel confrontational. He also seemed to enable the resulting pyromania.

About ninety minutes out of Flagstaff, they arrived at Little Painted Desert County Park, so marked by a sign that had definitely seen better days. They turned onto a barren road and passed a few picnic tables and a building with graffiti on it.

"What are we here for?" she asked.

"Just about the best view you can imagine."

They drove a short distance, and then the rim became visible. It overlooked rolling, barren hills that looked like they'd been hand-colored by an artist's brush. Dramatic, bold strokes of red, ochre and faded purples. He put the car in Park, and she got out, moving over to the edge and just standing there. Letting the vastness make her small.

This beautiful, brilliant thing she'd never even imagined she might see.

The world was so big, and she was so small in it.

She'd seen little tiny slices of the grandeur of it.

She'd seen little tiny slices of what living could be.

She'd lived one life. One experience.

She felt so hungry then. For all the great and wonderful things she would never see. It was an ache in her soul. An admiration for the immeasurable complexity of it all. Both grief-stricken and heartened that one person couldn't see it all, do it all.

It made it all feel so big.

It made her and her problems feel smaller. More manageable.

Because what was her little tiny marital issue compared to mountains that had stood for untold amounts of time? Beautiful whether she was there to look at them or not.

Maybe this was what Will felt. This crushing awe for everything he couldn't be or see or do.

Except of course that meant when he'd stared into this void, he'd thought the mysteries were contained between a stranger's legs.

She thought maybe it was a little more spiritual than that.

"Thank you," she whispered.

Logan hadn't said anything. She hadn't looked to see if he was standing near her, though she knew that he was.

"I knew you'd like it. It's not crowded like a lot of the other viewpoints and national parks. It's a good place to just sit with yourself."

"Yeah. I love it."

It wasn't enough, but she didn't want to explain to him that she'd just had a whole existential crisis in the space of a breath.

Or maybe it wasn't a crisis. Maybe it was a calling.

To see more.

To be more.

Maybe that was why she'd danced with Jonathan last night. Not that he was comparable to the grandeur before her, but it was something she'd never done. A slice of a life she'd never lived.

Going out, saying yes to sitting and sharing a drink with a stranger.

Maybe that was the value in all of this. She could live different lives for a moment, imagine what it was like to live in the desert instead of the lush, green Pacific Northwest.

Imagine what it would be like if she was the sort of woman who went out dancing.

Or didn't take her morning shower, but just loaded up the car and ate breakfast burritos on her way to stunning natural vistas.

They left, and she realized she hadn't taken a picture. But she knew a photo could never capture that. The colors, the scale.

It wasn't so much about what she'd seen. It was about what being there made her feel. That would stay with her whether she took a picture or not.

They rolled into the Silver Saddle Motel in Santa Fe in the early evening.

The building was a bright yellow, the doors painted turquoise, the office denoted by a big wooden sign and a very large wagon wheel out front. On the side of the big pueblo-style building was a bull and a big bucking bronco. It was truly the stuff of her kitschy dreams.

She followed Logan inside while he booked two rooms for them. This time, instead of being at the opposite end of the building from each other, they were side by side.

She let herself into her room and looked around. There was a cinder block wall, painted white. A patchwork quilt was on the king-sized bed, and there was an oversized painting of a horse, and a cowgirl hat hanging on the wall over said bed.

She realized she really hadn't looked at her phone all day, and when she did, she had about fifty messages from Elysia and Whitney, who had clearly spent a good portion of the day concocting very strange scenarios to explain her silence.

She decided to video call them both without warning as revenge.

"You're alive!" Elysia shrieked.

"Yes, yes," she said. "I was communing with nature. Now I'm communing with this awesome motel room." She turned the camera around and showed the room.

"How is it going?" Whitney said.

"Great, honestly. The sightseeing is amazing, and we're in Santa Fe now, and I can't wait to look around. So I'm thinking dinner out and then time exploring tomorrow."

"Sounds amazing."

"Here's hoping." They chatted for a while longer before hanging up.

Sam did not surprise video call her kids, because she was nice like that. Instead she gave a text check-in to each of them, and they responded at varying times, in accordance with their personalities.

Her oldest responding first, in spite of the fact that he was probably busy with his girlfriend and his adult life.

Then her youngest, who gave her a half-hearted thumbs-up emoji, though in fairness to him, it was late in Madrid.

Then finally her middle, who responded to her I'm safely in Santa Fe with: k

So of course she responded to Aiden with: Thank you, my love, your verbose appreciation of me is always the highlight of my evening.

Lol

Little asshole.

Love you tooooooo xoxox

That earned her a skull emoji, and she considered that a win.

She also considered it a goal to keep moving. Her realizations earlier had felt like they might swallow her whole. That moment had been enough for now.

She had felt it. That yawning divide between what she was, and what existed.

Between Samantha Parker and possibility.

She didn't need to exist in the void. She'd looked at it. She'd acknowledged it.

But tonight she was in Santa Fe. So she would be Sam in Santa Fe, and not Sam in existential dread.

There was no reason for dread, anyway.

This was the perfect opportunity to address some of those regrets. Those feelings of lives unlived, without committing to anything permanent.

Because in the end, they would meet back at the beginning.

She was sure of that.

She texted Logan and told him she was going to find food. Then, without waiting for him, she took the short walk to historic Santa Fe, and left her problems back at the Silver Saddle.

thirteen

She spent the day hunting around Santa Fe, and found some beautiful jewelry and more clothes she didn't need, but she was sightseeing. So.

They'd packed the car up that morning, and Logan had gone off to do whatever he found enjoyable while he'd dropped her off in a central, walkable locale at her request.

He'd offered to leave her the car, but she liked walking.

She went to two different art museums that she never would have been able to go to if she was traveling with her family.

It was mostly very enjoyable, though she decided she still didn't get modern art. But she'd come to that conclusion without her kids shrieking about it looking like a sneeze or a penis, while she tried not to laugh and Will "rested his eyes" over on a bench by the water fountain.

Always nice to confirm those things for yourself.

Around two, Logan texted her.

Time to head to Amarillo.

She gave him her location, and he came by to pick her up

fifteen minutes later. She was wearing her new earrings and necklace, all made from rough-cut gems.

"Those are nice," he said.

"Thanks," she said. "I got the necklace at the last art museum I went to."

"I wish I would have known you were doing museums."

"You…like museums?"

They started down the highway, and he put the top down on the car, the wind whipping hot and dry around them.

She took her hair band off her wrist and quickly tied her hair up—she'd learned that was a must in a convertible, at least for her sanity—and took the top-down wind tunnel sound as her cue to enjoy the scenery rather than the conversation.

But to her surprise, he answered her question over the sound of the wind. "Yes, I do."

"Really?" She turned to look at him.

He shrugged. "Life is weird. Museums are often a nicely displayed collection of that weirdness."

"I never thought of it that way."

"Yep. Bagged and tagged strangeness in display cases."

She thought about the time she'd been to a museum display up in Portland that'd had mummies, and how distinctly it'd hit her that it was such a messed-up, wrong thing to have displays of. It was grave robbery. If it taught her anything about human beings, it was more that they were considered acceptable displays.

"That is true," she said. "These were art museums, though."

"Even better. What people decide to paint or sculpt is very telling. Not just about them, but about humanity."

"I guess the same is true for what articles a person writes," she said, circling back to their earlier conversation about her writing.

It said a lot about what her life centered around, that was for sure.

"And the cars they choose to collect," he said. "What we spend time and money on is who we are."

"I guess today I'm art and overpriced jewelry?"

"Or just yourself."

They spent most of the rest of the drive to Amarillo not talking, the soundtrack the noise of the road and the breeze as they went down the highway.

They checked into the multicolored Big Texan Motel. The facade was painted to look like an Old West main street, each section a different color and shape to look like they were all different buildings. The rooms had wood paneling and wooden-framed beds, horses racing across the bedspreads.

I'm taking you to a honky tonk tonight.

Logan sent a text from wherever his room was. He was far enough way that she hadn't even seen.

I feel like that might be a Big & Rich song I'm not ready to jump into yet?

You're in Texas.

That was a good point. She was in Texas, and like…when in Texas you had to honky-tonk? Or something. She knew it was a huge state and the amount of experiences to be had were likely vast, but standing in this particularly cowboy-looking motel room, this seemed like the next logical experience.

Okay. What time?

Be ready by nine.

She noticed Logan didn't actually ask. Not for anything. He told her how it was going to be and when to get ready, and there was absolutely no softening to make things more palatable.

She was bemused by that.

The way that he just…was himself. Sometimes abrasive, and totally okay with it. That was a man thing, she was pretty sure.

She always cared what people thought. Her mom had drilled that into her.

A woman's job is to make her home comfortable.

Making other people feel good is a strength.

Being able to put your own needs aside isn't a weakness. Look at all the people who can't manage to do that.

Was that a woman thing or a her thing? She had no idea, but what she did know was that she'd never issued demands for anyone to join her at a honky-tonk.

Though apparently now she was going to one.

What did one wear to such a thing? She'd packed limited options, but she had bought a few dresses at the store in Santa Clara, so she decided to pick between the new ones. And did so without outsourcing opinions. She did it with her own opinions.

Which was not easy, and she had to actually just stop looking at herself after a minute because she was picking her body apart like it was carrion for her vulturish issues.

She wasn't usually quite so insecure. But there were circumstances.

That thought projected an image of Logan into her head. Tall and muscular, grinning at her at the gas pump.

A hard pang hit her square in the stomach.

It had *nothing* to do with him.

She was going out with him, she wasn't *going out* with him. They were on a trip together, and it was incidental that he was her tour guide.

They were getting along, but they often got along. It wasn't a total inability to get along with him that made him difficult. It was…

She frowned.

He was difficult, that was all. She was unsure of what to wear because she was unsure about herself, and she'd lost the way she would normally screen an outfit for going out.

Yet you had no issues in Flagstaff when you went to dinner alone.

She needed a less pushy internal narrator.

What's your point?

There. She had no rejoinder for that. She finished getting ready and then walked outside the motel room, looking down at her phone.

Okay, she texted. Ready to honky tonk.

He pulled up less than ten seconds later. "I don't think *honky-tonk* is a verb."

"I disagree."

The only light was from the parking lot lamps that poured harsh blue light straight down from above, and no one looked good in that light.

Except Logan managed to look like the bad boy date she'd never had come to get her for an evening out.

She felt like the good girl. The lamb being led to the wolf's den. Not a forty-year-old woman who knew well the ways of the world, and men, even if just in the abstract sense.

It was not a line of thought she wanted to be having about him. She didn't want to be pondering his adjacency to the big bad wolf in any regard, thank you.

"I've picked out a true dive bar to give you the full experience." He looked her over in a way that made her feel touched. "You might be overdressed."

Great, so she'd made the wrong call after all that. "I didn't know, and I liked the color, so…"

"You look beautiful."

The way he said it, rough and low and like time had suddenly gone slow, made her stop. Made her take a hard breath in.

He shouldn't be saying that to her. They were friends, if they were even that, and they didn't go commenting on each other's looks. She didn't want to be validated by a man, anyway. She was supposed to be validating herself.

Those words weren't supposed to make her hot, and restless, and happy all at once, but they did.

The fact was, Logan was a man who dabbled in debauchery (his words), and so didn't his opinion on her beauty mean something?

Will had always said she was beautiful.

But until this week (she wasn't thinking about that), he hadn't had practical experience of other women. Logan did.

He thought she was beautiful, even if she was overdressed.

She realized she'd been standing there saying nothing for too long. "Thank you."

She should have scolded him. Or something. But she didn't. Or maybe she should say it back? He was beautiful. But it felt too weird to say, so she just didn't.

Instead she got into the car and tried not to project any of the flustered feelings rolling around inside of her onto Logan, because while she might appreciate the compliment, she really didn't need him to know how much.

"So, where is this place?"

"Up the road apiece." He looked at her. "There's a mechanical bull."

"I'm not having a midlife crisis. You must have me confused with my husband."

"Is a midlife crisis necessary to ride a mechanical bull?"

"You don't have to have a midlife crisis to act a fool in a bar, but it helps. You can also be twenty-one. But I'm not twenty-one, either."

He laughed. "I wouldn't want to be twenty-one again."

"Really?"

"Yeah."

"I don't know. I feel like I kind of got dumped back into my twenties…though a twenties I never actually lived since I had three kids and a house by then."

He cleared his throat. "I wouldn't want to go back because of what I would have up ahead."

The comment felt electrified in the moment. She knew why. She just tried not to think about it.

"I didn't mean it in that way," she said. "But in the way that things are shiny and new and you have possibilities. Not that that was the case for me back then. My choices were already made. They still are."

She visualized next September. Meeting at their house, in their driveway, the hot summer air all around them.

I missed you, Will would say. *You were right. I went looking out there, and there was nothing better than us.*

"They don't have to be," he said.

"No, Logan, they do. They are. I made my choice when I was eighteen. I made my choice. I had kids with the man. I built a life with him."

· "When I was eighteen, I went down to California, pissed as hell at my old man, bound and determined to have a whole different life. If I were stuck in that choice, I'd be living in a shack down by a beach somewhere, surfing, drinking beer and trying to pick up college girls. We shouldn't be held to the decisions we make when we're eighteen. Hell, we aren't the same people this many years on."

In some ways, she agreed. But that wasn't how a long marriage worked. You grew and changed together and made a life around those changes.

Isn't that what Will is doing? Growing and changing, and you just don't like it?

No. She maintained that if your changes violated your marriage vows, they weren't fair game.

"I get that. But I don't want everything to change. I want my life back."

"What life, Sam, the one you had or the one you pretend to have?"

The words landed hard, like a bullet to the gut, right as they entered the neon parking lot of The Painted Lady. There was a classic cowgirl neon sign, a woman kicking her leg up as she reclined in a skirt and boots, her hand on the hat on her head.

The building itself wasn't as fancy as the sign.

"I don't know what you mean by that," she said.

"For God's sake." He got out of the car ahead of her and slammed the door behind him without bothering to wait for her.

She scrambled out and followed after him, into the building.

It was dim and disreputable inside. There was a jukebox and a cleared-out section of floor where people were line dancing. In the corner was the mechanical bull, which had drawn a crowd of balding men and young drunk girls, which seemed to draw a firm line beneath her earlier point that she was back in her twenties. Or someone's twenties, anyway. Since she'd already been a wife and mother at that point.

Logan was at the bar, and she saw him hold up two fingers while he was talking to the bartender, as if he was ordering two drinks in spite of the fact that she had clearly pissed him off.

The place was packed full, and she looked around, seeing that if she wanted a breather from her tour guide, she was going to have to line dance or ride the bull, and she wasn't feeling especially keen on either one.

But she decided, with all the cash in her pocket, that if she was going to do something…it was ride the mechanical bull.

So she waded through the crowd and went to stand in the line, behind a tall wiry cowboy type with gray hair. Older. Except she was forced to admit, probably not that much older than she was.

"First time riding the bull?" he asked.

"Yes indeed," she said, watching as a lithe blonde mounted

the back of the beast and drew all eyes for what was more of a simulated sex show than anything else. Until she was unseated, and went flying onto the mats below.

"Still want to do it?" the man in front of her asked.

"Oh yeah. I'm ready."

She watched the bull brutally unseat many a middle-aged man. She realized she was a near middle-aged woman signing up for the same, but *oh well.*

Then it was time for the cowboy in front to go, and he conquered the bull, to the cheers of the crowd.

"Just keep your focus," he said to her as she paid for her turn. As if she was playing in a championship game and not about to do something usually reserved for drunken shenanigans only.

She walked over to the bull and gripped the leather strap, hoisting herself up. "Don't embarrass me," she said, patting the headless beast's shoulder.

It said nothing. Of course.

It wouldn't have even if it'd had a head and was an actual bull.

Then it started moving, and she gripped it as tightly as she could with the one hand, and her knees, and she tried her best to keep the other arm thrown up in the air like she was a real bull rider, when what she actually wanted was to lie across its back and wrap both arms around it and cling to it like she was a baby possum.

She could feel herself starting to slip, and then she went flying. She landed inelegantly on the mats below, and realized belatedly that the dress probably wasn't doing much of anything for her modesty.

Go her, for riding the bull in a dress. She wasn't even a drunk girl and she was giving high-key drunk girl vibes, as her kids would say.

Or at least it's something they would have said at one time. It might all be passé now. She wouldn't know.

She realized she was still on the mats, feeling a little dazed, and she got herself back up. The cowboy met her at the edge of the mats holding a five-dollar bill.

"I'll pay for your next ride."

"Yeah," she said, because she'd already done it. She'd already been thrown off unceremoniously in a dress. Why not try to emerge victorious? "Yeah, I'll do it again."

She got back in line and took a deep breath. That was when she felt it.

Him.

Looking at her.

She turned her head and saw Logan, sitting at the back of the bar at a table for two with a diet soda can in front of the empty chair across from him. He was drinking a beer, his gaze sharp as it cut through everyone in the room, hitting her with exacting accuracy.

She turned away and set her eyes on the bull.

She didn't want to see his anger.

His anger wasn't fair.

She was married to Will. There was nothing wrong with wanting that to work out. There was everything right with it. He was supposed to be Will's best friend. Why was he even Will's friend if he thought so little of *their* life?

He wasn't fair.

It was her turn on the bull again, and again she went. She was unseated even faster this time, but she was not deterred. Even before her cowboy friend held up another five, she'd been determined not to let it best her.

She didn't know why.

She had no idea what she was trying to prove. To herself. To anyone. But she was damn well going to prove it. She got on the back of the bull and went down again. Then took another five and went again. And again.

Finally, on try number five, she did it. She conquered that

bull. She stayed on the whole damned ride, and she didn't care if was stupid, she'd done it. She'd *needed* to do it.

She was sweaty in her victory, but she was completely okay with it. All of the hair and makeup she'd done had likely at this point been for nothing.

But she had vanquished the bull.

Which she'd decided mattered, and if she had to make challenges to also create victories, why the hell not.

That was when her cowboy…touched her.

Like full-on wrapped his hand around her arm. "What do you say we go somewhere a little more quiet?"

"Oh." She blinked. How was this happening to her? How was another man hitting on her in the space of a few days?

Well. She never went to bars. She didn't actually know what she could expect from a normal evening out.

She was creeped out by him touching her like that, and she pulled away. "I… No."

"I paid for all those rides for you."

Anger rushed through her, hot and swift. "I was unaware that was transactional. You didn't lay out your terms and conditions. I would have said no."

"No need to be a bitch."

She was about to do something, haul off and hit him, when suddenly a hand shot out from behind her and gripped the man by his arm. She turned and Logan was right behind her, his eyes icy, his lip curled. "Take your fucking hands off her."

"Hey, buddy, I—"

"Shut your mouth," said Logan. "Walk the other way."

She stepped out of the space between them, and the older man lunged at Logan. Logan punched him. Once. Just once. And laid the guy out flat.

She looked at Logan and down at the floor. "Did you just… Is this a bar fight?"

He looked around the room. "Let's go."

No one was moving to help the guy, presumably because they'd all witnessed his behavior.

"Let's. Go." Then he took her hand in his and started to lead her from the bar, and the combination of things was too much for her to come up with a way to mount a resistance.

She still couldn't believe any of that had happened—from the fight in the car, to the bull, to the punching—and now he had his hand wrapped around hers. Like he just could.

They got out into the parking lot. The air was dry and dusty and warm even with the sun long gone. She turned to him, all lit up in the neon and ready to say something, but he spoke first.

"That was just the dumbest shit. What the hell are you doing?"

"What...what?" she asked. "None of that was my fault, you victim-blaming asshole. What did I do?"

"You don't know anything, do you? I'm not saying you owed the guy anything, but I am saying that if some dude is throwing dollar bills at you in a shithole dive bar, you maybe don't keep taking the dollar bills."

"You were being an asshole, so I needed something to do."

"I was..." He shook his head and took a step back from her. "You're incredible, do you know that?"

"What?"

"There it is," he said. "The denial. The round eyes. The absolute picture of fucking manufactured innocence."

Her heart stumbled over itself. "Logan..."

"You know what I mean. You might have tried to forget, but you know. The thing you're in denial about is us."

fourteen

Hawaii Route 92
Rented Kia Sorento and Ford Mustang
Family vacation—three years ago

"Yes. Okay, that's good to know." She kept her eyes focused on the road ahead. They were in Hawaii, dammit. It was her dream come true. It was tropical. There were palm trees. The water was clear.

Her mother was dead.

That thought kept occurring to her at random moments, and had constantly since that day. It surprised her every time.

My mom is dead. How weird is that?

She's dead.

Patricia Kent is dead.

But the nurse on the phone had told her: Your ultrasound was normal. You don't have the *BRCA* gene. You aren't at a significantly elevated risk for ovarian cancer.

This call was a follow-up to the exam and internal ultrasound she'd just gotten done while in a fog of sadness and anxiety. Just to see if they could see something, anything, in her own body that she needed to be aware of.

She knew she didn't have the gene. She'd known it, but it didn't take the fear away. It didn't do anything to assuage the grief she felt.

"But what can I do?" she asked.

Because if she didn't have the gene neither did her mother. She'd gotten cancer anyway so how did Sam keep herself safe?

Her husband was driving. The kids in the back seat were oddly quiet—a side effect of the six-hour flight, she supposed. It was rush hour. She hadn't thought Hawaii would have a rush hour.

"Dr. Ross anticipated that you would have some questions. She did say that you are a good candidate for a salpingectomy. You get your fallopian tubes out, and then, when you're actually in menopause, we take the rest. We know now that ninety percent of ovarian cancer starts in the tubes, so…"

"Yes. Schedule me for that." She wasn't using her tubes anyway.

She needed to feel like she was taking action. Like she was doing something.

"The surgery center will call with a date for the appointment."

"Okay."

"Sam… I'm sorry about your mother." Did she know the nurse on the phone? Maybe she did. It was a small town. She must have missed it when she'd said her name.

Or she'd heard.

She just didn't care.

It was so hard to care right now.

"Thanks."

Suddenly the nurse sounded emotional. "She was just such a lovely woman."

"She was. She was, but you know, she was very…very at peace." She did this a lot when confronted with the grief of others. She had to make them feel better.

She hadn't yet found the person who could make her feel better.

But life was relentless. It kept moving. The boys still had sports and homework and school. She still had all of her volunteer hours at the schools. She had articles to write. Lunches to make, dinners to make.

It was like she'd been shot in the stomach while running on a treadmill, and she couldn't turn the damn thing off, so she just had to press her hands over the wound and keep on running.

"That's good to hear."

Oh good, I'm glad I could make you feel better.

"Yeah. Well. Thank you. I'll…wait for that phone call. I'm on vacation so…you know, just have them call. Thanks. Bye." She hung up and looked out the passenger window.

"Who was that?" Will asked.

"Doctor's office. Everything looks normal."

"Well, that's great news," Will said.

She didn't feel like it was great news. She didn't know what was wrong with her. "Yeah, she said I can get my tubes out."

"Your… Oh."

"Yeah, I guess most ovarian cancer starts there? I said to call and schedule me."

"Do you really need to do that if you don't have a genetic risk?"

Yes. I have to. I feel like I might have a ticking time bomb inside of me, and why don't you just know that?

"It feels like it'll…help. With anxiety and all of that. If nothing else."

"Isn't surgery its own risk?"

"I guess," she said. "But I need to do it. I need to…"

"How long will recovery be?"

She didn't understand why he couldn't just support her. Why he had to question the decision. She liked to agree with Will. She liked being on the same page.

In all things, she tried to have harmony in their relationship.

But she really felt like this was important.

"I'll have a consult before I actually get it done."

"I just don't want you doing anything crazy because you're…"
He looked back briefly, then lowered his voice. "Because you're
grieving."

Even she, who valued peace in her house above all else,
would have raised holy hell at that statement if she weren't just
so…so tired. So foggy. Such a mess.

On her vacation.

In Hawaii.

Patricia Kent is dead.

*But you're in Hawaii. So suck it up. Everyone else doesn't have to
be miserable just because you are.*

They were unloading everything from the cars when she realized she forgot swimsuits. What the hell mother forgot swimsuits on a trip to Hawaii. She just sat there, staring into the void
that was her brain, trying to go over how she'd packed. She had
lists. She had checked them off. She couldn't even remember.

She never did stuff like this. Ever.

There was an ABC Store across the street, and there was a
high likelihood she'd find board shorts there, and she'd just
have to go as quickly as possible, before the boys wanted to go
down to the beach or get in the pool.

"Shit shit shit," she said into the emptiness of the living room.

"You okay?"

She turned around and saw Logan standing there in the
doorway.

"No," she said. "But we're in Hawaii, so I'm going to get
okay real quick."

"What's wrong?"

"I forgot the boys' swimsuits." She kept digging through the
suitcase. "Oh, and sunblock. For God's sake. This is like mom-
of-the-year status."

"There are stores," he said. "Also, your kids are grown up
enough to pack their own swimsuits."

"They won't, though, and you know that."

He took three steps across the room and reached out, putting his hand on her shoulder. She wanted, very suddenly, to lean on him. To sink into him. She had no right to do that. For one, she shouldn't be wanting to lean against Logan when she was married to Will. For another, Logan had lost his wife.

It might have been seven years, but it was... There was an order to things. A time frame. You were supposed to lose your parents. Maybe not when you were thirty-seven. But it wasn't like she was a child either.

She was done being...parented.

She blinked back sudden tears.

The problem was, she hadn't felt finished being mothered.

Who was going to take care of her after her surgery?

No one took care of you like your mother did.

She wanted to sit down and cry like a motherless child, because she *was* motherless and she hated it, but she had to go buy sunblock and swimsuits.

"Let's go to the store. We can get whatever you need."

"Oh, no, you don't have to go."

"How about just I go, and you sit for a minute."

She thought about that. She wouldn't sit, though. That was the thing. She would end up doing other things. "You don't have to come."

"Let me go with you. We might need some things too. I'm not the organizational mastermind you are. Chloe might not even have shoes."

"She had shoes to get on the plane. Also, she's sixteen, not six."

He smiled, and it felt soothing in some way. "Don't remind me."

"Yeah, I feel your pain."

"Come on, we'll go to the store. You'll see that you can get everything you need, and it doesn't matter if you got everything packed just right."

"I should tell Will."

"He's messing around with the grill. The kids are in the game room downstairs. I know, with Hawaii outside the door. Let's go."

There was something about the gentle authority that made her want to go right with him. She was buried beneath the weight of all of these decisions all the time. Of everything she had to do always.

Of all the organization. She wasn't able to keep track of it right now. She didn't even know what she didn't know.

They walked out of the vacation rental, three floors of glory with a wide deck overlooking Waikiki, and walked from the gravel driveway across the street to the store.

It was more than just a convenience store—though it was very convenient. It had everything. From clothes to sushi to tourist-trap-level merch and everything in between. They got a cart, and she put four masks and snorkels into it. "Just in case," she said.

Suddenly she felt the need to stockpile any and everything she might need. Just in case.

She grabbed three pairs of board shorts. Kukui nut necklaces. Food for the barbecue.

Logan didn't say much of anything. He just pushed the cart. But there was something steady about him being there. Like he was anchoring her.

Not expecting anything from her, just being there. It was sort of a radical experience. To walk and breathe for a second and just look mindlessly at the rows of Oahu-specific bottle openers and hula girls.

He took over at a certain point, getting all the food they needed, and remembering sunblock when she'd nearly forgotten it. He put everything on the belt when they went to check out, and he paid, which she didn't need him to do.

"You planned the whole vacation," he said. "Like you always do."

They stepped outside, all of their items in reusable bags, Logan holding every bag.

"You don't have to be okay," he said.

She stopped there on the sidewalk, the warm, fragrant breeze wrapping itself around her, a stark contrast to the moment. To what he'd just said.

"I do," she said. "If I'm not okay, then who am I?"

"You're still you. But you're a you who's been through a really shitty thing."

She looked at him, and in spite of herself, she smiled. "You know, that really does help. It's been shitty. I don't know what to do about it. There's nothing to do but keep going."

"You can stop sometimes. Catch your breath."

"I can't. If I don't keep on… The boys lost their grandmother. I can't abandon them too. I can't destabilize their lives more than they already have been. I…"

"Sam. Breathe."

So she did. The air was different here, and so was she.

"Thank you."

"You're welcome. Let's go barbecue."

"Honey."

She jerked and turned toward Will. They were lying on a very beautiful beach, and she kept feeling like she was floating off somewhere else.

"You've been really distracted," he said. Like that was a shock.

"Yeah. I was…thinking about… I don't know."

"Good thing we waited to come here when the kids are older so we aren't having to constantly make sure they aren't wandering into the tide."

There was something about that image that made her ache. She wished she were back there. When her mom was alive and the kids were little, and if they had a problem, she could scoop them up into her arms and kiss them and it would be fine. Jude was going to college at the end of the summer, and he'd had his heart broken horribly three months ago.

She couldn't go with him to school.

She couldn't keep him from getting hurt.

"Are you listening?"

She turned to Will, and she could feel it. His impatience with her pain. With the changes this was carving out inside of her. She wanted to be her old self too. She wanted to come out the other side of it fine and whole and exactly who she'd been before, but she didn't know how.

She wanted to yell at her mom about it.

You left me unprepared for this.

Smiling and being kind isn't fixing it.

Being good isn't getting me anywhere.

I want to yell and scream, and I don't want to make other people feel better, but all the platitudes just come out of my mouth even when I don't plan it.

I'm like a robot with a soul that's dying inside, and I don't know what to do.

Logan had been a comfort. Steady and just there in a way she couldn't quite describe. He made her feel like someone else was paying attention. Like someone else was there to handle things if she missed them. There was a steady strength to his presence she'd noticed for the first time when Becca was sick.

She found him sort of challenging a lot of the time, but she could see that there was something to that. He was a strong man. A hard one sometimes. Not always the most effusive.

But he was there when it counted. There for the hard things.

She swallowed.

"I'm listening. I'm sorry. I'm just having…a hard moment. It's okay. I'm okay."

She stood up and started walking toward the ocean. Maybe she would go for a swim and it would get her mind off of everything.

She just wished she could take a break from being herself. And she didn't know how to do that.

It was late and she was outside in the yard, listening to the sounds of the ocean on the beach. She couldn't sleep.

She could never sleep anymore.

So she stayed up and moved until her eyes got too heavy for her to stand it. She leaned against the porch rail and closed her eyes.

"Somehow I thought you'd be up."

It wasn't Will. It was Logan.

She wasn't even surprised.

It was intimate, though, the way he'd said that, his voice low and knowing. Certainly no man other than Will had ever spoken that way to her before. It made her stomach feel tight.

But she kept remembering. All the moments. When he'd seen her. When he'd known her. And right now they felt huge. Magnified.

"Yeah. That's me. Not sleeping again."

"I meant what I said earlier, Sam."

"What? That the cost for the snorkels was outrageous?"

"No. That you don't have to be okay."

It hit her hard this time. She tried to take a breath. "Logan... I do. What if... I don't..."

"Come here," he said.

She saw him, solid and tempting as he'd been earlier, and if he was offering, she was going to take it.

She moved toward him, and he folded her into his arms. He was strong, solid and hot, and he smelled like the sea and skin she wasn't familiar with.

Then all the tears she'd been holding back since that phone

call came. And they came from somewhere deep. Wrenched from her body. Pulled from deep within her soul.

She was shaking with it, but he was more than able to hold her up.

"I have to get surgery," she said, the words miserable and pouty, and she didn't know why she'd said it to him. His wife had gone through multiple surgeries. And worse. But everything she'd held in on the car ride over was bound and determined to come out now, because he'd offered her a place to rest so she didn't have to be strong. And she needed it. Needed to be small and terrified and sad for a minute. "I'm scared and I don't want to, and at the same time I can't…" She sobbed. "I can't leave my kids without their mother. I can't." She looked up at him from where she was pressed against his body. "Oh, I'm so sorry. I'm sorry. I didn't mean that Becca…"

He lifted his hands and cupped her cheeks, wiping her tears away. "Samantha," he said, the name like a caress. "Don't. This is about you. You need this. You don't need to protect me from how hard grief is. How sharp it is. I know." She looked into his blue eyes and was sure she was drowning. "I know," he said again.

She pressed her head into his chest again. His heart was beating so hard she could feel it against her cheek.

Even in the middle of all of this, that stood out.

Even in the middle of her despair.

She lifted her hand and stared at it for a moment, like it belonged to someone else. Then she pressed it against his chest. Against the beating of his heart. She looked up.

There was an intensity to his expression. Something sharp. Determined.

His eyes dropped to her mouth.

She could feel him. Looking at her. Like he was touching her there.

She moved her hand over his chest, and he made a short, masculine sound in the back of his throat.

She knew he wasn't offering comfort anymore.

He was offering something else. Something much, much more dangerous.

It was something she never thought she'd be tempted to take.

But she kept her hand there, and he shifted the way he held her face. Her breath caught.

On the exhale, her sanity returned.

Reality returned.

She stepped away from him, when everything in her resisted.

"Thank you," she whispered.

She couldn't acknowledge it. Neither of them had moved toward the other. They hadn't leaned in. Nothing had happened.

Nothing.

It could have easily all been in her head. She needed it to have been in her head.

She was grief-stricken and she couldn't even remember swimsuits.

Her husband's best friend had offered her comfort.

She had seen something more in it that wasn't there.

That was all. That was all.

fifteen

Now

He'd said it. He'd said it out loud. Her heart was pounding now like it had done that night out on the lanai.

"Logan…"

"I've waited. And waited and *waited* for you to ever acknowledge that."

"Why? Why would I?" she asked, the words exploding from her.

The absurdity of everything with this man. They'd nearly kissed on a Hawaiian island, and now she was screaming at him in a Texas parking lot.

The complexity, the unwanted complication, spanned a country. Spanned years.

"Because it happened."

She shook her head. "I just thought…"

"You're a liar. Most of all to yourself, Samantha Parker."

She felt like he'd gone and bodily thrown her off the back of the bull himself.

"I… I'm not. I… What I was—am—is a married woman,

Logan, and I had a moment of insanity. I had a moment of it, and I didn't do anything. You… Maybe you misunderstood."

"Oh, that is bullshit. We both know I didn't *misunderstand* anything. We both know you wanted me."

"The *misunderstanding* was in the fact that I wasn't prepared to cheat on my husband. I was *tempted*, but I didn't do anything. Even Jesus was tempted. Isn't that what they always say in church? Temptation isn't the sin, it's what you do about it, and I walked away. I think you would have too."

"Do you? I guess we don't have a way of knowing that for sure."

"He's your best friend."

"And you're *you*." He said it with such ferocity. Such conviction. Like she mattered.

"Logan…"

"Samantha. For the love of God. I don't need you to kiss me. I don't need you to… I just need you to stop lying. To *yourself* if not to me."

Panic fluttered in her chest like a trapped bird. "What good does it do?"

She couldn't say why it scared her so much except it felt like she was holding something back. A wall of understanding. She didn't want it to give. She didn't think she wanted to know more.

There was already too much. Life had already changed too much.

It was the ridiculousness of what he'd said earlier that stuck there.

The one you had, or the one you pretend you have?

"I don't care if it's good, bad or indifferent, it's the truth. I don't understand how you think you're going to spend this summer away from Will, and go back to a marriage where neither of you knows the other, and it's just fine."

"I know him," she said.

She knew it was a lie, because she'd have never said her husband would ask for an open relationship, and she frankly still didn't know why he had.

He talked about new experiences and freedom. But why? What did it mean to him? Why was sex freedom?

He doesn't know you want his best friend.

I do not want him. I almost kissed him once. I am not immune to his good looks, but what woman is?

"Sam," Logan bit out.

"Fine. I don't know him. Not how I thought I did. He doesn't know everything about me, and I don't know how… I don't know how the hell you're supposed to have a happy, smooth relationship and share everything. Like, I was supposed to go to him and say, 'Will, so I think I maybe almost kissed Logan'?"

"You could have talked to me about it."

"You aren't my husband."

"I'm clear on that."

She felt enraged and small. She wanted to curl into the nearest alcove and disappear into a ball of frightened outrage. But given that wasn't possible, and he was her ride, she had to have the conversation.

Or get an Uber.

She was starting to think that sounded like an okay solution.

"I don't need this," she said finally.

"I think you do. I think you need to face what your life actually was, so you can figure out if you want to go back to it. The truth is, you didn't know what marriage you were in."

"And you do?"

"I'm saying I fucking do. I didn't know he wanted to sleep with other women. But I knew you wanted to sleep with me. Three years ago, you wanted me, and if I would have kissed you…"

"I said no," she said. "I didn't let you."

"But if I had."

The image nearly brought her to her knees. His mouth meeting hers. All that heat and strength wrapped even more tightly around her. What would she have done?

She didn't have a clear answer to that because she'd been certain she would never be close enough to a man other than Will to be on the verge of kissing him, much less wanting to kiss him. So how could she say for sure what she would have done if he'd actually kissed her?

"It's a dead-end hypothetical because that's all it is. A hypothetical."

"Were you as happy as you think? That's my question."

The question didn't go down easy. It was like a spoonful of frosty dread, going all through her body.

"I was happy," she insisted. "I will be happy again."

"It doesn't matter to you at all that this is an intellectually bankrupt exercise?" His words were just so...hard. There was no attempt at ease or companionability or niceness. It was all just truth. Unvarnished. Awful. "You're using your separation as an opportunity to double down on everything that was wrong before."

"You don't know. You don't..."

But she couldn't argue. She found herself angry mostly at herself. Because she knew the truth. The truth was, you did not let a man get that close to you when you were married if there wasn't something wrong. She had confided in Logan because she didn't feel like she could confide in Will, and that meant nothing good. That meant something was wrong.

She saw it. The first crack in the dam. That little bit of water bursting out. The truth. Then it all just began to crumble. All of it. All the little things that she had ignored. All the ways in which they hadn't been able to communicate.

She was flexible. So flexible.

But just because she could didn't mean that she should be contorting herself into all of those shapes.

Will wasn't awful. She couldn't rewrite that. She didn't want to. He was a wonderful father. He was a good husband. Somewhere along the way, she had gotten so obsessed with being a good wife for him that she hadn't remembered to be the right woman for herself. Hadn't remembered to look after herself and her own needs in any regard. She had surrendered her hold on what she wanted so long ago that she didn't even know what it was.

When her mother died, she hadn't known how to speak up for herself. Hadn't known how to not be okay because it was so imperative to her that she be perfect. Because Will's wife was perfect. She handled everything. He had an important job, and she was the type A homemaker. She had a job that fit around raising kids than was more of a showcase for her skills as a homemaker that it was anything else. Will was endlessly proud of that. That he had a wife who was smart enough to turn homemaking into an income stream.

But it was all bending. Bending to fit. Into a mold that she had fit perfectly when she was eighteen, but that she didn't even know...

Suddenly she felt like she was standing out there alone, a tumbleweed in the middle of the parking lot. What would she have been if she hadn't put herself inside that box when she was eighteen years old?

Like a goldfish in a bowl. Who could only grow as big as the bowl she'd leaped into when she'd been too young to know there was a sea out there.

She had loved the bowl.

She did love it.

She had chosen it.

But she had chosen it at a very specific time in her life. What did that mean for her now?

Well, clearly what it meant for Will was breaking it. What he was doing didn't fit neatly into the fishbowl life. He'd clearly known—seen, felt—the issues in their relationship much more clearly than she had. How long? She had been so angry that he had blindsided her with that, but how was that fair?

She had nearly kissed Logan. That should have been a clue.

It should have been, and if she had kissed him, it would have been undeniable. But she hadn't kissed him. She'd wanted to. Her whole body had been heavy with her desire to do it, and she hadn't done it.

Because what she and Will had was more important to her than physical lust.

Suddenly a spark of fury ignited in her gut.

"You know what," she said, realizing that while conversationally, she might be on the same highway, she was making a left turn. "It just makes me want to punch him in the face. Because I do know what it's like. I know what it's like to feel like I want someone else. I said no. I said no because we were married. We *are* married."

"Well. Presumably he said no until the moment that he decided he would rather risk your anger to get the sex that he wanted."

Again, it was like a slap. Why was he so…him?

"Are you defending him now?"

"You're acting like I'm trying to manipulate the situation, and I'm not. I'm just making you look at it instead of pulling a blanket over your head. Something happened between us, and more than that, we were friends. You acting like you don't like me and you don't get why is some high-level bullshit, Sam. You know what happened between us. Pretending that you don't takes denial to a whole new place. And you know what, I was content to let you sit in the denial of your marriage. But the thing about denial is it all blows apart eventually. Look at you and Will."

"We're not blown apart," she said, pressing her hand to her chest. "We're separated."

A sharp groove carved itself between his eyebrows. "Why is it so important to you? Why is being with him so important to you?"

"Because I love him. He's the father of my children. He is… the love of my life."

"Right. Still."

"That's the thing about being with somebody for a long time. Things happen. They aren't always perfect. They change. You change. But in the end, you make the decision that it's worth being together."

"What if he wants an open marriage at the end? Then you won't want to be with him. Then there's a limit on the change."

"Just stop. Okay?" She closed her eyes. "I like you. I do. You're right. I did pull away from you. Because our…friendship strayed into dangerous territory, and I needed to remind myself exactly whose friend you were. And why I even know you. Really know you. Because of Will. The fact that I was attracted to you made it impossible for us to be close to each other. So yes, I dismissed it. More than that, I pretended it never happened because there was no room for it. I figured it was one-sided anyway."

"Did you really?"

She closed her eyes. "I'm going to be completely honest with you. I haven't thought about it. For years. There was a while, right after it happened, during the vacation, my surgery, all of that, I wasn't myself. I wasn't okay. The *most* okay that I felt was when you…" She closed her eyes. "When you held me. Part of me was grateful for that. For the way that I felt safe. But it was grief, Logan. I absolutely told myself that I was the one that turned it into something…"

"Sexual," he pressed.

"A near kiss isn't *sexual*."

"Ours was."

His voice sent a shiver through her body.

She swallowed, her throat dry. "Yeah. Okay. Ours was. But the thing is… The thing is…in that moment, I had a choice to make, and I chose my life. My *real* life. Not my life when I was in a crisis point. Not my life when I was feeling outside of my body. You can't make decisions like that when you're…when you're barely hanging on. You just can't."

Her words resonated between them. Because wasn't that where she was now? Outside of her life. In a completely different situation than she would normally find herself in. With him.

But he wasn't offering her comfort this time. He was pushing her.

"Maybe not. But as your friend," he said, his voice curving oddly around the word, "it would be remiss of me to not ask you to take this as an opportunity to see who the hell you are. To be honest. About what your life was. Because how in the world are you actually going to create a marriage where either of you is satisfied if you don't actually dig into the bullshit? You're just going to go back to right where you were. Even if he says, 'Fine, I'm done screwing around.' He'll only go do it again. Unless you figure out what the actual *reason* is that he thinks he needs something else."

She hated that everything he said sounded right. "Are you a psychologist?"

"I've been to a fuckton of therapy."

That stopped her. "Really?"

"*Really.* Because when you have a small child and experience a devastating loss, you have to think of people other than yourself and sort your shit out, sometimes by talking to a stranger, even if you would rather die."

"I just didn't think that you…"

"I'm a human being, Sam. I'm a husband, even though I don't have a wife anymore. I'm a father. I have responsibilities." He shoved his hands into the pockets of his jeans and looked up at the sky like the stars might have answers. "I'm not just around when you're there."

That made her feel incredibly guilty. It made her wonder if she had…if she had used him. Because she thought of all the times that she had taken comfort from him…

But then she thought of when she had offered it back. She didn't think that she used him. Not all the way.

"I know that," she said. "I know that you're human being. You're not just a taciturn, difficult man that I cannot seem to find my footing with."

"You can't find your footing with me because you've got a blindfold on. It's hard to see the trail."

That hurt. Mainly because it wasn't completely untrue. She hated him for that a little bit. But she also couldn't deny it.

"Okay. So here I am. My eyes are open." It was such a dangerous thing to say. There in that neon glow. The devastating nature of his features too much right now. That bad boy date impression not fading away at all.

Except this was real life. And he was Logan.

She had nearly kissed him three years ago, and she had never addressed that. Not really. Certainly not out loud. Certainly not with him.

Maybe she had to.

"Okay. I almost kissed you. I almost let you kiss me. However you want to look at that. I felt very, very alone. You made me feel less alone. I felt like you understood me. Back even further than that, watching you with Becca… I just knew that… I could trust you. That anyone could. I knew that you were a good man. I was drawn to that. Because who wouldn't be. You…you had to handle your life after all of that. I think when I was unraveling on that vacation, it was because I was still carrying all the things."

Why did it make her feel guilty? To give voice to this. To

the ways in which she'd felt like Will failed her then. She'd tried to lock it away. She'd tried to blame her sensitivity on her grief. But it was there, apparently, because she could call it all up now far too easily.

Not dealt with. Unexamined. Like so many other things.

She took a sharp breath. "Will is so great at his job. That's all he does. He doesn't manage the household. Or the finances. The food, the vacations, the packing. All of that is on me, and he didn't mean to, but he doesn't know how to handle things when I'm not a hundred percent, and some of that is my fault."

That was truer than she'd realized. She was often her own unsupportive partner. The one demanding she push through.

"It is," she repeated. "It is. I trained him to be that way. I taught him that I would handle all of that stuff. I've packed his lunches every day like he was going off to school. He never learned to do that for himself. The day that I didn't pack his lunch after I had my surgery…he wasn't mad at me. Don't… Please don't get the idea that he's awful. He's not. But he wants everything to be okay. He wants it so badly that sometimes I don't feel like he can sit with the brokenness of it all. I was very broken. You were the only person who offered to try and hold me together. I will always be grateful for that."

He let out a long breath. "It wasn't a hardship to be there for you. Just so you know."

"It wasn't a hardship to be there for you either. Not that I did much."

"You watched Chloe. Three days a week. Do you have any idea how long the list is of people I would have let have my daughter for that length of time in the aftermath of her mother's death? A short list. It's you and Will. What you did for her was no small thing."

There was a hoarseness to his voice, and more emotion behind his words than she could dig into. Like there was a wall up in him too, but she didn't have the strength to contend with what might come out if his crumbled. She was still dealing with the aftermath of her own wall failing.

She just didn't have it in her.

She just didn't. So she let it go. She didn't press. Didn't ask. Didn't even come close.

"Thank you," she said again. "For being there for me now. Because I do appreciate this. I know… I know we're complicated."

We.

We're complicated.

Those words felt wrong, and illicit somehow, and she wanted to deny them and push them away, but that was part of the problem. Part of the issue with what she'd been doing.

She didn't like things that were sharp or jagged either.

How could she be disdainful of Will's inability to sit in brokenness when all she wanted to do was round off the edges? Make them easy. Make them palatable. It was what she did in their life. In their marriage. It was why she hadn't been able to tell him she wasn't okay. It was why she'd had to fold herself into Logan's arms and rest there.

Because they made their marriage such a safe space that it couldn't support anything difficult.

It couldn't support her not fulfilling her role. Couldn't support despair, or doubt or too much change.

She didn't know who she was apart from it either. She wasn't blameless. As much as Will's expectations had been too much for her to handle back then, her own had been the same.

She would have needed something from Will that she couldn't even give to herself, and it had taken somebody outside of that union to look at her and see that she was falling apart.

That was all it was.

When the quiet desperation was coming from inside the house, neither of the people in it could truly hear it. They were too used to it at that point. Too accustomed to ignoring things.

"I will always be there for you," he said. "Even when you are being a stubborn asshole and causing bar fights."

"I like to think that I do neither of those things all that often. That was, in fact, the very first bar fight I even witnessed, much less caused."

"But stubborn asshole is on-brand."

"It is not! I am a lady." She sniffed. "I keep my head down, and I make things easier and smoother for all. As Patricia Kent taught me to do."

When she thought of her mom now, it was no longer the sharpest pain. In fact, it made her happy. Though there were things that she still wished she could say to her, and if ever the pain was sharp, it was because of that.

"You," he said, "are a stubborn little cuss, who finds ways to get what she wants. Are you not out here on this road trip because you didn't accept what Will told you?"

"Well," she said, "sure. But…"

"Yeah. I thought so."

"He is also off having sex with other women," she pointed out.

Gross. She hadn't really thought about that for a couple of days. She had put it behind her. And suddenly, a strange thought occurred to her. "Are you in touch with him?"

He shrugged. "As much as I ever am."

"He's texting you."

"Yes. Occasionally."

"About what I'm…doing?"

"No. Believe me. I have practice not talking to Will about you."

The words were heavy and meaningful. For a moment, she sat there with them. She had written that moment off. She had definitely told herself that even if he was interested in the moment, it was a man thing. A function of his biology and nothing personal. But the way that he was talking about it now.

The way that he remembered it. It made her wonder what he had actually felt then. He actually sat across from Will knowing that he was attracted to Will's wife?

You figured out how to be around him for all these years without ever acknowledging that was your issue with him.

All right. She had done that. She was very good at that. She wasn't necessarily proud of it. Right now she felt childish and foolish. But the explosion had happened, and they had both survived it. So she supposed there were worse things.

"Well. Has he told you…"

"No." It was emphatic. "Even if he had, you're separated."

"Yes. I know. I said that I didn't want to know. I don't want to know. Maybe he decided to go back to church instead of whoring around."

"Yeah, I think you have to go through a ho phase first. You have to be a sinner before you can repent."

"Thank you for that."

"I'm just saying."

"Let's go. Let's go back to the motel. I'm exhausted. Riding that dumb mechanical bull was *dumb*." She wanted to flag her previous statement for word repetition and childishness, but sadly, she wasn't writing a piece. She was living her life. And doing it sort of badly.

"Did you actually just ride it to get away from me?"

"Yes." She started to walk toward the car.

"You were that afraid of talking about this?"

"I'll be really honest with you. I didn't even realize this was what we were talking about. I told you. I have very intentionally not thought about it for a very long time."

"Why do you do that?"

"I don't know," she said honestly.

Maybe it was because she didn't actually know how to be in conflict with herself. Let alone anyone else. Difficult truths were often too hard to swallow. Especially for a woman who had been playing nice and getting along for all this time.

Pleasing everyone around her was so important, and the one time when she hadn't...

Well, she had doubled down on making that okay.

"I was already a sinner, you know," she said, getting in the car.

"Do you mean you getting pregnant with Jude?"

"You know I do. It was very scandalous."

"I guess. I mean, it's the kind of gossip that people are really into. But I wasn't living in town at the time. So I heard about it, but I can't say that I..." He shook his head. "I did think about it. I was shocked. You were...with Will. Still. That was all."

She frowned. "You knew who I was?"

"Yes, ma'am. I knew who you were."

"I didn't really have the impression that you did. You were like the fantasy object of the school. I was kind of a dork."

"Oh, you were very much a dork. But also, isn't it always those girls having freaky sex?"

He revved up the engine right then, and it made her blood feel fizzy.

She pushed away the physical reaction with a forced laugh. "It was not freaky. It was awkward, furtive, guilty sex that we both knew we shouldn't have been having, and we didn't have a condom, because of course we didn't actually mean to any of the times we had sex, because we were told that only bad kids had sex. We thought we were good."

"There is a joke that I want to make here, but I think it would be skirting dangerously close to sacrilege, and I don't want to anger God when we have this much driving left to do."

"Yeah. I know. I get it. There was no holy barrier that stopped us. Surprisingly, good intentions don't keep you from getting pregnant. I'll just never forget that."

This was another thing she preferred to bury. The memories. The guilt. The shame. If she remembered every messed-up thing her mom's friends, her mom, her dad, her old youth pastor, had said to her during that time, she'd have no choice but to set the town on fire and leave in a puff of smoke and hellish destruction.

She didn't.

"It was so…awful," she continued. "Having everyone knowing that I made a mistake. Everyone. Because we had to get married, and I was visibly pregnant at graduation. Even in Jacksonville, nobody gets married before graduation. If you do that, you're clearly pregnant. Many people got married in order to have sex. But the pre-graduation wedding is only if you already had sex."

"It's a town full of busybodies. You shouldn't worry about it."

"When I was eighteen, it was all I worried about. I just hated that. So… I made my bed, and I was determined to put throw pillows on the damn thing. I was determined to make the most out of it."

"That is just like you. Sort of aggressively biddable."

She laughed. "That is maybe the nicest thing anyone has ever said to me."

"I am very nice."

"You're something."

She couldn't call this moment easy. She couldn't call anything between them easy. He was too rough for that. But maybe he was sandpaper to some edges she needed sorting out.

It felt like she had been able to finally let out a breath that she had been holding for three years. She had to tiptoe around the truth of it, even in her own mind.

She had complicated feelings for him. Well. They weren't that complicated. He was sexy. And she was…attracted to him. For the last three years, she let herself think he was attractive, but not that she was attracted to him. So, she could admit it now. She was attracted to him. But being attracted to someone wasn't the same as acting on it. What she'd said about temptation was true. Being tempted wasn't the same as doing. She had honored her marriage vows, thank you very much.

She would continue to.

But if Will could be honest about his desire to sleep with other people, then she could be honest about that.

It had kind of started when Will said that he wanted the open relationship. That honesty. She had been aggressively honest with him in that moment. Maybe this was the thing she'd been missing.

Because she could keep a whole lot of baggage at Will's door, but the dishonesty, that belonged to her. She needed to start telling herself the truth. About everything.

Logan was right. There was no point meeting Will back in the same place, if they were in the same place. She had to figure out what was wrong with her. Not what had made him want other women—she didn't blame herself for that. But what had been missing when she'd nearly kissed another man.

She needed answers. She was only going to get them with honesty.

sixteen

She woke up the next morning with what felt like a hangover. Or maybe she was punch-drunk from the bull riding.

It was hard to say.

Perhaps it was the altercation and surprisingly *gentle* aftermath that had occurred in the parking lot.

She pondered it over coffee and biscuits and gravy at a greasy spoon on their way to the highway that would take them to Oklahoma. By design they were taking this part of the trip a little bit quicker, and she could honestly say that she was grateful for that.

It had been good. She had decided that. It had been good to have the exchange with Logan that she had. But now she wanted a little bit of time away, a little bit of time to herself to reflect on it.

Or hide. In a burrow of blankets. With slippers and a fluffy robe. One or the other. She didn't think that she could be too strongly judged for that.

"You're quiet," Logan said, leaning back on the red vinyl bench, lifting his coffee cup to his lips.

"I haven't had enough caffeine," she said.

"Right."

"Also, you've given me too much think about."

"Not a frequent accusation that I get."

"Somehow I don't believe that. You are...you're not what you appear to be."

"And what do I appear to be, Sam?"

She was suddenly exhausted, because she realized how much time they spent talking about her. She was grateful for the opportunity to talk about him.

"Well. You are a grease monkey. A car guy. *And* you were a jock. Way too good-looking for your own good. You created waves of teenage longing throughout the high school."

He looked too satisfied by that. "Did I?"

"Logan. You were a one-man wrecking crew for a good quarter of the hearts at our school. And I think you know that."

"Nice to hear either way."

"*And,*" she continued, "you never seemed to care all that much. You had that rebel life. You could have been the all-American. That kind of jock. But you weren't. It was like you were getting aggression out on the field or something, not looking for glory."

"Are you a psychiatrist?" he asked, echoing the question she asked him last night.

"No. But I spent a lot of time thinking about people." *Other* people. *And making up stories about myself.*

"Yeah. Well. You're not wrong. So, what about that makes me unexpected?"

"Well, for one, you used the phrase *intellectually bankrupt* last night."

"My vocabulary is unexpected?"

"You're a deeper thinker than it appears on the surface. Or rather, than stereotypes would suggest."

"You like a stereotype, don't you, Sam?" His mouth worked into a half smile, and her stomach went tight.

Whether it was discomfort brought about by the facial expression or from the observation, she wasn't certain. But she was going to go ahead and let it be about the observation. "Why do you say that?"

"Because it allows you to make sense of things. You really want things to make sense."

"Who doesn't?"

"Me. I don't give a shit. Here's the thing. When you go through something in life that doesn't make any sense, that has no meaning, you either go insane, or you stop expecting life to be what you ask it to."

"See, this is what I never expect from you. The philosophy."

"I have a lot of time to think. Thankfully, my job means that I talk to people in a limited capacity. The rest of the time I spend in my head or..."

"If you say 'listening to podcasts' then you're going to move yourself back into stereotype territory."

"Audiobooks." He grinned.

"Just barely dodged the stereotype," she said.

"Are you going to eat the rest of your biscuit?" He gestured to the half a biscuit that was still swimming in creamy gravy on her plate.

"No. But I would like to take some coffee to go."

He polished off the biscuit while she got a to-go cup, and then they were back on the road.

They made empty conversation through Oklahoma, stopping at a hotel in Springfield, Missouri, that was affiliated with Bass Pro Shop. "Because you have to stay at the Angler's Lodge," Logan had explained.

"I don't know that you do," she said, wandering through the lobby, which was antler-heavy as far as the decor went.

When she got to her room, she found no different.

Though she appreciated that one of the throw pillows had antlers printed on it, just the right size for her to lay her head down and give herself the appearance that she herself had antlers. She took a selfie, sent it to her friends and her kids.

Her oldest son sent back a skull.

The other kids didn't answer.

Her friends gave appropriate acknowledgment LOL's and ha's. Fine.

She thought she was cute *and* funny.

The next morning, they drove through Missouri, up into Illinois, making the final push to Chicago in a particularly long and torturous day.

The city was a stark contrast to anywhere else they'd been on the trip.

The hotel they stayed in even more so.

The high-rise with a view of the river, close to the Magnificent Mile. While Logan made his exchange with the car's owner the next day, she shopped, and wandered along the edge of Lake Erie. She had never seen one of the Great Lakes before. It was like standing on the edge of the ocean.

She walked along the harbor there, and stopped when she heard Frank Sinatra. She smiled, listening to the music filtering from one of the boats tethered there.

It was one of those strange, surreal experiences that she knew she would always remember. It was funny. Those moments in life.

That were just a little too perfect. Almost as if they were scripted. Maybe it was strange to ponder the appearance of background music at an opportune moment on quite that level, but nothing in her life had felt scripted for the last few weeks. So it was just sort of nice to rest in the softness of the moment. The romanticism of it. That made her smile too. That she could feel a sense of romanticism, walking by herself.

She took selfies in front of the big bean at the park, and wandered through the Art Institute. She particularly loved the display of Western art, and for the first time in a while found herself reflexively thinking that she should text Will.

Because he probably would've liked the bronze statue of the cowboy on a horse, and she would've texted him and said it was an art museum he would probably enjoy.

Except she didn't. Because they weren't speaking.

Being away from home made it a little bit easier. Being outside of her experience. Her normal life. But it didn't erase those well-worn pathways, those habits that were more a part of herself, her subconscious, than she'd realized.

She met with Logan again at dinnertime, and they had deepdish pizza, and she felt wistful at having the new experience without anyone in her family here, and she didn't know why she was feeling quite so melancholy.

She missed her kids. She missed a life she didn't think she could ever go back to. She wasn't sure why it was so harsh right now. Maybe because she should have been on a family vacation this time of year.

But she wouldn't have been anyway since her kids were off having lives.

"You seem like you're already across the country," Logan said.

"No," she responded. "I'm just marinating in parental guilt."

"Why?"

"Because I'm a parent and it's what we do?"

"Fair. But you shouldn't feel guilty."

"I think you and I both know I actually have a lot of things to feel guilty about."

"I thought temptation wasn't sin?"

"Yeah. Well. Sorry. It's not that simple for me. I feel guilty about it. That's why I didn't want to acknowledge it."

"I don't think that's true. I think you didn't want to acknowledge it because then it would be an action item. You really didn't want to do anything about the issues in your marriage."

"Stop it. You don't have an insider's perspective on my marriage. Quit acting like you do."

"Would you say that to Elysia? Or Whitney?"

"No," she said. She took another bite of pizza. "I also have never even *nearly* kissed one of them."

"I see. So I don't get to say anything because I'm a man."

"A man that I almost kissed. Yes."

"Just casually using that in conversation now?"

"You wanted honesty, Logan. Here it is."

"Yet somehow not."

She rolled her eyes. "Well, it's all about *right now*."

"Fair enough."

She had trouble sleeping that night. She sat in a chair by her sixteenth-floor window, looking out at the river below. At the boats gliding across the water, and all the lights shimmering across the surface. It was a beautiful city, and she wished that she had built more time into this portion of the trip. She didn't have to leave for the West Coast at the same time Logan did. But they had booked flights on the same plane.

She was grumpy and underslept by the time they arrived at O'Hare, which was an absolute zoo. The TSA lines were unreal, and she was beginning to get worried they would miss their plane by the time they finally got to the front of the line.

When they got to their gate, they sat in the uncomfortable black chairs closest to the podium.

"What group are you in?"

"Four," he said.

"Four? You're flying economy?"

The amusement that pulled at the corner of his mouth was distracting. "Yes, Sam."

"Like, not to be gauche or anything, but you're kind of rich."

"I don't see the point of spending my riches on what is essentially a chair hovering 36,000 feet above the ground. I'm 36,000 feet above the ground whether I'm in a fancy chair or not."

"You get to board first. And they give you champagne."

"Are you in boarding group one?"

"Yes, I am," she said. "Because the whole rest of this road trip was paid for, plus part of this ticket as well. Also, it's fancy. So."

Now she felt the need to justify it.

"Right. Well, enjoy."

She got up when her group was called and sat happily in her seat. She lifted her glass of champagne when Logan walked by ten minutes later. He gave her that same half smile he'd given her at the diner a few days ago, and her stomach did the exact same thing.

Maybe that was why when she got served ice cream for dessert after what was a very lovely meal, she bought Wi-Fi for the sole purpose of texting him a picture. He sent back a middle finger emoji.

She smiled, and leaned back in her seat, closing her eyes.

The first journey was done. She would get a break now.

Yes, some of that involved facing parts of her life she didn't especially want to face. But she could handle it. She had to.

She had felt, often, that she was more grown-up than most women her age. Than most people her age. After all, she had thrown herself into adulthood as a teenager. Right then, she felt like this was maybe her first step into something even more grown-up. She couldn't explain it.

Bringing up the past with Logan made the future feel a lot more precarious than she'd imagined it could feel.

She'd been totally certain of where she wanted to end up at the end of the summer.

Why did one memory have the power to change that?

seventeen

Oregon Trail route
1962 Ferrari Spyder
Now

A two-week break didn't help. She'd spent the time in a vacation rental on the Olympic Peninsula because it seemed like a fun place to go, and she'd written a piece about the first road trip—focusing on the sights and the car, and not the personal parts.

She ended up selling it to one of sites she worked with often, with the grabby header *I Went Cross-Country in a Classic Car—Here's What I Learned.*

She'd said she learned how to pack efficiently and where to get the best coffee.

She was lying a little. She thought again about what Logan had said—about writing a book.

The idea of putting her honest feelings out there made her feel so…

Ugh.

Her feelings were messy, and she did not present as having a messy life.

She didn't want to…admit that her insides didn't match the outside, and writing more than just a breezy article would force her to do that.

Logan seemed bound and determined to force her to do that.

It wasn't just the attraction that she had been forced to acknowledge, but the intensity of the way that he forced her to examine things. The honesty with which he approached it all.

She'd spent the night at Elysia's the night before she was set to leave with Logan, and she hadn't even come to terms with the reality of all that time with him. Again.

They were taking the Oregon Trail route, heading all the way from Willamette Valley to Boston.

It was *a lot* of him. A lot.

When he pulled up with the gleaming red car, she felt determined, and also a little bit apprehensive.

The time that she had spent by herself seemed so much less intense than the time on the road with him.

She'd had a little bit of reprieve. While she had been working on certain things, she hadn't felt quite so steeped in the most intense of the emotions.

Suddenly all of the emotional intensity seemed to hit her, and the conduit seemed to be Logan's blue eyes.

What was she doing reacting to a man's gaze like that? Like a middle school girl.

"You ready?" he asked.

No. Not really.

"Yeah. Ready."

He gave her first driving shift. The Ferrari was much smaller than the previous car, with tan leather seats, a spindly gear shift and the kind of power that made her heart race.

This experience might turn her into a car person yet.

There was something wildly unsettling and exciting about that thought. Because it was admitting this was going to change her.

That it already had.

He set the map for Multnomah Falls, and they drove up I-5 for five hours, mountains turning into fields of sheep and clover before becoming mountains again, the Columbia River flowing broad and slow beside them.

It was impossible to miss the falls from the road. Even from the parking lot across the street, the sound was thunderously loud, the water spilling down over a sheer rock face into a pool below, which spilled over again, cutting through lush ferns and moss-covered stones.

There was a restaurant and lodge near the falls and the hiking trails. It had the look of a storybook cottage with a steep pitched roof and walls made of gray stone. They went into the dining area, the back wall all windows and sunlight pouring in, counteracting the heaviness of the stone.

They sat and ordered, and when their food arrived, Logan looked at her.

"How's Ethan doing?" he asked.

"Good." She nodded. "He's doing good. Probably doing things I wish he wouldn't do, but every time I talk to him, he's happy."

"Glad to hear it."

"And Chloe?" she asked.

"I hope not partying too much. But she is my kid. So it's hard to say, and I can't be too judgmental."

"I'll let you in on a secret," she said. "You can be as judgmental as you want. You don't have to be fair. You are allowed to have hideous double standards when it comes to your kids."

He laughed. "Thanks. It does often feel hypocritical that I don't want her going out and doing the things that I do."

"It isn't hypocritical," she said. She frowned. "The thing is, when you're her age, you don't have a concept of things. You don't know what you're getting. Take that from somebody who grew up too quickly. You think you know so much. But you just don't. I thought I did. Now...now what the hell do I know? Logan, honestly, I don't know anything."

"That makes it tough. Trying to launch these kids out. We know everything we don't know. We also know that we know years' worth more than they do."

"I wonder if that's the only way to survive your teen years and your twenties. Thinking you know everything. It's what makes it fun. Livable. Not terrifying."

"Agreed. A feature, not a bug."

"Definitely. Though it's hard to watch."

He leaned back in his chair. "We're going to stay at Skamania Lodge tonight," he said. "It's nice. You'll like it. Then we'll get back to your regularly scheduled roadside horrors. Once we get a little further along. But I thought there's nothing wrong with enjoying some of the natural beauty in style."

She was happy enough with the subject change from heavy things, and liked the idea of nice accommodations.

"I figured it'd be good," he continued. "Since a little birdie told me that you like fancy."

"Why are you suddenly concerned with my enjoyment of things that are fancy?"

"Your first-class booking."

"Honestly, I thought you would be flying first-class too."

"And yet you weren't concerned about it enough to make sure that you were sitting next to me."

"No. I wasn't. But I'd rather sit fancy than sit with you."

He raised his eyebrows, then shook his head, letting out a slow breath as he ate the last of his french fries. "Well. Yeah, apparently."

She had been teasing. She hadn't meant it to have any kind of seriousness. But he had clearly taken it a little bit deeper than she meant.

"Well, then, since you're such a fancy lady," he said, making a clear effort to lighten his tone, "you probably aren't going to go on the zip line."

This irritated her. Sure, she'd never considered zip-lining in her life, but that didn't mean she was opposed, or never would. He didn't know her. "A zip line?"

"There's a big zip line course at the lodge."

"That sounds terrifying. Tell me more."

"Well. Considering you are after adventure, I thought you might appreciate the opportunity to try something new."

"But a zip line involves heights." That scared her.

"And speed. You do seem like kind of woman who likes speed. We *are* in a Ferrari. After all."

"All right. Well. Maybe. Maybe I'll try it."

"We can ease you into it. We can start with the bridge up there."

She wrinkled her nose. "The bridge gives me anxiety."

"It's got a beautiful view." She felt like this was some weird turning point. A gauntlet. "Come on."

So she did.

They finished their lunch and paid, then went back outside to the main part of the park, the trail that led up to the bridge. Two tiny children, probably four and six, scampered toward them, heading to their parents.

Emotion knocked her right in the chest, stealing her air. Her breath. She turned and watched as the mother and father each lifted one child up off the ground, the mom stroking her little boy's hair.

"Aw…that's… It's sweet," she whispered. They continued walking up the trail, and she pressed her hand to her chest, a spot right at the center suddenly sore.

She looked down at her feet. At the trail.

She was looking now. At where the eroded parts were, the rocks buried halfway in the mud. She was paying attention to why she lost her footing sometimes.

They both knew why now. So why not be honest. Why not tell him exactly what she was thinking about.

It was what had drawn her to him. Before.

Before she'd gotten scared of that connection.

She could say things to him and he didn't really try to solve the problem. He didn't seem desperate to make it go away.

"Do you know..." she said. "Sometimes I see something like that. Families. Small children. I can't tell if I ache for when my kids were little...or when I was little. It's all the same thing. It's time I can't get back. It's... I miss mothering in that way. Some days I really miss being mothered. Everything changes, always."

"Yeah. It does."

"It just feels sad sometimes. To know so profoundly that that part of my life is over. At forty. My kids are grown. My mother is gone. I just..."

They stopped walking, and he turned to face her, grabbing hold of her wrist. His grip was firm, not painful. Steadying. "You have life left. To be who you want. Whatever you want."

He released his hold and walked ahead.

She felt...destabilized.

Whatever you want...

She felt like she was holding on so tightly to her idea of what her life *should* be. It was all tangled up in those sharp moments that made her chest hurt. The things that she wished she could go back to.

She was accepting that her marriage wasn't what she'd believed it to be. What she'd wanted it to be, so desperately.

They traversed the switchbacks of the trail until they came to the bridge. They stood there, the pounding falls so close that the mist brushed her face.

The mist felt like a metaphor in a way she couldn't quite work out. All this water. Pouring down the rocks. There was always more water, but it wasn't the *same* water. It couldn't flow backward.

She was trying. Trying to meet Will back around again at the beginning. But the problem with a circle was that you ended up back where you started.

You might as well be going backward.

She took a breath. "We can go."

"Let's go up the trail. Come on. You came all this way. Let's see the view."

She was kind of over how deep every comment was making her think, but there was something to that too.

They hiked up a trail that went straight up the side of a hill, overlooking the valley below.

"You know," he said. "A lot of people have this freedom on the front of their lives. With all that rashness of youth, like you were just talking about. But you...you have it now. No one gets to tell you what to do with it. Don't leave it up to Will. The final decision. That's all."

He turned away from her and started back down the trail without waiting for her.

She couldn't argue with him. Not this time. Not now. She just let his words play over and over again as they hiked back down the trail and got back to the car.

The Bel Air had been a special sort of nostalgia, the kind that they were both too young for, but that evoked strong imagery of movies they'd seen. The Ferrari was just pure fun.

They drove over the Bridge of the Gods, and traversed the narrow roads to Skamania Lodge, which was over the border into Washington.

The room was simple and tasteful, and she only felt slightly disappointed that she couldn't unpack and settle in. It was all kind of grueling. This living out of a suitcase. But it was different. Maybe there was something to what Logan had said. It was up to her now.

She had these three remaining months to sort this out.

To make sure she didn't go backward.

She didn't have anyone else to take care of right now. It was all her.

She loved her kids, just like she cared about her friends and wanted to be in contact with them. She would still do things for her kids. But she wasn't bending her life around anyone else right now.

She had never lived alone.

It was an interesting experience, being by herself in these rooms. In the vacation rentals. Sometimes it felt too quiet, and sometimes she enjoyed it. But it was new. Yes, she ached sometimes, for time gone by, for small, bouncing children, or even back further to her own childhood. To family TV on Sunday nights. *Dr. Quinn, Medicine Woman*, and *America's Funniest Home Videos*, a bowl of popcorn, followed by some fudge pops.

Yeah, she missed those things.

But maybe wanting to get back to Will was like wishing she could rewind all the way back to that.

It was so funny to realize she had never lived by herself. It had only just now occurred to her. Maybe it was because she felt like she was being, and not really living.

She needed to be living. Every moment of this time. She couldn't wish this summer would go faster, couldn't will it away.

Otherwise, just like Logan said, she'd be right back where she started. Right in the same problems.

She met Logan down in the lobby area. "All right," she said. "Take me to the zip line."

"You're really going on it?"

"Yes. I thought about what you said. Well, I think about a lot of things that you've said. But I mean recently, just what you...just said. You're right. I have so many opportunities to do anything. As someone who knows more than they did, and also knows how much they don't know, that is pretty amazing. I would be silly to miss this opportunity."

They went and bought passes for the zip line, and were luckily in time for an upcoming group. Their two guides greeted them and a group of about six other people, and walked them across the street and up a trail to a yurt that was nestled in the trees. They were brought inside, with harnesses laid out on the floor for them to step into.

It all seemed unwieldy and unfamiliar. But they also gave her a helmet, which she found comforting.

They walked along the trail, and one of their guides unlocked a gate to a flight of stairs that led up, up into the trees, closed off from people who weren't in the tour. The stairs led to the first platform. Once they were on the platform, one guide hooked a harness strap with a carabiner on the end of it to a line that was attached to the tree that supported the platform. There were two hooks like that on the harness, and one was always attached to a line, even when the rider was transferred from one network of cables to another. Even if you fell, you'd be safe.

As nervous as she was, even she was relatively satisfied that there were enough safety mechanisms engaged, that it would require a pretty catastrophic failure of all of them at once, and that was unlikely.

She wasn't a terribly anxious person, but she liked to have all of her i's dotted and t's crossed. Thank you.

"Have you ever done this before?" she whispered out of the side of her mouth to Logan as the instructors continued on with the overview.

"Nope."

"But I thought you… I was so certain that you…"

"It's a new adventure for everyone," he said, far too chipper and not nervous. Given the fact that they were like twenty feet off the ground and were about to go careening through a forest. The first instructor went—they explained that one would spot them on that end, and the other would be on this end—and after an interval, the next person was clipped into the ready position, and off they went, screaming at high speed along the course.

"You want to go first?" Logan asked.

"I do not," she said.

He grinned and stepped into position. They watched as the guide transferred his hooks to the main line that ran between the platforms, and then Logan lifted his feet and went blitzing down the line.

She took a sharp breath, and looked down, and felt the resulting impact of looking straight down like that shoot up between her thighs. She squeezed her knees together, trying to stop that sensation.

"Are you ready?" the instructor asked.

"I'm not sure."

"Just hold on. You'll be fine. Keep your hands here."

"Uh...like this?"

"Yes. Just remember, hands on fabric, not on metal."

Great, now there were instructions.

"Hands on fabric."

"Keep your feet up so when you get to the other side, you don't hit the platform. But don't hold them out. You don't want to kick your other guide."

That was when she knew. She would never be ready. She just had to go. She lifted her feet and launched off the platform. Then she went flying. At first it was terrifying. She was weaving through the trees, clearing them easily, picking up speed as she went.

Then terror turned to joy.

It was like flying.

She slowed when the other platform came into view and stepped onto the landing pad there.

The other instructor unhooked her, one clasp at a time, moving her over to him.

"That was amazing," she said, looking up at Logan.

"Yeah," Logan agreed. "It's pretty amazing."

She loved it. The whole experience. Maybe she was a thrill seeker. She never had been. Everything she had ever done had been about being safe. She had worked so very hard to be safe.

Now she'd done something sort of daring and had enjoyed herself. When they finished, they went back to the resort and sat on the expansive deck overlooking a field and mountains.

She ordered a beer, which she never did, because she felt like maybe it paired well with zip-lining and facing fears.

It didn't. She ended up ordering a Diet Coke and letting Logan finish the rest of the beer.

"So," she said. "Honest question. Since you'd never tried zip-lining before...why did we do it?"

He looked out over the field. The mountains. "Because. I figure I have a lot of life left to live too."

eighteen

They headed down south toward Idaho the next day, yet further proof that route had nothing to do with efficiency and everything to do with whatever this was.

This exploration of life she had to live. That he had to live.

They followed the Oregon Trail route, and she couldn't help but get lost in thought pondering the people that had chosen to come out West. They had left everything behind. Uprooted everything they had ever known in order to start a life somewhere with opportunity. Maybe. There was no way they could have known if the life that they would find out West would actually be better than the one they had left back East. She marveled at that kind of bravery. She wasn't sure she had it. Sure, she had started the new life. Well, a new season of her life. But it wasn't something she had really chosen.

You have to stop thinking that way. Will didn't decide that you should go zip-lining. Or any of the other things that you're going to do.

No. He hadn't. *She* was out driving a Ferrari in the middle of nowhere in Idaho. She had never seen that coming. She really liked driving the Ferrari. They stopped in Idaho for dinner, going to a restaurant that billed itself as a french fry place, serving them as the main course with burgers on the side. Famous potatoes and all. Then they spent the night in a rather nondescript hotel—nothing like the kind they'd found on Route 66—and headed out to Wyoming the next morning.

She was overawed with Wyoming. The expanse of it. The scope of the mountains.

One thing she liked most about seeing all these different places was that it made her feel like she had a different perspective. Or maybe it was just a different view. Trying to imagine herself as a pioneer, as someone who chose to be brave. As someone who took the risk...to try something new, not knowing how it would turn out.

She hadn't been able to do that. All these years, she hadn't been able to do that. She had wanted to be a good daughter, a good wife, a good mother. Those things had come before everything else.

"Want do you want to do?"

"Probably find a burger soon?"

She shook her head. "No. I mean... Is there anything that you want to do that you haven't done?"

He looked at her for a moment and she felt it, down to her toes. "Well. That is a loaded question."

"It doesn't have to be. We can be honest. With each other, right?"

"I guess," he said. "All right. I haven't ever traveled overseas. I've been to Canada, but it's the only other country that I have been to. I sort of figured that I'd like to do that someday. But responsibilities, Chloe at home, and then work. I just haven't ever done it."

She breathed out, and it sounded more wistful than she intended. She felt more wistful than she'd realized. "I've always wanted to do that. I haven't either. You know... There's some things that I just... They sit there, in the back of my mind, not pressing, but when I think of them, they make my stomach feel like it's hollowed out. I get this excited feeling. The sense of anticipation. Then part of me just thinks… I think I have to do it the next time around." She laughed. Because until she'd said that out loud, she hadn't really realized she thought that, in those terms. But she did. "But there is no next time around, is there? I don't even believe in reincarnation. I just… That thought just popped into my head. It placates me when I think of something that I can't have. I… I have to figure out how to do it all *this* time around. This only time."

It was sobering.

"Okay," he said slowly. "What is it that you want?"

"I just said something that I wanted."

"You said something that *I* wanted back to me. You share it. That's fine. But you tell me something right now that you've never been able to do, that you've always wanted to do. Big or small."

"Ummm… I don't know. Get a tattoo." She said it, stream of consciousness, and hadn't fully realized how much that was true until she said it either. "I *have* always wanted one. But Will doesn't like them. My mom hated them too. You know, I couldn't really take *two* no votes against that."

He looked at her, a sidelong glance from the driver's seat. "It's your body," he said.

"Yes. And my mother created that body, and my husband… Well."

"Do you hear yourself?"

"I do. I do. I don't act like it, but if people aren't happy with a choice that I make… I mean, the people that are closest to me. Then I'm not really going to be happy with it either."

For so long, one of the most important things to her had been making the people around her happy with her. Getting along.

"I just… It seems like, you know, given we do only have one life, you want to be in harmony as much as possible." That might have been more impactful if she wasn't questioning every single thing about her life. "But then, what do I know? I wasn't actually doing myself any favors, was I? I thought I was."

"You're not wrong, really," he said. "We've all done it. Made a decision because it was the easy one. Because who wants to live their life on a battlefield?"

"Nobody," she said. "But…you know, it's the kind of thing that sticks in my head even now. That my mom would hate a tattoo. You know what, I wanted to get one for her. I wanted to get lavender. Because she—" She stopped for a moment, looking out at the scenery, blinking back tears. "When she was in hospice, she would rub lavender oil on her hands. The smell was soothing. I love that it comforted her. I love that there was something that did. Among all of the hard stuff, I was just glad that she had something, and it felt like a way to remember without, you know, getting a portrait or something. Which, if that's what people want to do, that's fine."

"The tribute's not for *her*, not really. It's for you. If you want it, you should get it."

"But it's in the back of my head… Her voice. Being disappointed in me, and I…" She stopped herself. Guilt washed over her. She didn't know how to explain that. That she still wanted to please her mother, as much as she sometimes resented that her mother had so many rules. Even swearing was something she never would've done in front of her mother. She did it sometimes, because Will did, and the boys certainly did.

But she felt a kick of guilt. Guilt was just so easy for her to access.

She felt guilty when she didn't have dinner ready for Will. She felt guilty when she didn't make her bed. Most of all, she felt lingering guilt over the pregnancy that had been her reason for marrying Will in the first place.

They'd had to get married, before high school finished, because she was pregnant, and for so many years she'd told the story differently. Who admitted to a shotgun wedding? She talked about their marriage as if it had been a certainty—pregnancy or not.

But she didn't know that. It was impossible to know that. Maybe she would have gone away to college. Maybe he would have too. Maybe they would have been a casualty of the distance. Of time. Of age.

If they'd waited, they might not have followed through with it at all.

That was too many dark and hollow thoughts for a road quite this lonely.

"Does it ever feel like you still have to do the things that Becca would want?" Bringing up his wife wasn't really an escape from the dark and lonely thoughts. She probably shouldn't have done it.

But he was the only person she'd ever talked to about this. This honestly. On this level.

The question earned her another long, slow look from his side of the car. "I sincerely doubt my wife would approve of some of the things that I do. She would think that it was self-destructive. She would say that I was better than the things I do when I'm lonely and sad, angry at the world. But she'd be wrong. I can't be better than that. Because I do it. She wasn't right about everything." He stared out ahead at the road. "About me, about us. Just because she died doesn't mean she's a saint."

He didn't say it bitter, or mean. It was just a very simple, accepted statement. She wanted to know more. Wanted to know how he could say that, while holding all the love he had for her at the same time.

"Tell me more about that," she said.

"It's easy, to start glossing things over once somebody is gone. It would be easy for me to pretend that my marriage to Becca was perfect. That she and I didn't have problems. That we were a perfect couple, who would have absolutely been married forever, and would have been happy the whole time." He thumped his hand against the steering wheel. "But I don't know that, Samantha. I can't know it. Hell, watching you and Will has drawn a line under that. If we'd had ten more years together, who knows what those years would have been like. The ten that we had weren't perfect. I loved her, but we fought." He cleared his throat. "She threatened to divorce me a couple of times."

"Why?" she asked, completely blindsided by that revelation.

"Just regular couple stuff. At first she regretted getting married so young. That was a regular thread in the fighting until Chloe came along. Then she was a lot more settled. Content. I don't think she ever regretted being a mother that young. But I didn't make very much money at first, so we had stress over that. I wasn't as helpful to her as I should have been. You know, it is just what it is. In the end, she made sure I knew that she was happy. She said… 'Isn't it stupid that I used to regret getting so serious so young. When young was all I had.'" His voice had gone low, and her throat tightened, emotion welling up inside of her, her eyes glossy with tears.

"I'm so sorry," she said. "It's just awful. It's just awful."

"It is. We made our peace. With the time that we had. But we will never know what would've happened if there was more time. I'm grateful that we got to say the things that needed saying. That she got to clear the air. I got to apologize for not helping around the house enough. For staying out too late sometimes. Not understanding how stressful it was, staying home with the baby. Not at first. Feeling like I was the one doing the hard work, you know. That dumb stuff."

It hooked into something she recognized. Deep in her heart. An issue that she had often felt was simmering below the surface between her and Will, whether she wanted to think about it or not.

"Yeah. I know. The great workload conflict." She swallowed hard. "It has taken me all these years to begin to untangle what I wish I would've said to my mom. Positive and negative. But

I was too afraid to say it. I looked at her lying there in the bed, and the words just stuck in my throat. I couldn't tell her what she meant to me. I couldn't tell her how she made me afraid. Of the parts of myself that were strong-willed. The parts of myself that were difficult or angry. How she made me fearful sometimes of my own instincts. But how also at the same time I knew she loved me so much, and she was such a good grandma to my kids, and a good wife to my dad, and... I didn't say any of it. Then there was no more time. What the hell are you even afraid of when another person is lying there dying and there *is no more time*? What's the point of being placating? What's the point of being dishonest? What's the point of being silent? But I was silent. I couldn't stand the weight of it. I let it crush everything I had to say. I just don't get to say it now. So instead I'm just still afraid of tattoos and what she would think...what she would think if she knew that Will had asked for an open marriage. What she'd think if she knew that I left. That I almost kissed you." She rubbed her hands over her face. "If she knew that, in her name, I toyed with the idea of a tattoo, she would come back from the grave and slap me."

Logan shifted. "Well, if she did that, then you'd have a chance to tell her what you needed to."

"Yeah," she said, laughing in spite of herself. "So that would be the upshot." She blinked back her sorrow. "I guess I can't live for her anymore either."

"No," he said. "That's another thing. The thing I've accepted after a whole decade of living with loss. I want to make sure that I do right by Chloe, that Chloe remembers Becca. In that sense, I want to live a life, and raise our child, in a way that would make her happy. But when it comes to me, I can't live for her. Because she isn't here for me to live for. If I don't find other things, I might as well lay down and die. But I had Chloe."

"And zip lines," she said.

"Exactly. I wish she could see how successful the business became. That's the worst part of losing somebody. Someone you were trying to make proud. None of it matters. I would have bought first-class seats for her."

"I know," she said. "I meant what I said. Watching you with her was such a real expression of love. I will never forget it as long as I live. Actually knowing that you are like the rest of us, imperfect, makes it matter even more."

"But you thought you and Will were perfect until relatively recently."

She laughed. "Yeah. Don't remind me of what an idiot I am. Because I am an idiot. An idiot who really wants a tattoo."

"A tattoo."

"I *would* like a tattoo," she said, affirming it for herself.

"You *really* want a tattoo?"

"Yes. Because you're right. It's my body. My tribute. It's not to make her proud. It's to help me remember."

"Then we'll get you a tattoo."

"I appreciate it."

"It's a full-service tour. Traveling the majestic Oregon Trail, making stops for roadside attractions and body art."

They had to make an obligatory drive through Yellowstone, where she hadn't been since the kids were little. It was crowded in spots, and warm.

But neither thing inhibited her enjoyment of the natural beauty.

"You want to run around with the buffalo?" he asked when they were stopped alongside the road by some of the grazing beasts.

"I do not. Have you never seen viral videos of tourists getting tossed around?"

"I have. I just thought you were, like, doing new things."

"Roaming with the buffalo is not going to be one of them."

"That's probably a good thing."

"I always wondered what kind of person you have to be to do stuff like that," she said. "To totally disregard common sense and the rules."

"Someone who's in the moment," he said. "Again, I'm not actually advocating for the North American edition of running with the bulls. But you know, there's something to be said for being led by passion. By your impulses."

"Is there?" She wrinkled her nose. "I'm not sure that I believe that."

"No?"

She thought about that for a while as she watched the large, shaggy beasts grazing with their heads down. She tried to feel it. The kind of energy that would propel somebody to discard all common sense to run wild like that.

There was a sliver of it. She could *almost* feel it. The need to just let go. It was like wanting the tattoo. But it required her to unlock so many of these chains that she still had around her wrists. Chains she was often not at all conscious of.

But they were there. Who was she living for?

The list was long. She was not at the top of it.

She wasn't even sure she was on it.

She had created for herself a life that she found very, very livable.

The alternative had been dealing with the heartbreak in the community. In her family.

The judgment that both she and Will would have received if they hadn't gotten married would've been so much greater than the judgment they had gotten for that pre-graduation ceremony.

She'd kept that fear with her. If they split, then they would only ever be the couple who got pregnant in high school and got married for that reason...and failed.

Fear was very strong glue.

But it wasn't enough.

"I can kind of understand," she said. "I'm still not going to do it. Because I like living. But…" The words had almost come out. She had very nearly said it.

I'm afraid of my passion.

Her passion was how she'd had gotten pregnant at eighteen.

Her passion, her feelings, had led her to nearly kiss Logan when she was lost in the fog of her grief, and the loneliness that it created.

Both of those things had been a betrayal.

A betrayal of the values that she had been brought up with.

A betrayal of the vows that she had made.

What frightened her most was that it wasn't a betrayal of herself. Not really.

Not the deepest part of her.

The part of her she'd been training to be someone new, someone better, since she'd first realized she might be dangerous.

Somewhere inside of her was a woman who wanted to run around with the buffalo.

That was scary. She didn't like it, and she had spent the better part of the last twenty-two years suppressing it.

Even when she had been tempted with Logan, she hadn't done it. She hadn't done it because it was wrong. She hadn't done it because it frightened her.

She hadn't done it because you just…you couldn't. You couldn't do things like that.

On some level, she wondered if she was always policing herself. She was always afraid she would be that person. Who jumped out of the car at a national park into something idiotic.

Who wildly went against what she actually wanted in the heat of the moment.

So she was always on a leash. Always gauging her actions through the lens of other people.

It was why what Will wanted was more important than what

she wanted. Why her mother being proud was more important than her having what she wanted.

It was why she was Patricia's daughter. Will's wife.

Jude, Aiden and Ethan's mother.

A volunteer. A friend.

But not just herself.

Herself, she had decided, wasn't trustworthy.

Herself was a problem.

Herself was a drunk girl that was going to get herself tossed in the air by buffalo.

But you never have.

Your marriage wasn't you breaking the rules. It was you trying to be what everyone needed you to be.

"Sorry," she said, realizing that she had lapsed off. "I... I was thinking."

"Are you okay?"

"I don't know. I don't know if I'm okay. I don't know if I'm ever going to be okay again. There are just things you can't put back in the box, can you?"

She realized that that could be taken several different ways. "I mean, the thing with Will. The thing with our marriage. Now I want to get a tattoo. He doesn't like them, and I'm going to do it anyway." She laughed. "Because seriously, fuck everyone's opinions. *Fuck.*"

"Okay."

"My mom hates that word." She put her fingertips on her forehead and rested her knees to her elbows. "I'm still a child. I let all these other people tell me what to do. Even without them having to tell me. It's crazy. I know it is. But I do it anyway. I do it anyway because I'm afraid."

"That's fair. Fear keeps you safe sometimes. You know. From them."

She laughed. "I guess. I think I've always thought my fear and common sense were the same thing. I don't want to run with bison, though. Maybe I need to separate the two. Maybe sometimes fear is just fear, and I can trust my common sense more than I think."

"That's a pretty bold statement. I like it."

"We can drive away from the buffalo now. The longer we linger, the more I actually am afraid that I'm going to jump out of the car. Because I'm having revelations at a pretty lightning speed, and that is more or less terrifying. The amount of times a day I challenge my own worldview is getting exhausting."

"I bet."

"It's grief, in a way. When you lose somebody that you love, you find yourself completely disoriented. You have to find a new way that you fit in the world. A new way that your life looks. This isn't the same. But it's like I'm tearing apart every little piece of everything, which I was afraid to do. I was steadfastly not doing it on that first trip. Because I kept asking myself, 'If I tear it into too many pieces, at what point will I not be able to put it back together?'"

That was really when her stomach hollowed out. She wasn't sure anymore if putting it back together was what she wanted.

She wasn't sure she cared. She was beginning to wonder if maybe she had to keep tearing it apart. Because if it could be broken into so many pieces that it couldn't be recovered, then it didn't deserve to be.

But then, who was she?

She couldn't be Patricia's daughter, and she couldn't be Will's wife...

Samantha.

She would just have to be Samantha.

"I think I'm doing this wrong," she said. "I was doing it *at* him. Proving to him that I didn't need to change. That we didn't need to change. I knew what the outcome would be. I put it out there like it was hypothetical. Like we were going to see. I didn't let myself believe that at the end, he might choose that life. Away from me. I certainly didn't let myself believe that I would be the one who might want something different. I have been certain for a very long time. The disruption of that certainty is always difficult for me. My mom's death was that. This…it's a whole other piece. I hate it. So I needed to make it something that I could control. Something I can be sure about. You're right about me. I pretend to go along with what everyone wants, and externally I often do, but I also want my way. Pretty deeply. I thought I was going to be able to quietly and without conflict strong-arm my way into that. What would happen if I let go?"

"I don't know."

"Neither do I. I don't know. I don't know, and I'm not even sure that I want to. I don't need to. Dammit, that is really hard to say. I like to know how it's going to go. How it's going to end."

"It's okay if you don't," he said.

"I guess this is the part where you settle on that old cliché. That it's not the destination, it's the journey."

"Sometimes clichés are clichés for a reason."

"I'm sorry. You're not getting paid to be my therapist."

"I would hope, Samantha, that after all this, you consider me a friend. Friends don't need to get paid to listen their friends talk about their problems."

She nodded slowly. "Yes. You're my friend."

It felt momentous to say that. An admission of the independent affectionate feelings that she had for Logan, rather than putting it all onto Will and their friendship.

It felt like a step toward danger, and she wasn't quite sure why.

Maybe it was more of that distrust of herself.

She had to stop with that. She had to stop doing that.

They drove back to the main highway, continuing on down the road toward where they would be staying for the night. "I did it," she said. "I did not do anything stupid. I even let myself think about it."

"Is that an achievement?"

"I don't know. It feels like it. It feels like being able to trust myself is maybe something I need to work on. Or at least work on making myself the authority in my own life."

"Well, tomorrow maybe you'll get a tattoo."

"I have to research tattoo shops."

"Research away."

Because she was wild. More so than she'd ever been in this moment. Braver, maybe, too.

But she also had no natural inclination toward getting that body art.

Reckless abandon…but with the appropriate amount of caution.

Maybe that was who she was. Maybe, if she let the chains loose, that was exactly who she was.

nineteen

She actually found the tattoo parlor that she wanted in Iowa. It surprised her. But it was a small-town studio that had a reputation for good art. More hipster than it was biker, which suited her just fine. Deciding what she wanted for a tattoo had been easier than deciding where she wanted the tattoo. It was so difficult not to ask somebody else's opinion. It felt like growth, buying a dress and not asking Will or one of her friends if it looked nice. This was like an extreme version of that.

She had a lot of worries, about whether or not she would choose the wrong location for it, and then feel annoyed when it showed and she no longer enjoyed it. She thought about all these hidden places, but then she wouldn't be able to see it. She wanted it to be her reminder. Of her mother. Of an event that had changed her.

Of the simple comfort found in the scent of lavender. How even in the end, there was comfort. She knew what she wanted.

She just had to stop being insecure. About her own decision-making. In the end, she decided on the inner part of her forearm, near her wrist.

She booked an appointment with the studio online en route,

and they ate a quick lunch at a little hole-in-the-wall diner before walking down the street two blocks to the tiny shop. The receptionist up front clearly had no issues deciding tattoo placement. She had determined that they should go everywhere.

Her hair was bright purple, and she had big fluorescent-pink gauges in her ears.

Samantha had to wonder what it was like. To not worry at all about standing out like a sore thumb when you walked down the street.

Like a sore thumb or like a brightly colored bird?

She intentionally shifted the thought from the original negative phrasing.

Because of course in her world, standing out was a negative, so she applied a negative term to it.

But you sort of want to stand out. In some ways. You just want everyone to be happy with you also, so...

She was the author of many of her own problems. She was beginning to be aware of that. Sure, there were contributing factors. But she'd left everything as it was for so long, unexamined, unthought about, undealt with, and that was on her.

"Samantha Parker," she told the receptionist.

"Right," she said. "You're with Justine. I see that you sent some information in here, so you just need to sign the medical waivers."

Logan sat next to her while she did.

"I'm sort of surprised you don't have any tattoos," she said as she tapped the paper with the tip of her pen.

He lifted a brow. "Who says I don't?" She whipped her head to the side and looked at him, her eyes roaming over his body without her permission, and her heart started to beat a little bit faster as she took in...all the everything.

Broad shoulders, muscles that she could see through his T-shirt, hard-looking thighs...

She'd seen him shirtless before. Now she was thinking about that.

"Well. You don't have any that I… That can be…"

"Many people have seen them," he said, a smile tugging at the corner of his lips.

"Oh. Many people have seen. You didn't even bother to tell me about them."

"Privileged information. Usually for drunk girls in bars."

"Wow."

Now she wanted to know about the tattoos. Desperately. He really did look like the kind of man who would have them. But like a full sleeve, something very visible. They weren't. What was that about? Why hadn't he mentioned it when she had started talking about the tattoo?

"You keep a lot to yourself too," she said.

"I never said I didn't."

"You were all yelling at me about honesty," she said, scribbling her pen violently against the paper as she signed off on the fact that if she got hepatitis or died of tetanus, the shop wasn't liable.

"No. I said that I wanted you to be honest about what happened between us. It wasn't a demand of wholesale honesty. Or spilling of one's guts."

"Right. Well. I think that's made-up. A made-up double standard."

"Okay," he said, a shrug in his voice.

"Why aren't you bothered by that?"

"I never said that I had a burning need to be fair."

"But people should want to be fair."

"Why?" She could see that he was amused. She could see it in the way the lines by his eyes scrunched up just a little bit, at the same time the grooves by his mouth deepened. He was holding back a smile.

"Because good and decent human beings care about fairness, Logan."

He looked at her, and she felt it, wicked and illicit, down in her stomach. "Who said I was decent?"

"Samantha?"

She turned, and there was a woman with black hair and prominent cheek piercings standing there smiling at her, the silver balls in her face making dimples.

"That's me," she said.

"I'm Justine," the woman said.

Justine had intricate webs of ink all over her brown skin, and extremely creative-looking piercings.

She was almost otherworldly. Samantha found herself fascinated by the two women in the shop, and how they created their own standard of beauty that seemed to exist simply to please themselves. It was innately their own style.

It wasn't Samantha's. It wouldn't be, ever, no matter how much growth and change she went through.

But she was still in awe of the kind of self-possession they must have. Especially living in a place like this.

She was stereotyping, sure. But she herself was from a small town. People who looked like this stood out. They were remarkable.

It took a lot of courage to be remarkable.

"I've done a couple of drawings," Justine said. "So you can let me know what you think of the sketches based on your notes, and I'll do some revisions."

It was a line drawing, delicate and perfect. She didn't have any notes for Justine at all.

The back room had gold stars hanging from the ceiling and glitter on the walls. It was like being in a night sky. It was a great distraction, because her nerves suddenly kicked in.

"Do you want me to stay?" Logan asked.

"Please?" she asked.

He nodded and sat in a chair near the one that she would be sitting in. She wanted him here, because having him around felt right. Because being near him was a comfort.

Logan would always be part of this. As permanent as the ink. That scared her.

It felt like something too big to grab onto, but she was trying to step away from denial, so she did her best.

He mattered.

A lot.

"This is your first tattoo?" Justine asked.

"Yeah," she said, sitting down, a rush of anxiety rising up inside her.

"You'll be back for more. They're like that."

Justine looked over at Logan and winked.

He smiled. Then he winked back. He was far too good at that. It should have been both annoying and cheesy, but he just looked good.

Obviously Justine could tell that he was a man that had ink. She was also flirting with him. Not that she could blame her, but Justine was probably barely thirty.

Of course, she bet women in their twenties hit on Logan all the time. He was hot whatever age you were. She was taken aback to discover that she felt a little bit possessive.

Was it that obvious that they weren't a couple? Because that was a little hurtful. He was hot, yes. Hotter than her, she would grant. But ouch.

Justine prepared her for the tattoo, placing the guide on her arm and leaving behind an impression of what she would leave there permanently in a few moments.

Samantha wasn't especially afraid of pain, but she didn't go seeking it out either, and she always got just a little bit of tightness in her stomach right before getting a shot. This felt like that, but magnified. Justine turned the gun on, and it made a buzzing sound, and then she brought it to her skin, and Sam's breath hissed through her teeth. It hurt. It wasn't horrific, but it wasn't pleasant either.

But she watched, rather than looking away, watched with intense interest as the design was etched into her skin.

Those fine, delicate lines becoming part of her.

Like the loss was part of her. Like the need for comfort was part of her.

She wanted it there, because she wanted to remember. She wanted it there because she wanted to feel, deeply, what her mother had meant to her, and also not be afraid to be her own person.

It was like taking that relationship and making it something new. Progressing it even though her mom wasn't there.

Because Samantha was her own person. Not just the person her mom wanted her to be. It didn't mean she loved her mom less. It just meant she needed to be free. To be herself. To make her own decisions. She knew her dad would raise his eyebrows when he saw the tattoo. She was going to have to be okay with it.

She *was* okay with it.

It was a weird thing, this moment. Reclaiming. Or claiming, maybe for the first time, herself in a very interesting way. For her, it hadn't been the bikini. For her, it was this.

Deciding to change something about her own body that she wouldn't have done before. Because she had given some kind of broader ownership of it to other people. She wasn't doing that anymore.

Justine finished the tattoo, and gave her instructions for after-care. She paid, a kind of euphoric haze settling over her.

They walked outside, and she got into the passenger seat of the Ferrari. As soon as the door closed, she burst into tears.

twenty

"I have no idea what's happening to me," she said, wiping tears away from her cheeks.

"It's normal," he said. "That kind of thing is a release."

"I don't know. I don't think anything about me is normal right now. I really do feel like a teenager. Without the tight ass."

"Your ass is fine."

He said it so dry and matter-of-fact, she…laughed. Even though she was crying. "My ass is fine?"

"I mean, as far as I can tell," he said.

"As far as you can tell? Meaning you looked."

"Sure. Are you going to tell me you haven't looked at mine?"

Sure. She'd looked. Though she spent more time on his forearms. But she didn't feel the need to disclose that. She said nothing. She looked down at the tattoo. Shiny and new.

She took a deep breath, and it stuck in her throat.

"I can't believe I did that."

"You don't regret it, do you?"

"No. I don't. I didn't ask anyone's opinion." She wiped a tear out of the corner of her eye. "Or permission. That must seem like such a small, sad thing."

"It doesn't. Not at all."

She appreciated that. More than she could say.

So she didn't even try to say it. They drove through Illinois again, but this time skipped the city and saw some roadside attractions like the World's Largest Catsup Bottle and the Pink Elephant Antique Mall. She texted pictures to Elysia and Whitney, but not of her tattoo. For some reason, that felt really personal, and she didn't really want to talk about it yet. Which was silly. Except she felt very vulnerable, and it was really a whole thing that it had been Logan there to see it. And the subsequent breakdown that had occurred after.

Everything was light between them for the next few days, but nothing was light inside of her.

Somewhere back on that road, before she had gotten the tattoo, but the tattoo had been a kind of cementing of it, she had really acknowledged that her end point might not be Will.

She was willing to do something that he wouldn't like. To not consider him as the primary reason to do or not do something.

It was a major shift. A landslide inside of her soul.

Except when Stevie Nicks sang about such things, it was soothing and a little bit haunting, and when it was actually happening inside of her, it felt like perhaps she was going to be crushed to death beneath the weight of the boulders rolling through her.

It was momentous. Epic. She wasn't even sure if it was a bad thing. The realization echoed through her all the way to Massachusetts. That it didn't really hurt. Suddenly, imagining in her mind that it might happen, that she was the one who said… no. Or even that he was… It wasn't unimaginable. That was the thing. The notable, very different thing.

She had never been to Boston before, and she was overwhelmed by the beauty and history of the city. She and Logan stayed in a small boutique hotel on the edge of the North End, and she was really happy that they had built in a couple of extra days to sightsee. So far, it was her favorite place that they'd been. She had always been a little bit of a history nerd, and this got her.

While he facilitated delivering the Ferrari to its owner, she spent a day wandering around Beacon Hill, taking a slow turn about the brick squares, wandering through crooked alleyways and imagining the kind of life that you could live in a place like this.

She had never fully been able to imagine living in a city, but she was coming to the conclusion that with millions of dollars at your disposal, you could be very happy on a quiet street like this one, on the edge of something bustling, a world away from it all at the same time.

She enjoyed meandering through the little boutiques. She found herself wandering along the clearly marked Freedom Trail, the brick line acting as a map between many historic sites.

She stopped at a shoe store partway through her walking tour and had to get herself a new pair, something to mitigate the pain from covering so much ground in what she had on.

She laughed at herself, and the horror a younger version of Samantha would've felt over the absolute mom shoes that she chose.

Practicality outweighed fashion for her these days. It didn't make her sad. It made her *happy*. Happy again, for all the years that she had between herself and the girl who would've tottered around on uncomfortable shoes with blisters simply to look cool. So there. Maybe she had moments of feeling like a teenager. Everything was new and life was frightening and her emotions were too big for her to handle. But at the end of the day, she was forty. She really liked herself at forty a lot better than she did at eighteen. Even with all the uncertainty. It hit her then, standing before the church where the Founding Fathers had first met to discuss the drafting of the Declaration of Independence, that life had always been uncertain. She just hadn't known that it was.

Then her mother had gotten cancer. That had certainly been something that happened to her. Her loved ones. Her family. She had a taste of that with Becca, but even then, Becca had been a somewhat distant friend, not a family member.

Her mother's illness had been the beginning of recognizing that no matter how she organized her life, no matter how many bins she sorted her children's toys into, she didn't know what was happening tomorrow. Didn't have the slightest idea. No amount of organization could change that.

She hadn't realized how much of the illusion she had still been carrying with her. It was only now that the security of that house on that same street, with that same man, had been taken away from her that she recognized life for what it was. A series of events that she couldn't predict. Perhaps, here in the cradle of American liberty—this had been said to her multiple times by people at historical sites—she was on the verge of finding out what that meant for her.

She found a book, a picture book, about ducklings, and later saw a statue of those same ducklings from the children's book, and she ached slightly that she didn't have any kids to buy it for.

Then immediately felt some sense of relief that she didn't, because it was why she was out here with the freedom she had.

It was like anything, she supposed. She loved that she had the experience of motherhood that she did. She also loved that she had gotten to a place where her kids were independent. Where she had successfully raised them into the human beings that they were. She also missed them being small. She grieved that she couldn't gather them all up in her arms anymore. Well, she could try.

But just because it wasn't there anymore didn't make it a bad thing. It scratched the back of her mind. Made her think of Will. Their marriage. Who they'd been a long time ago.

Maybe it was just something they couldn't recapture. Something that had worked when it did, but wouldn't anymore.

They had clung to each other, to the family that they made. To the ease of the life that they had created together. Centered around their children.

They had, after all, gotten married because she was pregnant. They had needed each other. Needed each other to support that life.

Will was the primary breadwinner, and she needed him. She kept the house, managed the kids' schooling, made sure that everything was organized and that they were where they needed to be at all times. He needed her for that. Every time she watched him with their children, her love for him grew. Her affection. They could rest together at the end of the day and be secure in the knowledge that they had done their parts, and done them well.

They had needed each other then. That same need just didn't exist now.

There were no children to pick up. She could work full-time if she wanted to, because she didn't have kids to take care of. She didn't need his money. He didn't need her meal planning.

That was scary. For a whole minute, that acknowledgment was scary.

It was like the sky got lower, like it might crush her, fear pushing down on her. Then it just…went away.

The fear eased. She could breathe.

She and Will had been running a gauntlet from their first moment together. At first they'd been driven by teenage emotion and hormones. Then it had been fear.

Then it had been that need to keep together the life they had created.

If they were going to get back together, it would have to be something else. They would have to be doing it because they wanted it, because they were choosing each other, just to be with each other. Not for their kids or their community. The answer she didn't have right now was if she wanted him enough to choose just him. She had *needed* him enough when they'd had kids at home, when they'd had all that labor of running a household.

But she could see clearly now that this was the transition that broke so many people. Because it took marriage from *need* to *want*.

When Will had suggested an open marriage, she had still been mired in *need*.

Because divorce would mean that people in town would think certain things about them. Divorce would be admitting a loss. Divorce, she had felt at that moment, would undermine everything that she had done to be acceptable by marrying him in the first place. In an open marriage, especially when the people in town might be aware of… She couldn't even fathom that. All the labor that she had done to be seen as morally acceptable would be erased by that.

She had still *needed* it.

But here she was, a woman with a tattoo wandering the streets of Boston, and she just wasn't sure if she needed it anymore. With that out of the way, she was left looking for the *want* to. God help her, she wasn't sure it was there. She cared about Will. But what surprised her the most was how little she was thinking of him these days. How little the inclination to text him hit her, and how much she enjoyed talking to Logan about her revelations and problems and fears.

How she hadn't been able to talk to Will about them. How nothing about their relationship had been a place where she could identify those needs and seize them.

It was quite simply the strangest thing.

But it didn't scare her. Not anymore. It was just something she was considering. Just something she was opening herself up to.

She regretted that she hadn't been able to do it that first day they had gotten on the road.

Really embrace this moment for what it was. She had been so lost in her stubbornness. In being right for the sake of it.

Proving to him that he was wrong and she was right.

Her own stubbornness was often her very worst enemy. Something that hilariously would not surprise Will at all.

By the time she got back to the hotel, she was exhausted. She was also laden with shopping bags, and ready to collapse.

She got up to her room on the sixth floor and dropped all her bags onto the ground, then laid herself flat on the smooth white bedspread in the minimalist room. It was a stark contrast to the roadside motels. But she kind of loved it. Her phone buzzed, and she looked at it. It was Logan.

Dinner?

Sure. But you might have to carry me there.

Not a problem.

Her heart thumped a little harder than was necessary.

Just let me change.

She was sweaty from all the walking, and she put on something comfortable, and also a bit stretchy, so that when they ate she wasn't conscious of the waistband biting into her stomach.

She had enough uncomfortable thoughts today. She didn't need to be physically uncomfortable on top of it. They met down in the lobby, and she paused to really look at him. His dark blond hair pushed back off of his forehead, that black leather jacket that called to teenage dreams she hadn't even had back then, because bad boys had been a shade too scary for her.

Hell, bad boys were a shade too scary for her now. So obsessed she was with being a good girl.

Here she was, at a hotel in Boston with a man she wasn't married to, looking at his broad shoulders, his muscular thighs. His butt. It seemed fair for her to ponder his ass, since he had commented on hers a few days ago.

"Let's go get pizza. You'll like it."

"Of course I like it," she said. "It's pizza."

"No. When I say you'll like it, I mean it's special."

They walked across the street and into the North End, all red brick and glorious buildings. The charm of it made her ache. For lives she hadn't lived, and never would. For the vastness of life. It was a feeling she was getting used to. A feeling she was coming to love. Because as much as it was uncomfortable, it reminded her that she was alive. It reminded her that there was more.

It made her feel like the loss of that small, safe life that she had wasn't quite as devastating as she had originally thought.

Because there were so many lives that she could live. So many places to go. So many layers to who she could be. If she had stayed on that street, in that house, with Will for the rest of her life...she would have been a kind of happy. But she was beginning to think that the changes, the thoughts, the moments that she had since the separation were transforming her into a person who might not be able to find her way back to that sort of happiness. It was a cliché. A goldfish in a bowl that had been dumped into the ocean. Now knew how big it all was.

But it was the dominant thing that she kept thinking.

She wasn't sure she would be able to fit back into that life.

Hell. She had a tattoo.

Regina Pizza was on a corner packed full of people, and Logan went and put their name on the list. It was a decently long wait, but she didn't mind meandering around, looking at the buildings, the brick and the metal detail that had aged into a green patina with time. It was more frenetic here than at Beacon Hill, not like the stately, well-appointed town houses on utterly silent streets, but rather apartments above these bustling buildings, bags of trash brought out to the curb, waiting to be collected the next day, and people everywhere.

Even this life made her smile to imagine living it. What kind of person would you be? Living in the middle of all this activity, all this history. The energy would be inspiring.

When they got called for their table, they were ushered into a noisy, crowded restaurant with no pretense or conceit. It somehow felt nostalgic, even though she'd never been there. Maybe because it was in many ways the image of what a pizza place should be. It must've been in a movie, or maybe she had just absorbed it somehow into her consciousness. The booths, the pictures on the wall, celebrities that had been there, local police officers. It was somehow brand-new and familiar all at once, and she was delighted by it, and of course by the food.

But it wasn't just this place.

It was Logan. That stark separation that had happened inside of her today. That realization. That her endgame might not be Will. Then suddenly, the driving need to know... To know what it would be like to kiss Logan. If it would change something else.

Zip-lining had. The tattoo had. Just wandering around the city by herself in her absolute freedom had.

She hadn't kissed him all those years ago. Because of fear, yes. Also because she had said vows to Will, and whatever she had felt at the time, whatever he had failed to do for her in her grief, she had never taken those vows lightly, and she never would.

But the rules weren't the same now.

She wanted different things now. She wanted some kind of clarity on exactly what that meant.

Logan was beautiful.

And she had crossed that line, that barrier, from admitting

that he was attractive to the fact that she was attracted to him. Now she felt not simply preoccupied with it but compelled by it. By the lines on his face, and blue of his eyes. The sharp awareness of his jaw, and his mouth.

Everything about his mouth.

She could remember feeling compelled by it then. When he had looked at her with all that care and tenderness and intensity at the same time.

She could remember feeling overwhelmed.

But there had also been a barrier. A barrier that simply didn't exist now.

The pizzeria was amazing, but it was hardly romantic. Her judgment wasn't being clouded by candlelight.

It was just the natural conclusion to everything.

All of it had brought her here. To this moment. To the opportunity to have what she hadn't been able to then.

She was suddenly distracted by it, barely able to finish the last piece of pizza, and having difficulty carrying on a conversation. Her limbs were infused with anxiety that took root in her stomach and spread out from there. Her hands tingled. Her fingertips felt numb.

She was suddenly in a hurry, when she had been enjoying herself and happy to sit here endlessly.

"I think they want to turn the table over," she said.

That was true. She could tell that the line outside had only gotten longer, and there was a definite need to clear space. But she had ulterior motives. She hadn't felt this kind of excitement in…a very long time. The sense that she was about to do something potentially wrong, but that was exciting enough she didn't care.

It was in her head now, and she couldn't get it out.

You want to kiss him, and then what?

You two are staying in the same hotel, and you have another night here.

That made her mouth dry. She wasn't quite ready to contemplate that. But maybe that was the key. No thought. Just action. She'd had had her fill of thinking, after all. It had been good. It had brought her to a good space.

Now she was ready to do *something*. A little less conversation, a little more action.

Maybe living her life via lyrical content from Elvis wasn't any better than Michael Jackson, all things considered, but she had to start somewhere.

It felt like it took an eternity for him to pay. Felt like the moment had extended into its own era.

Finally, they were back out on the street. It was still teeming with people. But that added to the excitement, to the rush of the moment. To the feeling that maybe she was someone else, or herself for the very first time. They were in a city, where no one knew them. Where they weren't accountable to anyone. It was a rush. A thrill. Unmatched. It was him.

He had been the object of so many hard feelings. She could recognize them for what they were now. They weren't hard feelings. They were forbidden feelings. Feelings that she hadn't been allowed to have. Feelings that she hadn't been brave enough to admit.

How could she admit them? It was so important to her to be good. To be perfect. To be beyond reproach. Then it had been so important to her to live in her self-righteousness when Will had made that proclamation. She didn't want to have sex with a stranger. She didn't want the touch of any random man that she might find in a bar. But she could relate to wanting the touch of someone else. She did. She had wanted Logan then for far longer than she was comfortable admitting. She wanted him now.

Beyond reason, with no endgame in sight, with no plan. She wanted him with everything she was. Whether it made sense or not. Whether it was reasonable or not.

So she did something that felt brave. She did something that felt like a risk. More so than getting up on that platform at the zip line. Because at least there she'd had a harness. Something to catch her if she fell. There was nothing here. Nothing but this. Nothing but them. And hundreds of people crowding the streets, but they didn't matter. How long had it been since nothing but the moment mattered?

It was a rush, her heart pounding fast, and she took his hand. She felt him jolt, but he didn't let go. Instead, he let her lead him to a side street, where there were no people. Where there was nothing but the lit gas lamps, casting an orange glow onto the bricks. She could only just hear the chatter of the people around them over her heart pounding in her temples.

That was when she did it. She reached out and grabbed the collar of his shirt and pulled him up against her. At the same time, she stretched up as far as she could on her toes, used her free hand to curve her arm around his neck, and kissed him.

It was like fire. Like the sensation of striking a match against a rough surface. Igniting an instant and deadly flame that couldn't be controlled or contained.

She had meant only to test the waters. A simple press of her lips against his, but there was nothing innocent about the contact. Nothing at all. It was an uncontained, raging explosion. The heat that she felt at the press, the firmness of his mouth on hers, was unlike anything she could remember. It burned everything else away. She found herself releasing that clinging hold on his T-shirt and moving her hand to his shoulder, down the back of his shirt collar, shuddering as she felt his skin beneath her fingertips. He was still for a moment, and then the kiss was his. He wrapped his arms around her and pressed her against one of the brick walls in the alley, the hardness of his body a welcome sensation.

She had been waiting for this for three years. Maybe she had been waiting for it her whole life. This kind of passion. Not a frightened, desperate, teenage kind of passion, but something exceedingly adult. She knew what she wanted. She could imagine it. She needed it.

He parted his lips, his tongue sliding against hers, and a rough groan escaped her. She couldn't control it. She wasn't even certain if she wanted to. She wanted to surrender. She wanted this, and everything that could come with it. She wanted to be new. *This* was the way. This was it. Him.

She was wrapped in him, enveloped in his strength, his heat. And it wasn't enough. She wanted more of him. She arched herself against him, desperate to take it there. To take it further. Faster.

They parted, for just a moment, their breath harsh and jagged. His blue eyes contained something wild in them. Something she had never seen before.

Logan. This was Logan. This man that she had known—in some capacity or another—since she was in high school. This man she had watched love another woman. Marry her. Bury her. Care for his beautiful daughter all on his own. This man who had vexed her from the moment looking at him made her feel a tension, excitement, heat that she could not explain away. She couldn't put into a neat little box. Because she was a married woman. The feelings that she'd had for him, they didn't have a place. Not in her world. Not in her scope of morality. Not in her life.

Now in this moment, she wondered if none of it mattered. If it had been inevitable. From that moment their eyes had met on the lanai in Hawaii, and it had become clear, exceptionally clear, that there was more between them than there should be. She had resisted this, but maybe it had been pointless. Fruitless. A delay of something that had been destined.

She moved back in, desperate to touch him again, but he stopped her, holding her apart from him, his grip on her shoulders hard.

"Are you still going back to him?"

"I…"

"Answer me. Yes or no. Are you done with Will?"

She faltered. She had just accepted that there was a need to open herself up to the possibility that they wouldn't end up together, but how could she say that definitively about the man she'd been married to for twenty-two years, in this moment, in an alley? How could she even think of Will?

It was like trying to swim through some kind of sensual fog. She was trying to accurately think of him. Think of his face, think of their life.

Will was the only man that she had ever kissed, but she hadn't compared him and Logan when Logan's mouth had touched hers. It hadn't even occurred to her to do so. Because kissing Logan had been its own experience. New and intense, and the only thing she wanted to live in. She didn't want to think about the future. She just wanted to have him. She just wanted to have the experience.

"Logan, I… I don't know. I… I feel like this was something that had to happen. This thing between us, it needs to happen, right? Because why else is it so… For so many years, why else has it been there? I think we need to see. I think it's an experience we have to have."

His face went hard. Cold. "I am not a zip line, Samantha. And I am not a tattoo. I am not an experience for you to have, or a rebellion against your mother, or a fuck-you to your husband. If you want me, you can't want him. It's that simple."

She couldn't speak. Part of it was out of fury, fury that he was holding this over her head right now, when she had been living in the moment, and he wasn't letting her have that. And fear. Because how could she promise him something like that when she didn't know if it was true? She had no idea what she wanted. She had no idea where this summer was going to take her, and it had been a step to let herself not know. He was asking for certainty. She didn't want certainty right now. She wanted to revel in not knowing. She wanted to follow whatever path she saw. He wasn't being fair.

"What? You can hook up with any random woman in a bar, but you can't hook up with me? I have to be able to give you answers? Do you ask the twenty-eight-year-olds that you take back home with you at night what they want for their future? Or is that just something you've reserved for me, because you think that my life should just be hard?"

"You're not them. You're you. You know that. Don't fucking insult me."

"Fine, then, what about you? You get all this time, all this space to sort out your life without your marriage, but I can't be uncertain?"

"Don't."

He turned away from her and started to walk away. She knew that she was safe. She didn't need him to guide her back to the hotel that was only a few blocks away, especially not with all these people around. So she didn't follow him. She just stood there. Marinating in her hurt. In her anger. In the absolute disaster of that moment. She had put herself out there. She had thrown her body against his. Had shown him how attracted she was to him. It was embarrassing. Humiliating. He didn't seem to care. He was demanding more things of her. Nothing she did was right for him. Good enough for him.

Her denial wasn't right. Flinging herself headlong into it wasn't right. She refused to go back to the hotel. She wandered around the crowded streets until she couldn't decide if she was ready to cry or ready to fall asleep, went to an Italian bakery, waited in an endless line and got herself an Italian pastry with a name she couldn't pronounce. The man who owned the bakery had made her try, and then had laughed at her, though not unkindly. He had given her two for her trouble.

She took the pastries back to her room, and she did not text Logan. Instead she ate them in bed with an ill-advised cup of coffee, and then stayed up far too late reading an e-book on her phone. She wanted to write down some of her feelings, her fantasies, her fears. The feverish idiocy that had overtaken her when she'd kissed that man. But she had determined that she wasn't going to write about this.

Anyway, she didn't really want to remember it. She felt awful. Hollowed out and small. An absolute wreck of a person. This summer was a disaster, and so was she.

Why would she hasten to commemorate that? She wouldn't. That was the simple answer.

When she woke up in the morning, very late, she went to Logan's room and knocked on the door. She decided that she needed to try and talk to him about what happened, because if she didn't, then she was just…reverting.

Reverting for a while was understandable. Fine even. A few hours of pastry and hiding was acceptable. But now she needed to be an adult.

Except he didn't answer.

She texted him and didn't get a response.

She went to the reception desk at the hotel.

"Can I leave a message for Logan Martin? In room 380?"

"Oh," the woman said, tapping at the computer for a second. "It appears that Mr. Martin checked out at about six o'clock this morning."

She laughed. She couldn't help it.

She picked up her phone and typed in two words: fucking coward.

twenty-one

The Loneliest Road
1954 Rolls-Royce Drophead
Now

She didn't see Logan during her two weeks in Jacksonville. This time she stayed in the B.F. Dowell House because it was fancy and her whole childhood she'd been curious about it, so the minute it had been made a vacation rental, she'd fantasized about staying in it.

It was a large brick house with a widow's walk on the second floor and historic furnishings. Gorgeous. And still, mostly she thought of Logan. Which was silly since she never even *almost* saw him.

Of course, she never went anywhere that she knew he would be.

She avoided bars of all kinds and didn't go near Logan's garage.

But the day she knew they were supposed to leave for the road trip, she decided she wasn't backing down. She wasn't giving Logan the chance to disinvite her from the trip without doing it to her face.

At five thirty in the morning, she rolled up to the garage. She was taking a risk. It was entirely possible that he had moved the car to his house last night and wouldn't in fact start from the garage. But she just had a feeling and went with it. When she saw the lights on inside, she felt triumphant. She pulled into the space and walked up to the front door. He had left it unlocked behind him, because it was a small town, and there was no crime to speak of. But he hadn't counted on her invading his space.

She walked into the garage and saw him, bent over the hood of a big black-and-silver car that looked like something from a gangster movie, his broad, muscular back taking up quite a bit of her mental bandwidth as she watched him.

"What's up?" she asked, her voice a little sharper than intended in the silent space. "Fucking coward."

She decided to just lean into it.

The muscles in his back shifted, but that was the only indicator he'd registered her presence. "Good. You're here."

"Yeah. Because I didn't figure you were going to swing by to pick me up."

He turned around. "That's where you're wrong."

"How were you going to do that? You don't know where I'm staying. I'm not with Elysia."

"I actually know that."

She stared at him. "How do you know that?"

"Because I listen to gossip about town, Samantha." He rested his hands on the edge of the car, arms straight, and leaned against it. "As you should know."

"You're a liar," she said. "I don't think you do."

"You're a hot topic. Your apparent separation is much talked about by my customers. Amy Callahan came in. She let me know that you were renting from her. Asked if I knew anything about what happened between you and Will."

"You *told* her?"

His expression went bland. "That I don't know a thing."

She hadn't expected him to…lie. Not for her. Unless it was for Will. Will did sound like a dick in this scenario. She almost thanked him. Then decided…no.

"Wow," she said. "And yet you couldn't text me back."

"I didn't have anything to say. But we have an agreement. So I expected that you would come with me on this trip."

"You just couldn't be bothered to speak to me for two weeks."

His mouth settled into a firm line. "I thought space was in order."

Oh for God's sake. Space followed by time spent shut in a car together. That was such a male, not-thought-through bit of rationale.

"Look who's in denial now," she said. "I made a mistake. I can own up to that. I screwed up. I wasn't trying to use you, and I didn't do a good enough job of making that clear. I couldn't think fast enough in the moment, and I wasn't…in the right headspace for the turn the conversation took. But I was never using you."

"Thanks."

"I'm not apologizing for the actual kiss, though. Because I don't regret it. I needed to kiss you. I'm sorry if you thought I used you, and that hurt you. But I'm not sorry that I did it."

"So not sorry at all," he said.

"No, I am. About some things. Just not *that* thing."

"Let's get in the car then."

She slid into the passenger's seat and immediately ran her fingers along the shiny wood dashboard. "Wow," she said.

"It's a 1954 Rolls-Royce," he said, gripping the black steering wheel with one hand as he turned the key in the ignition with the other. "I hate to let this one go. But I'm not sorry I get to drive it across the country."

"Where's the final destination this time?"

"Miami."

"Miami! You didn't think to mention we were going to Florida?"

"We weren't speaking."

"*You* weren't speaking, asshole."

He grunted, and she wasn't sure if she was meant to take that as an agreement or not. "We're going on The Loneliest Road for a piece and then heading south."

"Well, good thing I packed my swimsuit."

"Like you weren't going to buy clothes along the way."

Fair.

"I hear Florida is one hell of a drug," she said.

"What?"

"It's a song... Never mind."

It was going to be another fun trip. Except of course she and Logan were right back at hostile square one.

Though this time they had actually kissed, instead of just almost kissed, and he was the one who seemed to want to push it to the side.

They cut east instead of heading straight south, going toward Lake Tahoe. It was a desolate drive, the landscape becoming increasingly volcanic as they drove on. They essentially didn't speak to each other.

It was icier than the very first road trip.

She just wasn't having it. Maybe she felt too impatient. Maybe the fact that there were only a couple months left of this weird period of time, this time where she didn't have any certainty, any idea of what would happen in her life, made her feel like she was running out of time. Maybe she was conscious of the fact that if she was going to live another life, she needed to start it sooner rather than later.

But whatever the driving reason, she was over this.

She wasn't going to let the silence keep going.

"I started writing," she said. "About this."

It took him a moment, but he responded. "Really?"

He sounded actually interested in spite of himself.

"Yeah. I was getting tired of *thinking*. I mean, I know there's a fair amount of thinking involved in writing. But it's a different way of processing it. I don't know what to do with it, though. Like you said, my organization tips were helpful to you, but I don't know if my messy thoughts about my fragmented twenty-two-year marriage and my make-out session with my husband's best friend are going to be useful to anyone else."

She wondered if she'd gone too far there.

"You're really all about that make-out session."

She shifted, trying to ignore how tight her stomach had gotten. "I'm all about facing things. I've been sitting in it for a few months. I didn't expect you to be the one that wanted to run away from it."

"What do you want me to say? It's not news to me that you're a fantasy of mine, Samantha."

She reached out and gripped the handle on the passenger side door, like it was going to keep her from melting into the floorboards. "What?"

"I've known that," he said, like she hadn't asked a question at all. "You might have been blindsided by your attraction to me, but I haven't been in denial for the past however many years. I've known that you were inconveniently attractive to me for a long time. So you can see how I take a dim view on being used as a path of exploration. If you want to have sex with a new guy, go to a bar."

Anger tangled around the attraction inside of her stomach. "You would be fine with that?"

"Hell no," he said through gritted teeth.

"Then you can't be pleased."

"I'm used to that. That's kind of part and parcel with having a thing for your friend's wife."

"Right. Right." But her cheeks were hot, and her body felt

unsettled. She wanted to know more. About why he felt that way about her.

He could have any woman he wanted. So why fixate on her? Her self-esteem wasn't so low that she couldn't imagine a man wanting to sleep with her, she just didn't understand why Logan of all people had been carrying any kind of torch for her.

Not that he'd said that explicitly. He was just attracted to her.

Though she came back to the kiss in the alleyway. What they had was an exceptional sort of chemistry. It had erased everything else from her mind. Everything but him. She'd been so caught up in the moment that she hadn't wanted to stop and think about anything. That was damned powerful. Because turning her mind off was not her strong point.

Denial, sure. But denial was accomplished by layering other things over the top of the truth. The trick was to never have an empty mind. The trick was to have lots of thoughts, so that you were constantly intentionally guiding them.

Certainly when it came to sex, her experience was that her thoughts just kept moving. She was loath to admit that occasionally she could be running through her entire week's meal plan and kinda forget that she was supposed to be trying to have an orgasm. So yeah. The experience with Logan had been something else. Maybe that was it. Maybe he felt it too. Chemistry that went further than it usually did. That was the thing. She'd heard.

"I'm... All right, I can't tell you what's going to happen," she said. "But I can tell you that all I wanted to do was keep kissing you. I can tell you that I thought about it more times than I can even count in the weeks since it happened. I can tell you that I...that I want more. That I think about you and..."

A muscle in his jaw twitched, and he kept his eyes on the road. "Are you telling me that you think about me and touch yourself, Samantha?"

Calling her Samantha instead of Sam was so deliberate. So effective.

She was trying so hard not to be embarrassed. She was not a kid. She was a grown woman. She had needs. She accepted that. But telling a man that when she got a restless feeling between her legs, he was the one she thought of, well, that was really outside of her scope of experience.

"Yes," she said quickly. "Once or twice."

"Once or twice." He laughed, but it was flat and bitter-sounding. "You've got better self-control than I do."

She squeezed her thighs together, now decidedly physically uncomfortable.

"Well. What's the problem?" she asked, because was there even a problem? They wanted each other. Why was he being like this?

"I'm not having sex with another man's wife. As long as you *feel* like you're his wife, I'm not having sex with you."

Shame rushed through her. Along with that, anger.

"What a convenient set of morals. You were fine with everything that happened three years ago. You wanted me to acknowledge it. But now, now you have morality about it."

"I'm older. Less interested in bullshit."

"Right. Great." It wasn't bullshit, not to her. It was her life. She hadn't asked for any of this.

She didn't know how to tell him she definitely felt like Will wasn't her husband. He *was* her husband. She couldn't just erase of all those years. Maybe it was dead on the vine, but her issues with Will needed to be worked out with Will. She couldn't do that right now because they were not talking to each other. She just wanted to make this not about him. She wanted to separate it. She was frustrated Logan wouldn't let her do that.

This was more sitting in bad decisions and mistakes. And the fact that there wasn't going to be an easy resolution with him. This was a problem, because she liked him. Because it meant she was in a place with someone that she quite liked, where she couldn't make him happy with her. She couldn't seem to get what she wanted.

She was stuck with him in a car for the next three weeks.

What a trip.

You have a crush on him.

Oh good God. She did. She had a crush on him. She was with him in this car, and he didn't like her back.

She was really trying to stay away from the high school parallels, but they kept on finding her.

She hadn't experienced this in high school, of course, because she had liked Will, and Will had liked her back. Then they had dated. And that was that.

She hadn't experienced a hell of an unrequited crush. It sucked. She didn't like it.

She realized that the unrequited crush, at this point, should really feel like it was on her husband, whose activities she was just profoundly disinterested in. Maybe she could just tell Logan she was done with Will.

But what if she was wrong? What if she was motivated entirely by her desire to make Logan happy? To smooth this over? To not sit in this weird middle ground?

She owed it to herself to sit in the discomfort.

To not just try to tell him what he wanted to hear. What would get her what she wanted.

Wow. Emotional maturity really was just the worst. She had to fill the silence. She couldn't sit in that anymore.

"Are we stopping in Tahoe?" she asked.

"Yes," he said.

"Cool. I haven't been there for a while. You're taking me to a casino, right?"

"No. You'll have to make those kinds of bad decisions on your own."

"You seem to be leaving me to make all the bad decisions on

my own. It's not really fair. You were advertised as being kind of a good time. Turns out that was a lie."

"Right."

"Right. Okay, so you're just going to talk to me in as few words as possible then?"

He was being a dick, because he was mad at her. But she recognized the truth to that. It was adjacent to parental guilt. It didn't have to make sense. You could even know that it wasn't true, but it didn't just take it away. She couldn't imagine how often he must've felt not just lost in his own grief, but what his daughter was missing. By not having her mother.

Constantly not feeling enough, because he was only one person.

"Do you need more words?"

"How was your visit with Chloe?" she asked. "Didn't you drive down to Santa Clara for a minute?"

"Yes. It was good. She was busy, but the time I got with her was…worth it."

"I really meant what I said about you and Chloe. I have always admired the way that you were with her. I have always thought that you were an amazing father. My issues with you were about me."

"Yeah. Well, thank you."

"It's just true. I'm sorry that you have to deal with that. I'm sorry that it haunts you like that."

"How long?" He didn't look at her when he asked the question.

"How long what?"

"You said you had difficult feelings about me. How long did you have them?"

She felt stunned by the question. Like she was being pinned to the passenger seat of the car. It was a difficult question, and one she wasn't sure she wanted to answer.

"Come on. We're in a pretty morally shaky situation as it is," he said. "Why not dig in?"

She wondered if he was punishing her. Maybe he was. Maybe she deserved it. She hadn't decided. She was mad at him, but that didn't mean that she was entirely in the right. It might just mean that she was defensive.

"I don't really know," she said. She swallowed hard. "I... I want to say the time we nearly kissed. But I think that's a lie. Sometimes I wonder if it's just been there. The whole time. But I didn't look at it because I couldn't. When my defenses were down, I couldn't not be drawn to you. I didn't sit there and envy your wife. Not consciously. But I noticed the way that you were with her. Maybe thought about it more than I did with anyone else."

"Good."

That anger was like acid now, eating away at her. *Good*. That was all she got. His satisfaction over her admitting something that difficult. That she been kind of in lust with him for a long time. But she hadn't done anything. She would never have done something to compromise his marriage, or hers. She had proven that. So he didn't really win anything.

"You're mad at me," he said.

"I don't understand why you want to embarrass me."

"I don't want to embarrass you. I just want you to be honest."

"You be honest, then. How long have you wanted me?"

"I wanted you in high school. I couldn't have you. Because he always had you. When I found out you were having his baby, I was sick to my stomach. Does that make you happy?"

"Logan, I..."

"I let it go. Like you do when the girl that you liked in high school ends up with someone else. That's all it is. You let it go. You find somebody else. You move on. I did that. I fell in love, I got married, and I had a child. That was real. But *attraction*, wanting someone, that doesn't just go away, and that has been the single biggest source of guilt and regret in my life. That no matter what, I always wanted you. To touch you, kiss you. Have you."

She didn't know what to say to that. It was shocking. She took in a breath, short and shaky, and then tried to take a longer one. It was almost impossible. Logan had feelings for her. Logan had had feelings for her for a while. Well, maybe not feelings, but attraction.

"Oh."

That response was not really as articulate as she would've liked it to be. But she didn't feel articulate. She didn't feel anything but blindsided. Wholly and completely.

"Yeah. Well," he said. "You shouldn't ask questions you don't want the answers to."

"I am not saying I don't like the answer. It's just a lot."

"I've waited for a long time. I can keep waiting." She watched as he adjusted his hands on the steering wheel. He had such nice hands. "I figured it might never happen."

She had to wonder if he was sort of comfortable with the *never.* There was something about that that resonated inside of her.

That when there was something complicated, it was easiest if you just didn't have to ever face it.

This was so complicated. Not just by her marriage to Will, but by the fact that his feelings had been a preexisting condition to even his marriage.

"You loved Becca," she said, not questioning it, affirming it.

"Yes," he said without hesitation. "I chose her. I love her still. She was the mother of my daughter. My wife. I was never in danger of straying in our marriage. I was committed. My feelings were real."

She nodded, thankful for the clarification, but not fully certain it was a clarification.

"I loved her. With everything I had. That didn't mean I ever stopped thinking that you were beautiful."

Because they were two separate things. Feelings and desire. But Logan was the only person she'd ever experienced that with. Still, she knew in the moment she'd nearly kissed him in Hawaii, she'd wanted him.

Had been tempted to break her moral code and her vows with him.

And had loved Will at the same time. Had loved their life and not wanted to lose it, and those feelings combined had been stronger than her attraction.

But it didn't make her desire for Logan less real.

Though she had feelings for him. But they were different. Different than her feelings for Will had ever been. Not love like that, but also the attraction was sharper. More intense.

Maybe it was age. Experience. A knowledge of what you wanted, and what you hadn't had, and might like to try.

She couldn't say for sure. She could understand complicated. So, there was that.

She was beginning to understand that feelings for someone else, different, complex feelings, didn't erase other feelings.

She knew that this admission didn't take away from his love for Becca. Or his grief at her loss.

In the same way that just wanting to kiss him three years ago hadn't made her want to leave her husband. Now it was out there. This truth. It felt glorious and hideous all at once. Because she was consumed with it. Her desire for him, but she also understood that…there were just things he wasn't willing to do. She wasn't willing to lie. Or to shortchange anybody. Least of all him. Well, and herself.

She was trying to be okay with sitting in difficulty so that she didn't go shortchanging herself.

He turned up the music then, and she didn't even object to it being Springsteen.

She endured classic rock as her penance for hurting him. Had she hurt him? She wasn't really sure. She didn't know how to classify this whole thing. She felt a little bit hurt. Bruised. Preoccupied by these new revelations, and building certainties about old truths.

The motel they rolled up to was rustic, on the Nevada border, boasting coin-operated beds.

She wasn't even sure what to do with that. It might have made her feel embarrassed, but she was basically filled up to the top with embarrassment. Or maybe it wasn't even embarrassment. It was something else. Something less juvenile. It was just a sort of unsettled feeling.

It's thwarted desire is what it is.

They checked into their separate rooms at opposite ends of the long, narrow building. Said vibrating bed had a woodsy vibe, and while she wouldn't be making full use of its capabilities, she liked the look well enough.

She sat down on the edge of the bed, her heart thundering hard. She tried to push everything away except for the feeling. This feeling of wanting a man and not knowing if she could have him. This feeling of uncertainty. It was a new experience. It just cut deep. She lay back and looked up at the ceiling.

Logan Martin had liked her in high school. She wondered what past her would've thought of it.

The answer was quick and definitive. Past Samantha would have been afraid of him. She would have been afraid of what she might do with that handsome, dangerous-seeming boy. Ironic, considering Will had gotten her pregnant at eighteen. Logan would've probably gotten her pregnant at sixteen.

That made her laugh. Uncontrollably. Maybe she was hysterical. It was entirely possible. There was a lot to be hysterical about in this present moment. It was so strange, and she would've said it wasn't her. Except it seemed to be.

She took a shower, even though she didn't really need one,

and changed into jeans and a T-shirt. She looked at her phone and saw that Logan had texted her.

Burgers?

Yes.

So maybe things were normal again.
But she didn't think she wanted them to be.
She was tired of normal.
She wanted something extraordinary. Even if it was a mistake.
God help her, she was willing to make as big of a mistake as it took with him.

twenty-two

She didn't bother to put any makeup on, and went outside, looking down the sidewalk, to see him standing outside his room door also. She waved, and immediately felt stupid. He did not wave back. But his lips did curve into a smile that she could see twenty doors down. He walked out toward the car, and when they got to it, he tossed her the keys.

She smiled and turned the key, noticing that the engine sounded different than the Ferrari. She was picking up all kinds of things about the cars.

"You do all of this by hand?" she asked.

"Yep," he said. He put some directions into his phone, and they started off down the road toward Izzy's Burger Spa.

"You must feel like they're art projects," she said, moving her fingertips over the steering wheel. All the cars had been great, but the Rolls was particularly ornate and glorious.

He looked at her like she was strange. "I wouldn't say I think of them that way."

"Well, there must be some emotion in it," she said. "You put pieces of yourself in work like this. It's like writing. Even my articles, it comes from me. That doesn't necessarily make it emotional or anything, but it is a little bit of myself on the page every time. This is physical work. You got the blood, sweat and tears thing."

"I guarantee you I have never shed a tear about a car."

"You know what I mean." She moved her hands idly up and down the steering wheel, stroking the glossy black. "It's basically you."

He looked at her, their eyes clashed, and suddenly the sexual nature of both the comment and the way she was touching the car hit her. She swallowed and looked away.

Thankfully, they were saved by their arrival at the restaurant. The seating was outside, ordering taking place at a little window in front of a small shack-looking building.

The smell of charcoal barbecue was strong, and it made her stomach growl.

She ordered a hamburger with extra avocado, and Logan got one with mushrooms. They sat down across from each other, and she dug ferociously into her fries as a distraction.

She really needed the distraction. Because she was just looking at him. Her stomach was all tight. As she had acknowledged, it wasn't actually embarrassment. It was that she wanted him. Was it wrong that she wanted him and also didn't necessarily want to concede to what he'd asked for? It wasn't like she wanted to test him out to see.

She just didn't want being with him to be about that. She wanted what they were to stand separate from the past, the baggage, their other *stuff*, and maybe that wasn't fair. Maybe it wasn't a realistic expectation. But she didn't see why she should have to be the one to give everything. She wasn't using him. She was not using him to have an experience. In that she was confident.

What she felt for him had nothing to do with Will. And that felt like something big.

"Why classic cars?" She genuinely wanted to know.

Because it was something she didn't know about him. Really, there was a lot she didn't know about him. It was the funny thing about living in a small town and having a lot of connections to a person. You could put together a picture of their life, but it was through the lens of a collective group of other people. It made you feel like you didn't have to ask them everything about themselves. In many ways, she knew Logan's biography. But she didn't know his story. She wondered if the same was true of him and her. Less so now. He knew quite a bit about her now.

"My uncle," he said. "It was his dream. It wasn't what he was doing. But it was his dream. He exposed me to cars like this. I got the bug. It felt like something that connected me to a part of my family I otherwise wasn't very connected to. Now I have my own interest. It's like a connection to history."

Of course it was something deeper than just thinking they were cool. Not that there was anything wrong with that. But every time she went down a layer with him, she found out there were more. It just seemed to be how he was.

"What about you? Why writing?"

"Do you want the answer that I've given everybody for the last twenty-two years?"

"No. I want the truth."

So she wouldn't be telling him she did it so she could stay home with the kids. Because it complemented Will's work, and brought in a little extra. All of that made it not about her. She wasn't that big of a martyr.

"Well, I've always wanted to get along with everybody, and yet wanted fiercely to be understood. Writing is a way to do that. To take my feelings and put them somewhere neutral. Give me a way to unravel them. Unpack them. I think that's part of it. Well, and I could do it while the kids were little. So there is some truth to the convenience part of the story. But *I've* always gotten something out of it. When I was staying home with the boys, it was a way to connect with other people. Even if it wasn't totally interactive, I was able to share pieces of myself and my life. It felt satisfying."

"You know, keeping your house clean when you have kids is an uphill battle. I only had one kid. But I always felt like I wasn't making progress in general. With being organized. With being emotionally what she needed. Every day I felt like I did a little something, and then I would slide right back. You don't do that when you're restoring cars. You plan, you order everything, you get the project outlines, you make progress every day. In the end, you have something perfect and finished. Then you ship it off, and you start something else."

He picked up a french fry and looked away, at the highway next to the restaurant, his blue gaze faraway. "Nothing in my life felt like that when Chloe was little. When Becca was sick, and then after she died... It all just felt like no matter how hard I tried, I was falling short in some way. That I wasn't as far through my grief as I thought, and it would all hit me at unexpected times. That I wasn't as good at supporting Chloe emotionally as I thought. That I couldn't get her lunches packed right, you name it. I always felt like it was one step forward, two steps back. But then I could go to work and do something concrete. It was like therapy in that way."

She nodded. "I get that. I do. Kids are rewarding, but you're right. It's a lot of endless work. For little thanks."

"I didn't need her thank me. I know that isn't what you meant. But you know, she was going through her stuff. She was a kid who lost her mother. I was always very aware of that. Of the fact that I was inherently not what she needed sometimes. That was hard. But that was where it was good that we had you."

We had you.

She was swamped suddenly with an ache in her chest. She had taken care of Chloe, but maybe in that way, she had taken care of Logan too. She wished she could have been there for him more. She could have comforted him. Physically.

Conflicted heat rioted through her.

That was the wrong way to imagine comforting someone who had lost a wife.

Yet she found the regret was real. The need.

But it made her feel good to know that at least by extension, she had been there for him. They finished their food and went back to the car. It was getting dark, the air blue and heavy. They parked and got out of the car, and she moved toward him, extending her arm and handing him the keys. He took them, and she turned to walk away. She made it half a step when he gripped her arm and pulled her back to him, up against his body, his blue eyes burning into hers.

She had a moment to move away. A moment to take in a breath. But she didn't move away.

Then, his mouth was on hers. Fierce and hard and knowing, there was so much knowing.

That she wanted him, that he wanted her. That things were not settled between them, and this was something driven by desire, and not really a concession, or a decision.

She was okay with that. Well. That was putting it mildly. She was a slave to it. This was pure need. Desire, want. This was everything. He was so strong, his hands knowing as they roamed over her body. They were still standing outside where anybody could see them. But she was having trouble caring about that. She didn't want to think. She didn't want to care about anything. Anything other than his hands, on her waist, her hips. Anything other than the insistent move of his mouth over hers. Other than anything at all.

Just him. The taste of him. The feel of him. They had kissed that one other time. But this time, she knew they wouldn't stop.

His arm still wrapped tightly around her waist, he held her against his body as he worked to open the door to his motel room.

When he closed it behind him and locked it, drawing the chain slowly all the way to the right in its golden cradle, she nearly wept with relief.

She wasn't alone. He was right there with her. He couldn't stop. Didn't want to.

As soon as that chain clicked, they might as well have been the only two people in the world. This might as well have been the only moment in time.

She knew what it was like to be a horny teenager, at the mercy of this clawing wild thing that took over your thoughts, your reservations. This wasn't the same. It was better. Made richer by experience and self-confidence. She might not have perfect body positivity, but she knew that Logan thought she was hot. That left her with absolutely no insecurity. She felt bold. Powerful. Excited. To let Logan see her. To see him.

He pulled her back into his arms and kissed her again. She pushed her hands up beneath the bottom of his shirt, her palm making contact with his hard midsection.

He was perfect. Need tore through her, and she found herself pulling his shirt off, her touch greedy, her need taking on a life of its own. She knew what she wanted. She knew that his body was exactly the kind of playground she wanted to play on.

But seeing him... She hadn't been prepared for that.

He was perfect. Toned and hard, and...tattooed.

It had been a while since she'd seen him without his shirt. She had in Hawaii, and had done her best not to hyperfocus on that situation. He had a tattoo now, over his shoulder, mountains that faded down into a bear. She reached her hand out and touched it, where the bear roared, just over his heart. "What's that?"

"A mother bear," he said. "Because she's still watching over Chloe."

It was perfect. It wasn't her name. It wasn't a scrolling, perfectly lovely tribute. It was the visceral, intense, aggressive love of a mother, permanently etched into his body because of the love he had as a father. A reminder not just of the softness that Becca would have brought to Chloe's life. But the fierceness. He carried it with him. She loved that. In that moment, she loved him for that.

"It's perfect," she said.

"I understand waiting a while to figure out what permanent tribute you want."

She nodded slowly. "Tributes are tricky. Because you're right. They're for you."

He nodded slowly. "Yeah. They are."

She was glad they'd stopped to talk.

Because it gave her a chance to think.

She still wanted this.

She moved her hands down his chest, over his stomach. He sucked in a sharp breath, closing his eyes. She wondered if every woman that saw him naked asked about that tattoo. She knew that they did. She also knew just suddenly, as deep as she knew anything, that he didn't tell them. He didn't tell them what it meant, because it was his heart. He might share his body with all and sundry, but she knew that Logan Martin didn't share his heart with just anybody.

Maybe he didn't share it with anyone at all.

She undid his jeans, sliding the zipper down slowly and pressing her palm against the hardness of his arousal.

She bit her lip, excitement breaking out in pinpricks all over her body.

It had been a while, months now, since she had been intimate with another person, the longest she had gone in more than twenty years. But this wasn't that. It wasn't just a response because of sexual deprivation. It was something more. Something deeper. Chemistry. Chemistry that had burned low and slow for all of these years. She might not have known everything about him or what he wanted, but she had known that he wanted her. She had known it was there.

He growled, moving her palm away from him and pinning her wrists down low behind her back. "Don't get ahead of yourself."

"With all the time we've wasted, I'd say we're behind."

"We are exactly where I say we are," he said, that stern, bossy tone sending an arrow of need straight down between her thighs.

This was him. The man who calmly, quietly pushed that cart through a grocery store in Hawaii as she gathered items that didn't matter much at all, except they meant everything to her. Had watched slowly as she had put herself back together in that way. Had been the strong, steady presence while she did so.

That man who had held himself together to care for his wife, who hadn't given in to despair because Becca had needed to see hope, and Chloe had needed to see strength.

She would take any orders that man gave. Who wouldn't? He kissed her mouth again, along the line of her jaw, down her neck. Then he released his hold on her just long enough to pull her shirt up over her head before pressing her back against the wall, this time with her wrists held fast above her head. He looked at her, his gaze hungry as it raked over her skin.

"We're not going to rush this," he said, his voice low. "I've waited too damned long. I'm going to savor every inch of you."

She shivered, the sensual promise affecting her so deeply she thought she was going to climax there and then.

He didn't touch her. He only looked, but that gaze was like a trail of fire over her skin. Then he lifted his hand, brushing his knuckles slowly down her cheek, moving his thumb over her lips. She rocked her hips forward, desperate for something. She was so wet. So needy for him. She ached with it. She knew sex. The mechanics of it. She knew arousal. But she didn't know this.

This was singular. They were singular. And he was going to drive her insane.

"Please," she begged.

"I like it when you beg," he said. "But you don't get to run the show here. Like I said. I'm not a zip line. I'm not an experience, not a ride for you to get on." Her cheeks felt hot, and she thought about that fleeting comparison she made earlier to him in a playground. She supposed that she deserved the scolding.

She maybe even liked it a little bit.

"Do you understand?"

"I understand," she whispered.

Slowly, maddeningly so, he undid the button on her jeans and lowered the zipper, still holding her fast as he managed to push them down her hips, taking them all the way down to the floor. She was left in only her quite unspectacular flesh-colored bra and seamless, no-creep panties that she had chosen for comfort, and certainly not because anyone was going to see them. He did not seem turned off by the practicality of her underwear. Quite the opposite. With that same featherlight touch, he moved his knuckles down the valley between her breasts, and she arched into him, cruelly denied a more intimate touch as he made his way down to her belly button, and lower still, following that centerline all the way down between her thighs, the brush of his knuckles there making her cry out with need.

"You are very impatient," he said.

"Yes," she said. "I am very impatient." Maybe if she agreed with him, he would go faster.

"Good girls learn to wait their turn."

Her hips bucked, searching for firmer contact with his hand. She'd never been so turned on in her life.

Her nipples were hardened to painful points, and she ached between her legs. Felt hollow. Desperate to be filled by him. She would have been happy, more than happy, with hard and fast. Foreplay, in this instance, was definitely overrated. And she didn't require it. He moved his hand away from her and she whimpered. Then he gripped her chin, holding her face straight and steady as he went in to kiss her again, slowly this time, his tongue sliding meaningfully against hers.

"Please," she whispered.

"What do you want?"

"You," she said.

"What do you want?" he repeated.

"You inside of me," she said, making eye contact with him.

"Good," he said.

She nearly melted with that affirmation. She wanted him so much. She couldn't even see straight. Couldn't think. Couldn't do anything but obey his commands and beg. Since he liked the begging.

"*Please*," she said again.

Then suddenly he released his hold on her, hauling her into his arms, the hard, hot press of his body against hers almost more than she could stand.

He kissed her. But more than that, he consumed her. She wrapped herself around him, giving herself over to the full force of her desire. He lifted her up, encouraging her to wrap her legs around his waist, and she did, and he walked them both over to the bed, laying her down on it, his body over hers, his eyes intent.

She reached up and pushed her fingers through his hair, gripped his face as she lifted herself up to kiss him. He reached behind her and undid her bra, pulling it off and flinging it onto the floor. He moved his hand to cup her breast, sliding his thumb over her nipple, making her gasp at the firm contact of his skin against hers. Then he lowered his head and took her nipple into his mouth, sucking deep.

Her hips bucked up off the bed, and he curved his arm around her, holding her up against him as he sucked her deep, biting her gently before releasing her again.

"Logan," she cried out.

He pushed his hand beneath the waistband of her underwear, moved his fingers between her slick folds, finding her entrance and pushing two fingers into her, pressing his mouth to hers as he mimicked the thrust of his fingers with his tongue.

She was lost. Utterly and completely. At some point, he removed her underwear altogether, though she wasn't overly conscious of when or how. His mouth was hot and knowing as it moved over her body, as he moved between her legs, licking and sucking her, holding her firm, his broad shoulders forcing her thighs apart as he ate her like a starving man.

She shattered. Utterly and completely. Then he moved away from her, getting rid of the rest of his clothes before joining her on the bed. She only had a moment to enjoy him visually. It wasn't enough. She would need more. He reached back toward his jeans, and it occurred to her just then, what he was going for.

"I can't get pregnant," she said.

"I know," he said.

She'd wept in his arms about that surgery, so of course he knew.

"Well. You don't need one. As long as you…"

"I'm good," he said.

"I trust you. You're you."

It was a big deal, she realized, not using a condom. But she didn't want to. She wanted him. As close as she could be. She wanted everything. As much as she could have.

This was the most fully honest moment of her life, and she didn't want anything to come between them. This might destroy everything. It might break apart that cul-de-sac life that she'd lived for so long. She wasn't going to be able to claim innocence. She wasn't above anything. She didn't need to be.

She'd lasted two months into the separation.

Her willpower was nothing.

But maybe it had nothing to do with willpower at all. Maybe

it was just honesty. For the first time, and not turning away from it. Not hiding behind a shield of needing to be good.

She wanted to weep. As he moved back to her, kissing her mouth, settling between her thighs.

She wanted to weep because all she cared about was how good it felt. Not what anyone would think, not what it would mean tomorrow. She didn't want to know what it would mean tomorrow. Or in a week. Or in a month. She really didn't want to know what it would mean in five months. It didn't matter. Nothing mattered but this. The slow press of him into her body, the uncomfortable, delicious stretches, the way he filled her.

She moaned, arching up against him, and he began to move. Hard, short strokes that hit her in all the right places. He whispered things in her ear. The kinds of things no one had ever said to her before. Dark and illicit, and something out of a fantasy she'd been too afraid to have.

This was a fantasy. One she had never allowed herself. How could she have? But she hadn't wasted time on the fantasy. It was just reality. Sharp and honest. Glorious in its friction. In its honesty.

She was so aware of everything. All the messy things. The things you edited out in a movie. It wasn't soft or gauzy or easy. It was teeth, and fingernails digging into his shoulder. It was a sharp sting as he thrust deep, bigger than she was used to. It was sweat and grunting and ragged breathing. It was all the glorious and filthy things that she had never allowed herself to want. It was truly beautiful.

When her release took hold, everything in her mind went blank. There was nothing. Nothing but this. Nothing but him. She felt free.

When his own need overtook him, when he clung to her as he growled out his climax, she shuddered again, a new wave of sensation overtaking her. The deep satisfaction of knowing that she had given him pleasure almost as good as her own.

They clung to each other. Breathing hard, the wreckage of so many decades of forbidden desire taking the shape of an up-ended bedspread and clothes all over the floor. It didn't seem like quite enough. It felt like the whole room should have come down around them. Or like lightning should have come through the roof, God smiting them for transgressions.

But no. They were whole, and so was the room. So was everything.

For a brief moment she was sort of disappointed they had survived the thunderstorm. Because that meant consequences. But not just yet. Instead, she pressed her head to his chest, resting her hand over his raging heartbeat. Over the bear. She traced those dark lines with her fingertips, and then he pressed his index finger to the inside of her forearm, doing the same, making a path over her tattoo. They were tracing each other's grief. Looking at it. Acknowledging it.

Her eyes filled with tears, and she pressed her face more firmly against his chest, trying to cover them up.

He wrapped his arm around her, and kissed her head.

The simple, comforting, nonsexual gesture tangling up her insides.

If she'd had a chance to think about this ahead of time, she would've said that being naked with Logan would be awkward or strange. But it wasn't. It just felt like a long time coming. Because this was the truth of it. The full exposure of all the lies that she had told herself for all these years.

They wanted each other. They had each other.

It wasn't enough. It wasn't going to be. Something inside of her chest cracked. Because one thing was perfectly clear to her. Her marriage was irredeemably broken. She was never going back to him.

She wanted to laugh. A little bit. Because this was just another example of her epic denial. Of course she wasn't going back to him. Of course it had never really been an option from the moment she had really started digging into everything.

But she couldn't... She couldn't just jump into another relationship. She had been married for twenty-two years. Had been in a relationship since she was sixteen years old. There was just... She had needed this. But it had been a dead end. Because what could she possibly get from this? She had to go eat and pray before she could love, right? That was the thing. Everybody knew it was dumb to rebound. It sold everyone short.

She had lived her life beholden to somebody else for so long, and she...

"Stop," he said, his voice firm.

"What?"

"Thinking. Planning. Trying to spin out every last damn implication of this."

"How can I not?"

"Well, that means I'm a failure, because my intent was to fuck your brains out."

She couldn't help herself. She laughed. "I mean, my brains aren't intact. Trust me. Though..." A pulse started to beat at the apex of her thighs again, and she marveled at the fact that she could be so confused and get aroused at the same time. He had that effect. "I can go again."

"Give me a minute," he said.

"But see, if I have a minute, I'm going to start thinking. I can't help it."

"Just don't."

"How?"

"It's a trick I learned," he said. "When Becca was sick. I knew what the future held. I knew she was going to die. But I didn't think about that. I counted the breaths that she was taking right now. I would make myself conscious of the air, the position of the sun in the sky, the feeling of my clothes on my body. Anything and everything to ground myself in the moment. There is nothing more than the moment. Everything else is a what-if. Nothing else is real. The past is gone. The future doesn't exist yet. This," he said, his blue eyes so intense she had to fight not to look away. "This is the only thing that's real. Right now. We are all that's real. Everything outside that door is only a possibility." At this, he dragged his fingertips along her lower lip again. "This is the only real thing in the world."

He lowered his head and kissed her again, and she let herself get caught up in that. In that seductive promise. In everything.

The only real thing.

twenty-three

She woke up pressed against an unfamiliar masculine body. It all came back to her. Quickly and in stunningly vivid Technicolor. Logan. She didn't know quite what to do. She needed to go back to her room. She didn't know what time it was. She hadn't texted anybody who was expecting a text from her, and they would probably think that she was dead on the highway somewhere. She needed to get back to her things. To her space so that she could…breathe. So that she could text her kids and her friends.

She slipped away from the warmth of his hold and out of bed, collecting her clothes.

She didn't want to call Elysia and Whitney.

It was a weird thing to think, except when she'd first had sex, she'd been ashamed and horrified at herself…and desperate to talk to her friends.

She wasn't horrified or ashamed, not this time.

But she didn't want to share it either.

Which was inconvenient in some ways because she was also confused. She didn't know what to do next. She didn't know anything. It would have been helpful to talk to her friends, to share the moment. But the moment felt like hers and Logan's. Like it didn't belong to anyone else. It was wound around too many other personal things.

Becca, her death, his tattoo. His feelings for her in high school.

Her fears about her own wickedness. Her shortcomings as a wife. Her cowardice. Her audacity.

She didn't know how she managed to find herself a wicked coward who also had audacity, but she did.

In the middle of all that, though, was satisfaction. And the knowledge she wouldn't take last night back even if she could.

There was a lesson in all this, she supposed. The same lesson that had been there from the beginning. This lesson about uncertainty and discomfort. About being okay with being messy and wrong and not having any idea what she was doing. But while she was accepting that it was her lesson, she still wasn't entirely comfortable with it.

That was its own lesson.

She stepped outside, and realized that the sun hadn't come up yet. She hadn't even bothered to check the time. She took her phone out of her purse and saw that it was four in the morning.

She clutched her chest as she walked down the sidewalk toward her room. She was doing a very short little walk of shame. This was a new experience.

She wasn't ashamed though. Not really. At least, that wasn't the dominant feeling. It was, as ever, more complex than that. She growled quietly as she let herself into her room. She was a little bit tired of complexity, honestly. She took a shower, and as the warm water washed over her skin, she tried not to imagine what it had been like when he touched her.

Her head was full of him. She felt like she was failing her assignment, only recently given to her. To see about this new life on her terms.

That was on your terms. You wanted him.

It was true. She had. She was taking points from herself for involving another person, but the truth was, she and Logan were involved. They had been.

They were just being honest now.

She found some pajamas and put them on, climbed into bed. She lay there with her eyes closed for two hours. She didn't sleep. Not at all.

Then she got up and grabbed her phone, texting the kids to let them know that she had arrived in South Lake Tahoe, and then texting Elysia and Whitney the same.

It was Elysia who was awake and responded immediately.

Good. I was worried.

No need to worry. Just got distracted.

It felt disingenuous. But she couldn't talk about what had happened.

She waited in her room. And paced. Waited for him to come and knock. But he didn't.

Finally she gathered all of her things and walked down toward where the car was parked. She could text him. He could text her. Finally, in a fit of frustration, she knocked on his door.

It only took a second for him to open it. Shirtless. He was only wearing his jeans, and she knew they were the same jeans that she had taken off of him last night, and there was something extremely intimate about this morning after she had tried not to have.

So this was what it was like. To be intimate with somebody when you weren't in a relationship. When you hadn't professed to love each other or made any promises about the future, and in fact actively couldn't make promises about the future.

"I thought maybe you'd taken a bus back to Oregon," he said.

"No. I just went to take a shower."

"At about four o'clock."

"You were awake?"

"I was a single dad. Everything wakes me up. Hyper-vigilance."

"Well, then, don't go calling me a coward if you didn't try to stop me from going." She didn't know why it irritated her. That he'd done that. That he hadn't tried to have the conversation then. Maybe if he'd done that, she just would have let him talk her back into bed.

The thought made her warm.

"I wasn't going to tell you what to do."

"You had no trouble with that just a few hours before."

"Different contexts," he said.

"I wasn't running away. I needed a shower, and I needed to text everyone and let them know I wasn't dead."

"I see."

"I forgot. I text Elysia and Whitney and the kids every time we get to a new location. I was distracted. They might have thought I was…serial killed or something."

They stared at each other for a long moment. She could tell that he wanted to have a fight with her. She sort of wanted to have a fight with him. She wasn't entirely sure why. But she felt something intense burning in her chest, and she needed to let it out. She just didn't know exactly what it was. What it meant.

The easiest way seemed to be yelling. Or maybe sex. But neither one seemed like an easy thing to reach for while they were standing in that motel doorway, her on the outside, him on the inside. She could feel them both trying to manufacture reasons. So instead she took a step toward him and wrapped her fingers around the back of his neck, stretched up and kissed him. Just light. More of a friendly kind of thing really.

She slid her hand down his bare chest, and he growled. She liked that. It was a little feral and ridiculous, but it was really hot. Suddenly the kiss felt deeper than it had when she'd given it.

"See," she whispered. "I didn't run away."

He looked at her, and she could see the question there. If she wanted to go right back into that hotel room and do more of what had happened last night.

"Yes," she said softly. "But I suspect that we should talk."

"I was afraid you would say that."

"Me too. But maybe let's get coffee. I hate morning sex anyway."

The look he gave her spoke volumes. He had taken that as a challenge. She thrilled at that. Great. She was doing such a good job with the rational adult thing.

"*Coffee*," she restated.

"Let me get my things."

They drove through a coffee place. They didn't stop. She figured that was for the best anyway. Better to have the conversation in the confines of the car than to actually talk about what had happened surrounded by a bunch of men who fancied themselves entrepreneurs, shouting into their phones, and college students and parents who had just completed school drop-off.

She was certain that was who would be in the coffee shop on a weekday morning. Coffee shops were the same all over the country. Probably all over the world.

"Why did that happen?"

"You don't know?"

"I mean, I know from the standpoint of failures and self-control and human nature. But after what happened when we kissed, I don't know. I don't know how to do this. I'm not you, Logan. I haven't had years' worth of one-night stands bolstering me. I haven't had time to explore the idea of sex without a relationship. Anyway, you were pretty dead set against doing anything like that with me."

"No, I was dead-set against being something you wanted to

do to get back at Will. But it turns out I wanted to have sex with you more than I wanted to make sure that wasn't happening. Apparently I can be bought. I didn't realize my self-respect was for sale, but there you go."

She felt bad about that. She didn't want him thinking that. And at the same time, she found it flattering that he had abandoned his principles for a chance to have her. That was a new feeling. She felt so specifically wanted by him, and it did things to her.

"I didn't think of him at all. I just want you to know that. Not what he would think, and not how it was different. You know he's the only man I've been with. Other than you. I'm still not comparing. I can't."

"Because you're in love with him?"

"Because it's not the same thing. This thing is not… I know it sounds crazy, because you also know that I got pregnant when I was in high school. Which speaks to a lack of control. But it isn't the same. It's not the same as being a teenager, and being led around by your hormones. It's not hormones for me now. It's chemistry. I've never experienced that with anyone but you. There's a reason I almost kissed you when that went against everything that I believe in. Because I would've stayed with him. Until the end, I would've stayed with him. I never would've turned over any of those rocks. I wanted to kiss you so badly, Logan. I don't want you to think that me turning away shortchanges what we had. The fact that it happened at all demonstrates how much I wanted you. How different it is. There is not another man on Earth who could have enticed me into that position. I was always so careful. I didn't want to be careful with you. I remember all those moments of my family vacation with so much clarity. The moments where it was you and me. Where knowing you started to turn into something more."

He made a grunting sound and accelerated.

"It's true," she said. "Look, I have no idea where I'm headed. But I do know that I'm not going back to Will."

He turned to look at her. "You know that?"

She felt something break inside of her. "Yeah. I know that."

For the first time since all of this started, she really felt like her marriage was over. She really knew that it was.

She couldn't help it, a sob rose in her chest, and she didn't even bother to hold back as tears spilled down her cheeks.

"I know he thinks him wanting to be with other people, or wanting more freedom, doesn't mean he isn't in love with me or our life. But…it does for me. This isn't the same thing. I don't want other people. I want you. Very specifically you. That doesn't work. I can never have an open relationship. I'll tell you that much. I can't want two men at the same time. I can't be with two at the same time. I can't… I also need for this to be… I don't know where I'm headed. That's the thing. I eliminated the destination that I thought I was going to. It's not with him anymore. I know that. But I don't know where it is. I need to be okay with the uncertainty, and I am trying. I got so angry at you when you demanded to know after the kiss in Boston. I didn't want to tell you that I wasn't going to be with him just because I wanted you. Does that make sense? I didn't want to lie. I didn't want to choose something that felt good at the time, but that I would regret later. I wanted to give it space."

She swallowed hard. "I wanted to make sure that when I told you something, it was true. Mostly I didn't want to think about him at all. I'm just exhausted. From tearing my own life into pieces."

"Are you giving me the this-is-all-I-have-to-offer-you speech?"

"Maybe. Except that shortchanges it too. But I'm a mess. And so is my whole life. Lucky you, having a front-row ticket to the whole thing. I am uncertain. I'm trying not to rush to make myself certain. Because that's how I ended up where I am now."

"I can handle that."

"I mean, we'll save money," she said, looking out the window.

"How so?"

"We only need one room for the rest of the trip."

"You think so?" he asked.

"I mean, we can play games, Logan, but we both know we're going to end up back in bed. We might as well just accept it. I might not be able to see further ahead than tonight, but I know that I am going to jump you again."

"Assuming I'm fine with that."

She looked at him, hard, forcing him to look away from the road and into her eyes. "You're not going to say no to this."

"Yeah. Damn straight I'm not."

They were both just desperately human.

She might have no experience with this whatsoever, but she knew that you didn't have sex that good, spend another three weeks and forced proximity with the person you had it with, and resist it. She didn't even want to try. She felt like she'd had years of resisting all kinds of things. He was emblematic of that. She didn't want to resist. She just wanted to see what was on the road ahead.

No planning. Just being.

Not being afraid of herself. Or what anyone would think. Easy, when she knew they had miles of only strangers ahead of them. They took the long stretch that day, heading all the way to Utah. Then he didn't take them to a roadside place, but to a resort nestled in the mountains, with villas that each had a hot tub.

"Well, this is an upgrade," she said. "We're not saving any money."

"I wasn't thinking about saving money. I was choosing where I wanted to have you next."

The words sent a shiver down her spine.

Was this her life? Suddenly at this out-of-the-way place with this man who said those kinds of things to her. Who made her feel this way.

It was her life right now. She couldn't guarantee it would be her life forever. But it was her life right now.

The villas were nestled into the side of the mountain, with views, and privacy. Completely blocked off from each other, but open to the landscape.

So even with all the lights on in the place, as they trailed in with their bags, she embraced the boldness that overtook her, and pulled her shirt off, slipped out of her jeans, took off her bra and her underwear. She had been looking forward to this part of her life. Wandering around her house inhibition-free because that was what empty nesters were supposed to be able to do, and she could have it now.

Logan's short, low curse was satisfying.

"It's really too bad we don't have groceries. Maybe I'd cook dinner for you."

"I would be worried that you would sustain an injury to parts of you I really don't want wounded."

She laughed. "You're kind of basic."

"Hell yeah."

She liked that about him. That he was complicated most of the time, but basic when her tits were out. It was pretty comforting. She felt basic looking at him too. So it seemed fair. He sat down on the couch and watched her. She made a show of slowly moving their bags into the bedroom, and she knew that it was a game. Because he had historically helped her with bags on every trip they'd ever taken, it wasn't a lapse in chivalry. But maybe she needed this. This feeling of being admired. In a wholly sexual way. This strange, giddy sense of freedom as she was free from her inhibitions in front of him.

As she freed herself from inhibition in herself she hadn't been aware was there.

When she was finished, he looked at her from his position on the couch, lazy, but it was deceptive. He was more like a predator. Just waiting.

"Come here," he said.

Her body heated. She obeyed the command. She sat down on his lap, his jeans rough against her backside. Then he gripped her chin and kissed her, holding her right where he wanted her, one hand resting on her thigh, the other holding her face as he took the kiss deeper and deeper.

She shivered. The very deliberate way that he didn't touch her all over was beginning to drive her mad, his palm burning into her thigh, her whole body desperate for that kind of warmth.

She could feel his intense need to control the interactions between them. She wondered if on some level it was a punishment. For how long he'd had to wait. For some other failure on her part. Because there was a tension to all this that she didn't quite understand.

But it felt good. So she wasn't going to fight it. She wasn't going to question it. He took her hand and guided it to the front of his jeans, to where he was hard and ready for her. She knew exactly what to do with that. She undid his belt, the button on his jeans, the zipper.

He moved his hand over her hair, down her back, and she followed the unspoken instruction, sliding off of his lap and down to the floor as she exposed him.

He put his finger under her chin, tilting her face up so that she met his gaze. "You're gonna have to learn how to do this for me," he said. "Don't just do what he likes. Pay attention to what I like."

She didn't even want to think about that. Because how could she compare her previous experience to this? There was no way. She wouldn't lie. Typically, in her marriage, she looked at a blow job as a gift. For him.

But this…this felt like something for her. Like he was offering her the prize.

She leaned in, testing him, his responses, to her lips, her tongue. To taking him deep, to going slow or fast.

Using her hands.

She was so aroused she thought she was going to die from it. But what a way to go.

She couldn't complain.

Abruptly he gripped her hair and stopped her, guiding her back up onto his lap. He was still mostly clothed, but he guided her over his arousal, and she sank slowly onto him, biting her lip as he filled her.

He held her hips as she rode him, as they established a rhythm that worked for them both.

He gripped the back of her head, pressing her forehead to his, praising her, telling her how beautiful she was. How good she felt.

Her climax hit her before she was ready. Before she had even really felt it build. The cry that escaped her mouth was half shock, half deep pleasure.

His head fell back, his teeth clenched together, his jaw tight as he held her, and gave himself up to his own release.

"I knew I picked a good place," he said.

She laughed and moved forward, pressing her head to his chest.

They were going to sleep in the same bed tonight. All night.

She didn't know how she felt about it, but she knew it was going to happen. She wanted it. She just didn't know how she felt about it.

They got into the hot tub, and everything that happened there felt a little bit naughty and just plain fun. It was amazing, how being with him cut the way it did, but also was just so enjoyable.

By the time they went to bed, she was exhausted in the best way. She just felt satisfied. Boneless. Better than she had for a very long while.

It was so domestic, brushing her teeth in the same bathroom where he had just brushed his. She hadn't stood next to him while he did it or anything. She was in no hurry to make things too cozy. She liked the edge to this. The danger. She liked the way he was Logan, but also felt a little bit like a stranger. Because this was a whole new part of him. She didn't need to turn it into…

She deliberately didn't think about relationship words.

She walked out of the bathroom, and he was already in bed, shirtless, and she really would never get tired of looking at his torso.

She had put on some sweats after the hot tub, after their shower, which had been slick and wonderful, but now she was feeling a little bit overdressed. She took her shirt off and shimmied out of her pants, and got beneath the covers next to him.

The sheets were soft against her skin, and he wrapped his arm around her, his skin hot against hers.

It felt so deliberate, climbing into bed with him like this. Deliberate and sexy and also like an out-of-body experience. To be beside him like this.

She reached her hand out and put it on his chest, looking up at him. "I guess I didn't ask if you wanted me to sleep in a different room."

"Why would I want that?" He reached out and pulled her against him. "It would be inconvenient."

"Yeah," she said. "I guess it would be."

She had a lot of questions she wanted to ask. Like if he normally shared beds with women. Or if this was different for him. Strange. If this was something completely outside of his comfort zone.

Maybe he always slept with the women he was having sex with.

She stopped herself from going down that path. This was just the two of them. There was no room for anyone else in this bed.

No ghosts of marriages past or anything else.

She listened to the beat of his heart. Wondered if she was crazy or if it actually sounded new.

Well, it didn't matter what was true, she supposed. It felt true. This felt different. Like theirs.

She had been consumed by what the future might hold. She had been consumed with untangling the past and all of her issues. But she was determined to let this trip be about now. About the two of them.

About herself and this moment.

She could think of nothing she wanted more.

twenty-four

Where the other road trips had been about discoveries they made during the day, she found the key part of this trip—The Loneliest Road—happened at night.

When they found each other in new and interesting ways. There was part of her that wanted to tell herself she hadn't needed this. That it was fun, but that she wasn't such a cliché that sexual discovery felt like an integral part of her experience and who she was. But it did. It just did. There had been wounds, things that she had tried not to internalize in the past few months about her own beauty. Her own ability to satisfy a man, and he went to great lengths to destroy those insecurities. Just by being him.

But that wasn't all, or everything. Those parts of herself that had been afraid to step outside of boxes were being challenged here and now with him.

So much of her marriage had been defined by fear, and she would never have realized that if not for these recent events. In addition to that, there was still a lot of shame.

They had gotten married because they'd had sex. On some

level, she had felt like there were certain things that she could never ask to have changed. Certain things she couldn't ask for.

She didn't know why. It was only that there was a level of feeling like the sex that had brought them there was the sex they had to keep on having. Whether that made sense or not. That any more was a reflection of her...being wrong.

Dirty in some way. Maybe the reason Will had been forced into this life he hadn't been happy with in the end.

It was so loaded. So shame-filled.

Logan took that narrative and shattered it.

Because there was nothing that she asked for or did that shocked him. She couldn't find it in her to feel shame. She probably should.

By the standards of everyone who knew them, they were sinners now.

And so was Will. And so was everybody.

She tried really hard not to let those thoughts in. When she did, like now, what she tried to do was identify it, label it, and put it into a box for later.

She and Logan had made it to Colorado, and were literally parked on a mountaintop, kissing, and more in the back seat of the car.

They could go to the motel. They could find a bed. But there was something wonderful about this. There was something giddy about it.

Challenging the ghosts of her old self.

When they checked into the motel, she felt giddy, bringing it all down the mountain with her. It was wonderful. She blushed when he asked for one room with a king-size bed, and when he accepted the upgrade of the jetted tub.

She wondered if the kid working at the check-in counter believed that they were about to have crazy sex in that room, or if he thought they were more like his parents than anything else.

She wanted to tell him there was a lot of life left ahead.

But she didn't, because that kind of stuff was only ever annoying to hear from adults, and you couldn't ever really know it
until you knew it. They departed from The Loneliest Road and
went sharply south, heading all the way to Florida. To Miami,
where it was hot and full of neon and brightly colored buildings. They both made the decision to rebook their flights for
a week later, so that they could stay on the beach, and do the
things they hadn't when they were in Hawaii.

They still weren't talking about any kind of future. What
future was there to talk about?

She had made the decision to pour herself into this moment.
To make it entirely about them. Not about what was next.

But this was also a break in format, this week in a little villa
on the ocean.

She got a bikini, because she could see that he liked it,
and looking at her own body through the hunger in his eyes
changed something. It didn't feel like a power move, not the
kind she had been searching for that day back in the boutique
in California. It felt like a game between lovers. If she spent all
day out on the beach in the bikini, by the time they got back
to the room he was in a state of torture, and she couldn't deny
that she enjoyed that.

The element of delayed gratification was always going to be
a part of them.

Well, however long always was. She didn't really know what
it looked like at the moment.

Late in the day she would put on a cover-up, and he put on a
T-shirt, and they would walk down to a bar that was right there
on the beach. They were probably two of the most dressed-up
people there. They had fish and drinks, and sometimes they
would dance to salsa music, even though neither of them really knew what they were doing, and in general it was mostly
foreplay until they could get back to the room.

It made her ache.

It was another one of those buried truths. Another one of her maybe-the-next-time-around feelings that had echoed in her chest for longer than she wanted to admit, even to herself. When she saw couples who looked at each other like this. When she read books where the desire was all-consuming, or saw movies where people gave up every last inhibition to consume each other. She had never believed she would have it. She had wanted it. Having it with him now was a vague sort of torture. Beautiful, and sexy, but torture all the same. Still, she was willingly submitting herself to it.

It was warm and humid outside, and after they made love that night, they had the doors to the bedroom open out to the private deck, the sound of the waves crashing soothing and perfect.

Logan was holding her in his arms, her body curved into his.

"It's okay to put yourself first, you know. To think you're special."

It was so unexpected, and it hit her somewhere that was so sore, she nearly gasped in pain when he spoke the words.

It was like he had reached all the way down inside of her and found the smallest, sorriest piece of her insecurity, and pressed his palm to it.

Because at the heart of everything, of all of her fear, of everything she did, was the deep belief that she really didn't deserve all that much. That she wasn't good enough. She didn't trust herself, she didn't believe that what she wrote was unique enough or mattered enough to go anywhere, she hadn't thought that what she needed in her marriage was important enough to get in a fight about.

Her mother hadn't meant to, but she had taught her to put herself last and last and last again. Every time she had worried about what people in the community thought, people at church, she had been putting herself last.

She hadn't been miserable, but it had been little things, over the years, waves against rocks, wearing them down, making them smooth. Taking away everything sharp, everything interesting, everything that was theirs.

She had allowed that to happen. She had done it to herself, and encouraged everyone around her to pile right on.

She had a stake in her own unhappiness.

Logan had been the only person to identify the very root cause of it. Logan had been the only one to see. Even deeper than she had, exactly why she did it.

She couldn't say anything, so she just moved her hand along his chest, along his muscles, which were familiar now, but no less thrilling for it.

This hadn't been about discovering the landscape out there. She had been discovering the landscape of his body. In this moment, even more profoundly, the landscape of herself.

"I don't know how to do that," she said, her throat tight.

"Just like this. A step at a time, listening to yourself."

She didn't know what she did to deserve this. But maybe that was that same old thinking. Except she wanted to give to him, in the same way that he was giving to her. It wasn't about earning his affection, or earning the right to lie next to him in bed. It was just about…wanting to give him something. Wanting to give in equal measure to what he was doing for her, not because there were roles to fulfill, or because there was something she owed him. It wasn't like that.

It wasn't a series of payments. It was just need. But everything with him was. Maybe more than that.

Maybe it was want.

"Do you listen to yourself?" she asked.

"I do whatever I want all the time," he said, stroking her arm absently.

She knew that wasn't true.

But she didn't know how to say that. Or even if she had the right to. Because her life was changing in ways that were out of her control, sure. Or had been at first. Now they were changes

she was choosing, and embracing, changes that she was own-
ing. His changes hadn't been like that. She didn't know how to
navigate his grief on this level. Which made her feel unequal to
him. She knew what grief felt like. But the kind of grief that he
had experienced, the kind that disrupted your whole life, every
aspect of it, that she didn't know. So she just said what she believed to be true, because she didn't have platitudes. Sometimes
platitudes were useless anyway. Most of the time they were.

"You're a good man. A good father. You've just done everything so...so well."

It felt like a pale imitation of what she really wanted to say.
Of what should be said to a man like him. It was two shades
away from *that'll do, pig*, and that was pretty useless. But in this
moment, it was the best she had. She wasn't ready to leave. They
weren't even flying back to the West Coast together. She was
headed up to Vermont to visit with Jude and his girlfriend for
a week before she headed back.

They had a shorter gap between trips this time, and she
wanted to ask him if they would see each other. What they
would do. She wanted to know all kinds of things, and she
wasn't sure how to ask. She wasn't sure if he was going to tell
her. She wasn't even sure what she wanted to know. So she just
tried to leave it in the present. She wrapped herself around him
that night and hoped that everything would come together in
the end.

Whatever that looked like.

They went to the airport at the same time together the next
morning, but weren't even flying on the same airline and had
separated before security. He had curved his arm around her
and kissed her, and it was about the only thing that gave her a
sense of comfort as she walked to her gate.

He hadn't gone platonic on her just because the trip was over.
But she was stuck on the way they'd had radio silence last

time, and she knew the circumstances were different, but still. She worried about it on the plane, and she had to laugh, because here she was, obsessing about a man.

She stopped herself from thinking that. Because she was minimizing her own feelings. The fact that for the first time in her life she was having a sexual relationship without promises. Without parameters. That at forty years old she was having some kind of revelation. A revolution, sexually and emotionally, and she wasn't going to reduce it by telling herself she was just worrying about a boy. Because it wasn't that. She was a grown woman, and he was a man she cared about a lot. He had been part of her life for years, and had been instrumental in helping her realize certain things about herself. He was the only person who seemed to know and understand why she felt certain things. Why she did certain things. Not even she had understood them on the level that he did. She was not going to minimize her feelings just because she knew what an article on the internet might say. An article on the internet didn't know her. Didn't understand her experiences.

Now, she wasn't sure she trusted her own feelings. So there was that. But she wasn't going to deny them or pretend they didn't exist. She wasn't going to push them down and tell herself they didn't matter.

She never even got her laptop or a book out on the plane, because she was too busy policing her feelings, and then reminding herself not to.

She just needed to stop worrying about him. She was going to go see her son. She was going to focus on him and his new life, and not think about hers at all.

Right now, the idea of just being someone's mom felt like a relief.

twenty-five

She had Whitney and Elysia over to her apartment when she got back home. She didn't know yet if she and Logan were taking a breather until the next road trip or if she should just invite him over after they left.

She just didn't know yet. But that was a hallmark of the whole experience.

"So how was this trip?" Whitney asked, bringing a plate of cheese over to the table and having a seat.

"Good," she said. "Jude is great, and his girlfriend is darling."

"Did you tell him about you and Will?"

Will?

She couldn't even think about…about what she needed to tell her kids about Will for a full thirty seconds. All she could think about was Logan.

"I… No. I just told him Will was working."

She hesitated. But she felt like she needed to share this, not so much out of the friendship obligation or anything like that, but because she was at a loss, and tired of finding wisdom in herself to the best of her ability.

Sometimes she needed a little bit of help. That was another step forward.

Because she didn't like to admit uncertainty any more than she liked to expose cracks in her life.

But she had kept so much of her messiness to herself, even hidden from herself, and she felt like this was an opportunity to put it out there. On the table.

"I… Things are changing between me and Logan," she said slowly. "I… I slept with him."

She wanted to give thanks that Elysia and Whitney didn't squeal or act excited, or even look at each other in a knowing way. Or owe each other money like there was some kind of secret bet, like they both knew things about her that she didn't, because that would've been unbearable.

"Oh," Elysia said. "You… Well."

"Yes. Well. I mean, I slept with him more than once. To be clear. I slept with him a lot of times. That was basically the whole trip, and then also the whole extra week in Miami."

"What about Will?" Elysia asked.

"I don't… I don't know. I mean, I do know. I'm not getting back with him."

She had said that to Logan, the only other person. It felt good to say it again. "That was starting to become clear to me before, but really, once I was with him, I knew."

"Samantha…" Whitney looked deeply concerned.

"Look," Elysia said, her tone pragmatic. "The ho phase is necessary. Believe me. You have to kind of sort out what you've been missing, and how sex works these days, and all of that."

"I don't think it's a ho phase," Sam said.

Elysia winced. "Sam, it's not… He's Will's friend, and you've known him a thousand years, and he was married to Becca…"

"I am actually very clear on his biography," she said. "But I have feelings for him."

As soon as she said that, she knew how true it was. "I don't know what that means. I get why you're looking at me like I've committed a cardinal sin. Because believe me, I know. I want to be very, very sure that I'm not just leaping into this because I'm afraid of being alone. I don't want to do anything because I'm afraid. I married Will because I was afraid. I have never examined any of the issues in our marriage because I was afraid. I don't want to do things out of fear, not anymore."

"It is actually fair to do things because the man is hot," Whitney said. "Will did put all that on the table…"

"It doesn't matter anymore. The rules, or anything like that. I haven't talked to Will for almost three months. You know what, I don't miss him like I should. He was a habit. Like brushing my teeth. I mean, that's not fair, because that makes it sound like I don't feel anything for him, and that isn't true either. We were happy in many ways. But we were more comfortable than we were anything else. I just needed to tell you…even though I don't have it all figured out. I'm going to have to…deal with my marriage and tell the kids and…"

"Oof," said Elysia, putting her hand to her chest.

"Yes. Exactly."

She realized her friends didn't wholly approve either. She was going to have to be her own barometer. Like trying on a dress and not asking someone else's opinion. Because actually nobody else knew. She wasn't going to tell them. She couldn't dig into all the ways that she and Logan weren't a cliché, the ways that he wasn't just a ho phase, though he had certainly done a lot for her inner ho.

But all the clarity, all the certainty, was going to have to come from inside her. No one was going to fulfill everything for her, or give her the answers. She had to fulfill herself. She had to find the answers in herself.

Of all the uncomfortable things.

"You need to be happy," Whitney said.

"Yeah," she said. "I do."

But she knew that it was going to be up to her to decide what that looked like.

She decided that for tonight, she was going to sleep by herself, and get a feel for life in town. Life in this apartment she'd chosen for herself. Life on her own terms.

With or without the approval of the people around her.

She spent three days in that space. On the afternoon of that third day, she decided to go to the garage.

Logan was there, and she could see his coveralls-clad legs sticking out from underneath the silver car he was currently working on.

"Is this ours?"

He rolled out from beneath the vehicle, his eyebrows raised. "Yes. I wasn't sure if I would see you."

"Well, you know, you could actually come see me."

"I'm very aware of the fact that this summer is yours," he said.

"Yes," she said, looking around the garage. "This summer is mine. That's why I'm here. Because it's where I want to be."

He looked away for a second, then back at her. "Well, that's nice."

"Have you been down to see Chloe again?"

"She came up here while you were over in Vermont. Stayed with me for the weekend. I think she enjoyed being back. But I also think she was pretty ready to leave. It's tough. When they're just... They don't need you anymore."

"Oh, they need you. I know you didn't have the same kind of relationship with either of your parents that I did with mine. But I can tell you, as someone who had...has, parents that I felt close to, but who definitely weren't perfect, you need them. You feel the lack of them when they're gone. You don't need to be perfect for her to need you. I'm personally experimenting with imperfection."

"Yeah?"

"Have you talked to Will?"

"Oddly, sleeping with you made me feel not so keen to see what he was up to."

"Yeah. You would think, though, that he..."

"I think he's busy."

"Is he just having like a second life as a frat boy?"

"Do you care?"

"I really don't, actually."

He smiled and stood up. He had dirty, greasy hands, and when he put them on her face, she didn't even complain. When he leaned in and kissed her, she kissed him back, and it felt like coming home in a way going into that apartment hadn't. She looked up at him, her gaze questioning, but he didn't give her any answers.

"Come over tonight," he said.

"Okay." She looked back at the car. "You lied," she said, feeling breathless.

"About?"

"This car has no back seat."

"I didn't think the question was about a literal back seat, but more about whether or not I was planning to satisfy you, and thoroughly, throughout the trip."

"And that's a yes?" she asked.

He lowered his head, his forehead pressed to hers. He saw her. She didn't want to hide. "That's a hell yes."

"Good."

"I'll see you tonight."

This was another change. Another shift. But she was still working out what it meant. Because now they weren't even taking a break from each other. Now they were bringing each other into their life here.

They didn't walk around in public like a couple. They didn't go out to eat or anything like that. She slept alone maybe twice a week, but otherwise, they were at each other's houses, and even if they slept separate, that didn't mean they didn't hook up at some point during the day.

The drive between them to be physical was intense, and it was something that she refused to minimize. It was clearly something she needed. Something she was hungry for. This passion. The way that he was with her. Like he was discovering sex for the first time all over again with her.

It meant something to her because she had only been with one other man. Her experience was limited.

It meant something that he felt the same way, because he'd been with quite a few women, and had experience with casual sex. Somehow, the blend of the two realities made her feel like it must be real.

If he could feel this with his experience, and she could feel it with her lack, well, that had to matter.

When it came time for them to head north, to take the car up over The Great Northern road and go on their final trip, they drove from his house to the garage together. And that felt significant. It felt real. But so did everything else. The clock was winding down, and she knew that she would have to make some decisions she didn't necessarily want to.

But for just a little while longer, maybe she could just be lost in this. In him.

At first she'd been desperate for the summer to end, and now it felt like an execution date.

Except she wasn't a prisoner. She was in charge of her own life. Of what she did with her time. So she supposed it was up to her to decide what to do next.

It was time to stop living in the present.

It was time to figure out what happened next.

twenty-six

The Great Northern
1953 Chevy Corvette
Now

The drive north was lush and green, even in the heat, and when they got into Washington, it was a good twenty degrees cooler than it had been down in southern Oregon.

They didn't linger in Washington, but moved quickly through the state and into Montana.

"Are you going to tell me what your plan is?"

"I was thinking I'd keep it a surprise."

"Is it a very fancy villa where we can have sex in a hot tub?"

"No," he said. "I was thinking camping."

She frowned. "Camping."

"In Glacier."

She had never been to Glacier National Park before. She was interested in that. But she was a little bit skeptical about camping.

"Did you bring a…a tent?"

"I did. And a Dutch oven. And food."

"Well," she said, trying not to sound grumpy. "It sounds like you're ready to take care of me a little bit at least."

"You don't like camping?"

"I haven't actually done it since the kids were really little, and it was kind of a supervision nightmare. We never did it when I was growing up. And no, I don't think I like it. But you didn't ask."

"Sorry. I guess I should have…"

"We can do it," she said.

He had planned this. He had brought everything. It felt like he was showing her another piece of himself, and that felt like it mattered. It felt important. To say yes to this.

"Are you martyring yourself?"

She thought about it. Really. She was trying not to just go along with things, but she didn't think that's what she was doing here.

"Do you like camping?"

"I always wanted to do it when I was a kid," he said. "But my mom didn't like it. My uncle took me a few times. In some parks down in Southern California. They were crowded. I kind of wanted more wilderness camping experience. But I liked it. It was something that I… I thought that if I had a dad, we might have gone. You know, obviously I have a dad, just not one that cared. I'm over that." He looked at her from the driver's seat. She wondered if he was actually over it.

She wondered if you got over something like that.

Becca hadn't chosen to leave Chloe. It was a trauma, definitely, to lose your mother like that. But she could know, really know, how much her mom loved her.

Logan was missing that from his father.

"You took Chloe camping," she said.

He nodded slowly. "We did it a lot before Becca got sick. It was our thing."

"Then you just ended up going on our vacation rental beach holidays. Which must have been very not what you enjoyed."

"It was different," he said. "For a while that was what I needed. We got back into camping when Chloe was in high school."

He was giving to his daughter what he hadn't had. Something he'd imagined a good father would do. She hadn't appreciated until this moment just how much weight was on this man's shoulders. He wasn't just trying to be the mother Becca would've been, he was trying to be the father his own had never tried to be.

He had no guidebook for the past he'd been forced to walk.

"Logan, I don't think that I fully appreciated the work that you put into giving both Becca and Chloe what you didn't have. You are an incredible man. You weren't just there for them. The way that you were there for me after my mom died was so needed. Desperately. I don't know where you got the strength to do all of that."

"You remember when you told me that loss was just shitty sometimes? I needed that. You didn't give me platitudes or try to cheer me up. Try to tell me she was in a better place or that it was some divine plan. That I must be strong to have been given so much to carry."

She pressed her fingertips to her temples. "I would love to believe that that didn't happen, and that those things weren't said to you. But I of course know they were. I can even imagine which people said them."

"It's well-meaning. But it's pointless. It isn't pointless to sit there and acknowledge how hard something is. To support somebody like that. Will… He was the best friend I ever had, but things like that make him uncomfortable. Whether it's grappling with mortality, or just the fact that you can't always shape life into what you wanted it to be, I don't know. He was happy to have a drink with me. But he couldn't give me that. That acknowledgment that it was just bad. But you did."

"A couple of years after the fact, if I remember correctly," she said.

"It was almost more important to get it then. Because at that point, people have stopped bringing you casseroles and sympathy." He laughed. "At that point, people think that maybe you've moved on, and they don't realize that you having to live your life is not an indication that you've let anything go."

"It must be hard. Because I understand that even with my mom, I don't want to forget. You want your grief to be less sharp, but you don't want to forget the person that you loved. And sometimes it feels like pain is the tribute."

"Sometimes it does."

She remembered the women at Orcas Island, and Will's commentary on Logan's sex life. "Can I ask you something personal?"

"Considering the amount of personal things that we've done, sure."

"Okay. Point taken. But sometimes I think this is maybe more personal."

"This? This topic of conversation? Yeah. I guess it is."

"How long did you wait? To…to sleep with somebody else."

He looked out the windshield, and she thought she saw something like shame in his eyes. "Not as long as I should have. Probably. Because there's a point where you're not thinking clearly, and everybody walks away feeling used."

"Oh."

"Don't turn me into a paragon. I really don't deserve it."

"I don't think I've ever considered you a paragon. I think you're a good man. That doesn't mean I think you aren't a man."

"Well, sooner than I would like to admit, there were times when you or my former in-laws would have Chloe, and I would just go and lose myself for a couple of hours. With a woman I didn't know. It was a way to forget."

She didn't say it, not right then, but she had a feeling it was a way for him to hate himself too.

"I don't judge you for that. Hell, life is a lot more complicated than I ever give it credit for. I don't care if you did it the night after the funeral."

"It wasn't quite that quick. But I barely made it a month. I told you, I did a lot of things she wouldn't approve of."

"Maybe that's why you had to do it. It makes sense."

He nodded slowly. "Thank you. For understanding that too."

"It makes sense if you were angry. About a lot of things."

"I was. But maybe not quite in the way you think. But behaving well... I couldn't really see the point to it. As far as I could tell, there was no reward."

"So you were as self-destructive as you could think to be without compromising your relationship with your daughter."

"Just my relationship with myself."

"That's fair."

"I didn't keep that up. There were a few years there where I didn't really... I lost interest. It wasn't doing it for me anymore."

"When was that?"

"After the bonfire. Until Oahu."

"Logan..."

"I'm sorry. For the way you're tangled up in this. In my stuff."

"Don't apologize to me. You've been tangled up in all of this. It isn't particularly fair to you. You have enough...baggage and pain in your life without being in whatever this is with me."

"You're a good part of my life," he said.

"Okay. Well, then you need to accept that you're a good part of mine. Don't apologize to me. Not for anything. Definitely not for camping. Most especially not for sharing you."

He leaned over and kissed her, while driving, and the thrill of it buoyed her all the way to Glacier.

The campsite that he chose for them was near the water, nestled into the trees, and it provided a fair amount of seclusion in spite of the fact that the park was a fairly popular destination. The bright red car, all shiny and bright against the rugged landscape, made her smile, as did the way Logan gamely set up the entire camp himself.

"As the resident camping expert," he said.

He got out a lawn chair for her and handed her a soda can, encouraging her to recline while he put up the tent and unloaded all of the food.

"We will keep it up in a bear bag," he said.

"All right," she said, looking around. "There are grizzly bears here, aren't there?"

"Yes," he said. "There are."

"That's unnerving."

"Don't be unnerved. You're safe."

She trusted him. It was that easy.

He got a fire going and put the Dutch oven over the flame, announcing that he was making camp chili for them.

He looked up at her, the firelight spilling over his face.

It was the strangest thing. Because it didn't happen when he was telling her about his wife, or his wounds. It didn't happen when they were kissing.

It didn't happen when they were having sex.

It didn't happen when he was saying something particularly insightful or encouraging to her, which he often had.

It was just right then. Realizing that right now she would rather be here, camping with him, out here in the wilderness prepared to sleep in a place with grizzly bears, than anywhere else in the world.

She had fallen in love with him.

She didn't know if it had happened in the last three months, three years. She just knew that she had.

And she didn't know what it meant. Or what the right thing to do with that was.

She was still legally married to Will. What did a new relationship look like now? Between two people who had already raised their kids, one who had lost a spouse to death, and her, who had gone through this reckoning. Who had questioned everything, coming to the conclusion she wanted her life to change.

That she wanted Logan. For more than just sex.

Will didn't even know that yet.

Did Logan want to spend the rest of his years with her?

Should she make that kind of proclamation now? With things in her life still so messy?

Her kids would freak out.

What about Chloe?

They had time. They had three weeks of this trip. A month until the end of this. This summer apart from Will and her life.

She wanted to sit with this realization. Because it was beautiful and terrifying. She wanted to turn it over. What it meant. How it was the same to love as she had experienced it before. And how it was different.

Because she needed to be able to tell him. When she had kissed him in Boston, she hadn't been able to give him the answers that he wanted.

Now she wanted to give him every answer she possibly could. Every answer that existed inside of her soul.

She needed to create those answers. She needed to know them, so that when she told him that she loved him, she could say exactly what she wanted from him.

It terrified her. So she needed this moment to last.

This moment to be just about them. Nothing more. Nothing less.

She had realized that she needed to look to the future, but this was where the future was bringing her.

To this sort of terrifying place. That was filled with wonder and something she had never thought she would find.

This was a passionate kind of love.

This was something she thought was reserved only for movies. She wasn't rewriting her past.

She was not foolish enough to create a story about how she and Will had been unhappy. About how their love had been fake, or hadn't been real. But it had been young. It had been founded on immature feelings, and forced into a very mature place out of fear. They had been forced to grow up quickly, and because of that, they hadn't grown in a way that was intentional or on purpose. It had just been wild and desperate. They had needed to survive, and they'd done it. They'd created a life and a family, and they had created a measure of real happiness.

But she had fallen in love with Logan without boundaries. Without expectation. Without the influence of anyone else.

It was this mad, wonderful thing that she had never expected to find. That she had never in her wildest dreams thought existed for her.

No, she was not foolish enough to rewrite her life, for better or for worse.

She had loved Will. Their love hadn't faded. Not because of familiarity, or any of the things that you normally blamed waning passion on.

That wasn't them.

Their love was like a flower that had been put in a pot that was far too small.

The roots were stifled. It hadn't been able to grow. Eventually, a plant like that withered away.

It could never be all that it might've been.

But that didn't mean it wasn't real. It didn't mean it hadn't flowered. That it hadn't been beautiful. For all the seasons it had lived.

But it was done growing.

By the time it was dark, the chili was done, and she and Logan sat next to each other in lawn chairs while she made worried comments about bears.

"You're not going to get eaten by a bear," he said.

"You would have to sacrifice yourself for me," she said.

"I would?"

"That's chivalry, Logan. A man must stand when a lady enters the room, and he must lie down and allow a grizzly bear to eat him so the lady can run away."

"That's not very progressive of you."

"Well, when it comes to bears I'm very traditional."

"Good to know."

They went into the tent, and she smiled when she saw the sleeping bags were zipped together.

"I like your version of camping," she said, taking her clothes off and sliding beneath the covers.

"I'm a simple man," he said, taking his shirt off, and then the rest of his clothes, getting into the sleeping bag with her.

It was so quiet out there. When he turned the lantern off inside the tent, so dark. But she knew the feel of him now. His body had become familiar, and there was something exciting about that.

She moved her hands over his chest, and he wrapped her up in his arms, kissing her.

She made love with him, knowing that she loved him.

She remembered what he had said back in the motel in Tahoe.

That right in that moment, they were the only thing that was real.

She knew now that it was true. They were real. This was real.

It wasn't a break from real life. This was real life.

The way she lived it from now to forever was up to her.

twenty-seven

She hadn't thought such a thing would be possible, but the intensity between them increased as the days went on. He touched her more during the day, and at night...

She'd had plenty of sex in her previous life.

This was something else. This was fire and intensity and a total lack of inhibition. When he wanted something, she wanted it more. Every demand he made, she had one of her own.

There wasn't a boundary between them.

Every night they burned through that passion, and the next night it came right back. With breathless, sweaty intensity.

She wondered if it was so intense because he felt that deadline too.

But they saw a giant bison in North Dakota, and enjoyed the drive through Michigan, and then they got to break out their passports to head into Canada, going into Ottawa. It was beautiful. More like a European city than any place she had ever been. The architecture was stunning, the scenery was amazing. It was something new. Something else new that she was doing with him.

They spent the day walking around the city, in no particular hurry, and then had dinner in a place that overlooked one of the rivers.

She looked at him across the table, and her heart suddenly felt too big for that space in her chest. "This is what it would be like," she said. "If we went to Europe together."

"Too bad I can't drive a car over there."

She felt edgy and restless. Afraid. "We could just go. We don't need an excuse."

He looked at her, but he didn't say anything, and she didn't feel quite brave enough to keep going.

She wanted to go to Europe with him. That was the thing. All of these years that she had left to do things...they would be even better if she could do them with him.

"Happy birthday," he said.

She hadn't realized he'd known, and for some reason it sounded more like goodbye than a celebration.

"Thank you."

She was forty-one. She knew more what she wanted now than she had at the beginning of the summer. But it wasn't certain.

Dinner came, and then dessert, and she was still sitting with the weight of that revelation. She had thought she needed to be by herself for a while. That she couldn't afford to be in a relationship. She couldn't even think about marriage or anything like that. Because she needed to be... Open-minded or something. But the truth was, with Logan she was every bit herself as she was without him. But with him, she was happy. He gave so much to her. Then he took nothing at all. He was special. They might even be everything.

A partner in a way she'd never had before. But there was something sort of hard in his eyes and difficult to read, and it kept her from bringing that up. Kept her from saying it.

It made her feel like a coward.

Maybe she was one. But she loved him.

Now she knew she wanted more. Wanted all these years left to live to be with him. It felt so glorious and wonderful to know. It was like all the pieces of herself that hadn't quite matched up for all of these years suddenly did. There was no tension. She wanted him. There was no reservation.

She would disappoint people. They wouldn't understand. People would believe the worst of them. They wouldn't know that Will had asked for an open marriage. They'd think that she and Logan had an affair in secret, because God knew they would've had the opportunity at any point over the years. Maybe even Will would believe that. She could understand why he might since there had been attraction between her and Logan even then.

Her moral high ground would be shot. The truth of it didn't matter.

She didn't need the moral high ground. She just needed him.

In the disappointment, the complications, all seemed like a fair price to pay.

For this level of happiness. Once upon a time, she had loved Will. She had chosen him forever because she was afraid. Because it put her life back together. Because it made difficult things neat again. Because it allowed them to have a perfect nuclear family without custody arrangements for half siblings, or any of those difficult things. Because she cared for him, and she was attracted to him, and she had loved him the most that she had ever loved another person.

But this was different.

She was choosing Logan not because it would make life easier. But because it would make it better. Because he made her better. They didn't have kids together. They didn't have a mortgage. Nobody would think that by being together they were doing the right thing.

This wasn't for anyone else. This was a love that was between just the two of them, and she could honestly say that was not something she'd experienced before. She had let the weight of other people's expectations inform her decision-making back when she had been younger.

She wasn't doing that now.

Right now, she wanted this revelation to be hers. Only hers. They stayed in a beautiful hotel downtown, up on the top floor that overlooked the water and the city lights.

She took her time undressing, watching his face as he looked at her.

She still sensed a hardness there. Like a barricade. Like he was trying to hold something back, or keep her from saying something.

He probably was.

But he didn't need to worry about her talking. Tonight, she just wanted to show him.

She moved across the room and wrapped her arms around his neck, pressing her naked body to his fully clothed one. He was a revelation every time.

They were.

He moved his hand down to cup her ass, and she knew she would never get tired of that feeling. Him, rough and big and hot. He made her feel beautiful. He made her feel sexy in a way that lingered long after he had stopped touching her.

He had transformed the way she felt about herself from the inside out. No part of her was left untouched.

It was her body and her soul. And her heart.

She unbuttoned his shirt, moved her hands over his muscles, and she felt like it was the first time all of a sudden. So hyperaware of everything. Of the way her hand looked against his chest. The way his skin felt against hers.

Then suddenly, the control wasn't hers anymore. His kiss became hard, intense. He stripped his clothes off as he moved them back toward the bed, pressed her down into the mattress. He kissed her neck, down to her breasts, moving his way down between her thighs. He loved to do that. She arched up off the bed when his tongue met with the most sensitive part of her. She had never been the biggest fan of this—it always felt like a lot of pressure to her—but there was something about the way he enjoyed it that made her own pleasure in the act feel that much more intense.

He brought her to the edge, over and over again, but he didn't let her have release.

Usually he did, as many times as she could. But not this time. He kept her there, poised on the edge, torturing her. Until her skin was beaded with sweat, and she was panting, her version of begging because she couldn't even speak. She needed it to end, but she didn't want it to. She wanted to stay right there, where his mouth and hands were playing havoc on her sanity, and they were caught in the whirlwind forever.

Because release was wonderful, but that meant it was over.

Well, until next time. But still. She was caught in the glory of being suspended here.

When he pressed himself inside of her, she tried to stop herself from going over the edge. But she couldn't. When he thrust in, hard and deep, she unraveled.

She clung to him, wrapping her legs around his waist as he thrust hard and without rhythm. Before she could catch her breath, another climax took hold of her, and she dug her fingernails into his shoulders, her whole body on fire.

He found his own release on a harsh, feral growl and she let out her own in response, feeling more animal than human in this beautifully sophisticated hotel room.

Then when it was over, she pressed herself against him, and put her hand over his raging heartbeat.

She wanted to sleep with him like this forever.

She had thought of a lot of different scenarios for her future. Going back to sleeping with Will. Sleeping alone.

But this was the one that felt right. This was the one that felt real.

She wanted him. Whether it was in a tent in Glacier or a roadside motel in Tahoe, she wanted him. She would have him back in their hometown. She wanted him. She fell asleep knowing that. Also knowing that she couldn't say it. Because she could feel the hesitance in him, even if she didn't know why.

She and Logan had had a whole lot of honesty. But there were some stones left unturned. She knew that if they were going to do this, she had to be ready. Had to be absolutely ready to turn them over, and she would. But not right now. Right now, she was just going to sleep. Rest with him, and enjoy the certainty she felt in her own soul, because she had a feeling that when she got Logan's soul tangled up in her certainty, it wasn't going to be this simple.

twenty-eight

This time when they arrived at their destination, she went with Logan to present the car to its new owner.

On the other trips, she had been committed to that moment when they finally got some breathing room from each other. Even though she could sense that Logan actually wanted some space, she didn't want it.

She could feel the walls going up around him, and it was frustrating her, because it was like he was preparing himself for an end that they hadn't discussed.

They were both going back to Oregon. Her in first class—and she assumed that he would be in coach, and that was his prerogative. But the point was, they weren't separating, not necessarily. He knew that she wasn't going back to Will. He knew that she was headed toward the end of her marriage, not a new beginning. So why in the hell he wasn't just talking to her rather than shutting down she didn't know.

And in the past, she would've let that go. But this wasn't the past.

Now, though, they had an audience. An older woman whose

eyes lit up with absolute joy when the red Corvette convertible was presented to her.

She smiled, her eyes shining with tears. "This was what Howard and I used to drive around. Back when we were in high school. It was brand-new. Beautiful."

Samantha's heart ached.

This car represented something bigger than a car. It was tied up in her love. For Howard.

"How long were you and Howard together?" she asked.

"We were married for sixty-five years. Before he passed."

The way that the woman spoke of it, still with such a look of electric joy on her face, even in spite of the fact that there was grief there. Of course there was grief.

Samantha wanted that. To speak of the love of her life with that level of joy.

It was the kind of joy she felt when she was with Logan. Really even when he was being kind of a closed-off difficult piece of work.

That wasn't fair. It wasn't like he was doing anything. She just felt hypersensitive to his moods. It was the result of being with each other so much over these past months. But this was some certainty. Some clarity. Because she knew that she wanted that kind of love. The kind that made your eyes sparkle after all those years. That was what she wanted. It was just really great to know. To know what she wanted apart from what anyone else expected. To know what she wanted, without exhaustively checking for anyone else's opinion.

Even Logan's. It had been important to her to cement this inside of herself before she talked to him.

When they left the car, they got a ride service down to the beach. It was getting to be late, the sun setting and casting glorious colors over the water.

She took his hand in hers and looked at him.

"Logan," she said. "I need to tell you…" She could see him,

tensing, bracing. For what, she wasn't quite sure. For what she was going to say, or what he believed she was going to say.

She knew that she could stop now. That she could choose to not take a risk.

She wasn't going to do that.

"I love you. I realized that a while ago, but I wanted to be prepared to tell you what that meant to me. I love you and I want to be with you. Not because we have to be. Not because I'm afraid to be alone. Not because I'm afraid that people will judge me. Just because I want to."

She saw pain, deep pain in his blue eyes. Then that wall went up.

"Samantha," he said. "Don't tell me that."

Oh, she really loved this man. And he was being an idiot. Where did he think this was going? From the very beginning, it had been more. He knew that. He hadn't yelled at her in a honky-tonk parking lot over sex. Over temporary. Over lust or friendship or anything short of love, and she knew that. Deep in her heart.

Just like she'd known he was going to resist it.

She'd decided to go ahead with it anyway. Because she didn't hide from hard.

Not anymore.

It was his own fault. He'd helped bring her to this point.

"What else was I going to tell you?" she asked, trying to smile.

"You…"

"No. Really. You didn't want me to have you when you thought I was going back to Will, so where did you think this was going to go?"

"Exactly what you said back in Tahoe. That you needed time by yourself."

"I thought I did. But I had a lot of time by myself these last few months. I had a lot of time with you. You know what's funny? I'm the same person either way. It's not the person that I was when I was with Will, though. I've done different things, said different things. Wanted different things. With you…it's consistent. I am myself. When I'm with you, when I'm not. Being with you doesn't hurt my growth. It's been part of it. You have been part of showing me what I want, and who I am."

"I can't give you what you're asking for."

"So the thing is, you're forty-three years old, Logan. And that's the kiss-off of a twenty-year-old, and I think you can do better than that."

He pressed his hands over his face, and then he looked at her. He looked exhausted. He didn't have the words, she knew that. In the same way she hadn't had them. But that was months ago. He should have grown with her.

He should have arrived at this place with her, not just physically, but emotionally.

But he wasn't with her.

What bothered her the most was that she wasn't even surprised. Somehow she had known this was coming. Because he shared, he shared quite a lot, but there was something that he hadn't shared, and she knew that. There were things that he was holding back, and she knew that.

But she had been intent on doing this anyway. On laying it bare.

Maybe she would've been able to coast with him if she hadn't had to say it. If she hadn't had to tell him what this meant to her. What she wanted. But she had. Because she had spent twenty-two years not saying what she wanted. She had spent twenty-two years hiding from the truth, so that she would never hear a thing she didn't want to hear.

She couldn't do that. Not now. Here they were, in Maine, across the country from Oregon. Almost as far away from Oregon as they could possibly be. She wanted to take the love that she felt all the way back across the country, into that life, into that town, regardless of the consequences. She wasn't willing to let there be questions or silence. She wanted it all out in the open. She wanted it all clear.

"Tell me," she said. "And it's your turn to be honest. Don't lie to me, Logan, what did you think this was going to be? You and me. What did you think I would want in the end, if not forever. If not you."

"You were supposed to... I was never supposed to be able to reach you, Samantha. You were...my penance."

"I'm not anyone's penance, Logan."

"No. You were mine. Do you know why I had sex with a stranger a month after my wife died? Do you know?"

"No. Because you didn't tell me."

"I'll tell you now. It was because I couldn't have either woman that I wanted. Rebecca was gone, and you were married. It just felt like one hell of a cosmic joke, and the fact that I even thought that, that I thought...that I thought I wanted you. Right then, I knew that I was... I have never hated myself more. No, that's not true. I did after I slept with her. I couldn't tell you who she was. Because I didn't ask her name. It didn't matter. It was all just trying to put distance between myself and that...that trail of a thought. I will never be able to untangle that. Those feelings, that moment."

"So you can't be with me because you're punishing yourself?"

"No. No, it's that I... I can't do it. I... I just can't. That was the lowest point of my life. You are wrapped up in it, Sam, whether that's fair or not. I can never go back there. Caring for you while you were with him? That was its own kind of torture, but I kind of liked it. Then I wasn't strong enough not to pick at it when I knew that I could have you. When I could see it. I wasn't strong enough."

"What about Hawaii?"

"I would've kissed you. I would've slept with you. Fuck him.

I don't care. It was never about him. The only reason I didn't push it was because of you."

"And now we could be together, and you're still telling me no."

For the first time since that day he had come to their house and told Will that there was no way Becca was going to live, she saw fear in his eyes. Real. Deep.

"Tell me. Because this isn't honest. Is it guilt? You won't let yourself have this because you feel bad?"

"It's not that simple."

"Tell me in the simplest terms possible."

"She knew, Sam. She knew that I was somewhere else sometimes. That I wasn't the husband I should have been or could have been because I was never all the way with her." His blue eyes burned. "Because of you. But not because of you. Because I don't think I can ever really be there all the way for anyone. It's convenient, right? To marry someone, but keep part of your heart reserved for another man's wife?"

"You were a good husband to Becca. A great husband."

"In the end. When there was a time limit. When it was too late." He sighed, deep and hard and like it hurt. "I can't give you what you want. Or maybe I could. Maybe I could get you stuck with me instead of Will. But it'll only ever disappoint you. You've been disappointed enough. I can keep you happy. In bed. We're good at that."

"Stop it. Don't act like this wasn't a relationship. Don't act like we didn't share the deepest parts of ourselves. It was not just sex. Do not make it that. Don't do that."

"You need someone who isn't such a bad fucking husband, Samantha. I was a bad husband. I could never… I could never not want you. I could never give all of myself."

"And what? You're afraid that even if it's me, it's just going to be like that? It won't be. Because what if it was always us?"

"That's magic thinking. I don't believe in magic."

"Fine," she said. "Maybe it's not magic. Maybe we're not

meant to be. Maybe we're just two desperately human people who are deeply attracted to each other, and who felt things when we knew we shouldn't, and did the hard thing, the right thing. And we're here. Now. Where we can actually be together if we want. If we are just brave enough to reach out and take it. So be brave enough."

"I tried with Chloe," he said, his voice rough. "I am all she has, God bless that poor kid. I am all she has. I did better than my father there, but there's part of me… I've never been able to prove to myself I'm not him. He couldn't stay. He couldn't be there. Not for me, not for my mom."

"You aren't your dad. That's magic thinking, Logan. That somehow a man who donated sperm to your conception all those years ago has more to do with who you are now than the ways you've loved Chloe, the way you cared for Becca, the way you care for me."

And she could see him. Warring with himself. Trying to reason out whether or not he could do this.

She'd had a whole summer. To decide what she wanted. Where she wanted to be. That summer had brought her here. Standing here with him. Willing to take this risk.

He couldn't answer her. Not now.

Much in the same way she hadn't been able to answer him when he'd been all fury and thwarted desire in that alleyway in Boston.

Because something was holding him back. Something still owned a piece of him. She was demanding answers, and she could see clearly that he didn't have them.

"It's okay," she said, nodding. "You don't have to tell me. Not now. I love you, and…"

"Don't keep hoping," he said. "Don't hold out for me. Don't hold out for Will. Don't hold out for anyone. Go live your life."

"I don't actually need you to tell me to do that. I'm not putting myself on hold. But neither should you."

"It was a great summer, Sam."

"The best," she said around a hard lump in her throat and tears in her eyes.

"I'm better when there's an end. And this is the end."

She felt something inside of her shatter. That hadn't happened when Will had told her he wanted to see other people. When they had decided to take a break.

She had been hurt. But nothing had broken.

This…this broke her heart. Not just because Logan didn't love her back, not just because she couldn't be with him. But because he was trapped in some kind of personal hell, and he was not going to reach past it. He was not going to let her help.

"I turned over a lot of rocks in my soul," she said. "But I can't turn yours over for you. You have to do it for yourself. You have to want it. It's really hard work, to heal yourself. I was so lucky to have you with me while I worked on my healing. I am so sorry that I didn't see. That I didn't understand that you still had so much left to do. But I love you, Logan, and that's not contingent on you loving me back right away. Or giving me what I want." Tears welled up in her eyes as she turned away. Then she stopped and turned back. "I always think of you as Will's best friend. But you know what? That's not true." She didn't wait for him to say anything. "You're my best friend. Not his. I want you to know that no matter what, that's true." Then suddenly she couldn't hold it back. The pain. The tears. "But I really do love you," she said, tears spilling down her cheeks. "I really do." She turned away from him again.

"Where are you going?"

"I thought I would get a car. I might try to change my plane ticket. It's time for me to go home. Deal with the rest of my life. We have a lot of years left."

twenty-nine

This was heartbreak. And it really hurt. It hurt all the way back to Oregon. It hurt as she took a ride service to her house from the airport. It hurt as she got into bed and went to sleep without texting anybody.

Two days. In two days she was meeting with Will. In that time, she was going to have to try to stand there looking a little bit less broken. Or maybe not. She wasn't interested in anything fake. Not anymore.

She suddenly remembered her wedding ring. That it had literally been in her purse in a pouch for the last few months. She took it out and held it up.

It looked strange. Like it belonged to another woman.

In many ways, it did. She felt so much compassion for that woman.

That woman who had wanted her comfort beyond anything else.

Who had wanted what she knew. Who had wanted to be safe. Who had been ready to sit in her marriage, in her life, forever. She never would've questioned it. Never would've tested it. Not ever.

Now she had done more than just tested. She had shattered it.

She had taken that ring off her finger nearly four months ago with the full intention of putting it back on. She smiled through her tears as she realized that would never happen.

She swallowed hard and put it back in her purse.

She might keep it. She might give it back to Will. She didn't know.

Two days.

Elysia and Whitney texted her to make sure she was okay, and that she was ready for everything to come with Will.

She texted them reassurance, but she still needed to sit in her own feelings. She wasn't quite ready for her girls' night. Someday. Someday maybe this would all be one of those stories that she told while laughing and drinking a mojito. Except she barely ever drank, and she couldn't imagine laughing about this.

She would love it if she could. If she could talk about her crazy sexcapades with Logan, about how big he was, and how many orgasms he could give her in a night. But it wasn't about that.

It was too much hers to give to anyone else.

Especially now that she had no guarantee she would ever be with him like that again.

Everything hurt.

She hadn't even considered the fallout for their daily life. How could she have?

But there was Chloe…

She wouldn't let this hurt her relationship with Chloe.

Finally, it was time. Time for her to get in her lame-ass SUV and make her very last road trip. From this town house she was renting to the place she had lived with Will for all those years. The place where they had raised their children. She drove slowly, taking in the familiar sites, consciously looking at everything through new eyes.

She drove slowly down their street. She hadn't been on the street in four months.

The street that had been part of her every day. It felt weird to be here.

Slowly, very slowly, she turned into the driveway. Then she got out of her car, walked to the front door and unlocked it. She laughed when she walked in and saw it looked like they'd never left.

Like nothing had changed.

Everything had changed.

It was a good house.

It had been a good life.

But it wasn't hers. Not anymore.

It had only taken one cruel summer to unravel all of it.

One cruel, devastating, necessary summer to make her see that what she'd thought was happiness had been her own stubbornness. Had been denial. Had been fear.

She was standing there in the center of this room that had been her life, when the light suddenly flicked on, and she turned to see Will standing in the doorway.

She waited. For a kick of excitement. For attraction. Something.

It was just Will. One thing that was strange was it was almost like it was just a Monday after a weekend away, not a whole summer. He was that familiar.

They hadn't talked. Hadn't texted. Not once, through this whole summer. She had no idea what he had done. What he had lived.

She looked down and noticed that on his left hand, he was wearing his wedding ring.

"Sam," he said.

"Hi," she returned.

"This is weird," he said, stepping deeper into the living room.

"Yeah. It is." She looked down at her own hand, which now felt resolutely bare.

Then she looked back up at him. "How was it?"

"It's been kind of a long summer," he said.

Not long enough.

She thought of Logan. Of each and every trip. Each car. Each mile down the road leaving this version of herself who had lived in this home further and further behind.

"I know what I want," she said.

"I know you do. You were very clear about it from the be-ginning…"

"No," she said, cutting him off. "I know what I want now." She took a breath and dove right in, because she'd waited months. And she wasn't waiting anymore. "Will, I want a divorce."

She didn't have Logan. She had absolutely no certainty that he would ever come back to her. She loved him. She loved him with everything she had, even though losing him hurt her.

She loved him.

But she wasn't afraid to be alone. Whether she was with Logan or not, Will wasn't the right thing for her. This wasn't the right place.

"What?" He looked blindsided. Devastated. Perversely, she wanted to laugh. He might have been a mirror of where she was four months ago.

That idiot. What had he done with his summer?

"Yeah," she said. "I think we should see other people. *Only* other people. I'm sorry, that was a bad joke. I swear to you I didn't plan it."

"But you said that you wanted to be with me. You wanted to separate because you couldn't stand the idea…"

"I know. That was months ago. A lot has happened."

"What?"

"Do you want that kind of honesty?"

"You're asking me for divorce, why not?" he asked, sounding bitter and angry. How was that fair?

Of course it's not fair. It's feelings.

Feelings weren't fair.

And he'd been the hero of whatever journey he'd been on this past summer, the same as she'd been on hers. She didn't esteem his journey, but still.

"I fell in love," she said.

The words landed hard. She could see that. Like a fist to his face.

"You got so angry at me because I wanted to have an open marriage, and then you went and *fell in love* with someone else?"

"Yes." She didn't take his bait, or tell him to save his outrage, even though she wanted to. "I did. I learned something about myself. I can't love more than one person at the same time. Or rather, I can't be *in* love with them. You will always be the father of our children. You will always be the man that I spent twenty-two years married to. I care about you. I even mostly like you, even though I was mad at you before we split. But I'm not in love with you."

He looked like he was processing the speech, but slowly. Trying to grasp at her words as best he could.

"You're leaving me for another man?"

She shook her head. "No. It turns out that he doesn't want..." A tear fell down her cheek, and she wiped it away. Here she was, crying about Logan in front of Will. But it felt really honest. She was out of everything but honesty.

She couldn't offer easy. She couldn't offer fake. She couldn't offer anything but the truth.

"He doesn't want the same things I do," she said. "So I'm not leaving you for him. I'm leaving you because I don't think either of us should be in a marriage when we know we want something *more*. I shouldn't be married to you knowing that I can love someone more than I love you. And *you* shouldn't be with me knowing you want someone more than you want me."

"I was going tell you that I don't... That you were right," he said, his voice raw. "I don't want that. I tried it. At the end of the day, it's just sex, Samantha. There's no one to go home to. There's nobody to talk to. There's... None of them know me. You knew me. You knew me when I was a teenager, and you saw things in me that nobody else did, and..."

It was about him. All of it. What she gave to him, not how he felt about her.

She'd never been more certain of her decision. Of herself.

"I'm sorry," she said. "That it took you all that time to realize that what we had was special. But I can't be sorry that it took me this break to realize that what we had wasn't enough."

She was breaking him. In the way that Logan had broken her.

But this had nothing to do with her being afraid. She was being brave. Will was just going back to what he knew. Because it was all about him. He missed the way that she saw him. He didn't want to start a new relationship because he would have to get to know somebody. They would have to get to know him. He didn't want a new relationship because that woman wouldn't be the mother of his children, giving him allowances and forgiveness because of their history.

She had jumped headlong into a relationship that was hard, and he didn't want that, because she had spent twenty-two years making his life easy.

"You were right," she whispered. "I wasn't happy at the same time you weren't. We were on the same page, Will. I just didn't know it. You said it was..." Oh, she almost wanted to laugh. "You said you started feeling dissatisfied three years ago, and I can see now I did too."

When she'd nearly kissed Logan, that should have told her everything.

Something was wrong in her marriage.

There were cracks.

She'd been so filled with pride that she'd chosen herself and Will, but she'd never asked herself why it had felt like a choice.

"We can work on that," he said.

She would have wanted to four months ago. If he'd said he wasn't happy, and he'd said he wanted to work to be happier with her, she'd have done it. She'd have kept on pushing it all down.

"I can't. I spent the last four months working on myself. There are things I can't go back to not knowing. It changed me. It changed everything."

"Please don't leave me," he said. "I don't care that you were with someone else. I was with other people… It doesn't matter. It doesn't mean anything. It's just sex."

"It *wasn't* for me. It wasn't. I love him."

"If he doesn't want to be with you, then what does it matter?"

How had she ever not realized how differently she and Will saw sex and love? They'd never discussed it. They'd just done it. She'd assumed he felt how she did.

She could see now how wrong she'd been.

"Because I know I can be happier. Because I know that I can be more myself. Because I know that I can have better sex. Because I know that there is more. More out there. I refuse to take less. Don't take less, Will. Don't take less because it's easier. You don't love me. You're not in love with me. You loved our life. I get that. I loved our life too. But once I started going over everything that was wrong with it, I couldn't unsee it. Once I saw the cracks, I could never not know they were there. We were breaking. Before you ever told me you wanted to see other people, we were falling apart, but I wasn't brave enough to look at it."

He looked so hurt. So wounded.

But she was done making things easy.

"You started this," she said. "Have the courage to finish it."

"That's not fair," he said. "You were the one who said…"

"And you were the one who said, 'Why don't we see what else there is?' You were the one who said, 'Why does marriage have to be this?' Now I agree with you. With that question. We needed each other. For a long time. We needed each other to make this life, to make our family. But at the end of the day, do we want each other? All of each other. Because you can't just want me as a wife who supports you. As the wife who knows you. Isn't that just the natural completion of this little midlife crisis that you had? To go off and screw younger women for fun, and then to get to come back home to me? The woman who knew you back in high school. The woman who still sees you as you were."

She shook her head. "That's the easy way out, Will. You started this. Finish it. Find what you're really looking for. Deal with your mortality. Howl at the moon. Find some woman who's crazy about who you are right now. Find someone you have to try for. Work for. Find someone you have to be better for. Or don't. Spread it around. Sleep with half the county, I don't care, but don't convince yourself that I'm hurting you because I won't let you go back to what's comfortable. You started this. I was too scared to be honest then, but I am being honest now. You were brave enough to call it out. That we weren't happy. You exposed a bunch of things that I was too scared to look at. But now I have. Don't get mad at me because you dragged all that shit out into the daylight."

He looked down at her arm. "You got a tattoo?"

"Yeah. I got a tattoo. And a bikini." *And the best sex of my life.*

But she didn't say that last part out loud, because that was petty. She didn't actually want to be petty. Because there wasn't a whole lot of triumph from where she was standing. It was just growth. As she had established earlier, growth and self-awareness were honestly a little bit overrated. And mostly painful.

"Who is it?" he asked, his voice quiet.

Oh shit.

She took a deep breath. She wasn't sure she was going to tell him, because honestly, what was the point?

But there was something in the hesitation that clearly got to him.

"Sam…" His gaze was wary. And then…knowing. "Please don't…"

"If you're asking me not to… Well, you already know, don't you?"

His expression was dark then, angry. Angry like they never got at each other. Angry like they should have gotten sometimes and hadn't been brave enough to. This was really the end, and only now was she seeing this part of him. They had been so scared. They'd had to get here to be brave. "How…how can you do this?" he asked. "When you acted so outraged that I asked you for an open marriage?" He shook his head. "And how long… God. I knew that you wanted to fuck him. I knew it."

"Oh, did you?" she asked, anger spiking now. "You knew? You just sat on that bit of info and kept inviting him to dinner and all our vacations even though you thought I wanted him?"

"Then tell me it's not true. Tell me you didn't want to sleep with him." The denial stuck in her throat, and Will's eyes widened. He'd been angry, he hadn't actually believed his own accusations. Now he did, though. "You did, didn't you?"

She let out a breath. "I didn't *do* anything with him when we were together."

"But you *wanted* to. That whole time."

She shook her head. "No. I didn't. I was attracted to him, and I didn't acknowledge it. I pushed it away. Because you matter more to me. But then, when I didn't have an obligation to you anymore, when you were the one who said that we should see other people…"

"He's my *best friend*."

"Yeah, well, are you mad at me, or are you mad at him?"

"He didn't say anything. I texted him during the summer. I…"

"He was respecting *me*. The fact that he knew that I didn't have any contact with you. He didn't bring you into what was happening between us. Because you didn't need to be involved. You know what, you still don't. He doesn't want to be with me. But it doesn't change the fact that I'm in love with him."

"I feel like you're going to regret this," he said. "Breaking everything apart for Logan."

He didn't understand. He still didn't understand her.

But she wasn't going to spend the rest of her life with him, not anymore.

So she didn't need him to.

And that, well, that made her feel free.

"I'm not breaking everything apart for Logan," she said. "I'm breaking it apart for me."

thirty

They didn't leave things on a good note. But it was done.

She knew that someday they would be okay. She knew because they weren't passionate enough to despise each other. He would see that. He was mad because he had made a decision, and she had disrupted it. But he clearly hadn't been pining for her enough to not sleep with other women.

Or maybe she had broken his heart. But the truth was, he had never broken hers.

She spent two days writing about it.

The story didn't have a happy ending, but it had a lot of truth in it.

In the absence of happiness, she'd take truth.

So, she took her broken heart and walked it over to Elysia's, where Whitney met up with them as well.

"I'm single," she said. "And not at all ready to mingle. But here we are."

A cheese board was thrust her direction, and then a can of soda. She started to cry, because it was all a little bit much. Then she couldn't stop.

"So you told Will," Whitney said.

"I told him. I told him I was in love with someone else. And now he knows it's Logan. But Logan…he doesn't want to be with me." She couldn't bring herself to say he wasn't in love with her, because she suspected that in fact he was. It was just that he couldn't cope with it.

"I'm so sorry," said Elysia, rubbing her arm.

"I'm fine. I mean, I'm not fine. I'm experiencing my first major heartbreak, at forty-one. Yay me. But you know what, the fact that Will isn't my heartbreak tells me a lot."

"It does," said Whitney. "I really hope that you don't feel too broken."

"I do," she said. "But I'm not afraid of it. Because I got to love him really, really well."

She understood then why they said that. That it was better to have loved and lost than to have never loved at all. Because she was changed by loving Logan in this way. She wouldn't trade it for comfort. Comfort wasn't the answer. Not always. Comfort was sometimes just a way to slide easily through the years without ever feeling them.

At least now she knew she was alive.

She still couldn't quite bring herself to brag about her sex-capades, but she talked a lot about the trips, and the different things they saw, and she stumbled home and went to sleep, then woke up the next morning and FaceTimed the kids.

She should have brought them into all this sooner. But it had seemed like…why tell them when she'd been so certain things would go back to how they had always been?

She realized that she hadn't given Will back the wedding ring. Was she supposed to?

It was hers.

But she dug through her things until she found a little jewelry box she got from her mother. Inside were a couple of family heirloom pieces. She took the ring out of her purse and put it carefully in there.

Because it was part of her history. Like this other jewelry. It also wasn't part of her life. But she had no interest in erasing it or pretending it didn't exist.

Samantha, the Samantha who had worn that ring, had been pretty darn happy.

But it didn't fit anymore.

She heard the sound of an engine revving outside, and she went over to the window and looked down at the street.

There was a bright red Chevy Bel Air parked right out front, with aggressively large fins.

There could be only one man behind the wheel.

She frowned, because she was trying to keep herself from smiling. Because she was trying to keep her heart from leaping in her chest, even though it did it anyway.

Because she felt sixteen and forty-one at the same time. Desperately optimistic, but horrifically realistic.

She ran down the stairs to the front door and flung it open.

"Want to go for a drive with me?" he asked.

She was hurt. And she was pretty mad at him. But she was going to get in that car.

She opened up the passenger door and got in.

"What's this?" she asked.

"This? This one is mine. Because there have to be some perks of this job."

"It's beautiful," she said.

"The car is not really the point, though." He pulled away from the curb and started to drive up out of town, toward the hills.

"What is the point?"

"That I realized we didn't have any more of these trips coming up. I'm going to miss them."

"Whose choice was that?" she asked. "Is this a man thing? Being mad about your own choices?"

"Yeah. I take your point."

"I asked Will for a divorce yesterday," she said.

He cleared his throat. "Yeah. I may or may not have had a visit from him."

"He visited you?"

"Yeah. He took a swing at me. I dodged it, and he punched the side of my house. I feel kind of bad about that. I probably should've let him get one in somewhere on my face."

She pressed her hands down against the seat and leaned forward, turning toward Logan in utter shock. "He tried to punch you?"

She didn't even think Will knew how to punch.

"Yeah. He was pretty pissed off. Something about stealing you, but then…something about hurting you."

Wow. That was unexpected.

"Well. You did. Hurt me. But I made that pretty clear at the time."

"You did. I wanted to give you some space. But then Will came to see me, and… I figured space was maybe a little bit performative."

"I mean, you pulled up to the front of my house in this car. At this point the whole thing is kind of performative."

"It's not. I promise. I'm just trying to do this right." He pulled up to a scenic outlook that gave them a view of the whole town. It was weird to be above it. This place that held so much sway over her. And all the decisions she had made so far.

It seemed small. It all did.

"I'm sorry. You were right. I have been a fucking coward every step of the way. I wanted you for so long, and I felt so guilty about parts of it… But the biggest thing isn't that. It's the fact that you were such a fantasy that I was afraid I would never be able to live up to it. That I would never be able to give you what you wanted. Do you know how many times I told myself I would be better for you than him? But it hit me.

How can I really believe that? I wasn't perfect for the wife I had. But I convinced myself that I would be perfect for you."

"I don't need you to be perfect for me," she said. "I have changed so much in the last year, and I plan on changing more. How could I ask you to be perfect? I'm not perfect. I just want you to be with me. I just want you to love me."

"I do," he said, his voice rough. "I love you. I have loved you. For so long. I didn't know what to do when I realized I could have you. That I could *fail* you. That I could *lose* you." He turned to her, gripping her chin with his thumb and forefinger. "What if I lose you? Sam… I wanted you for so long. I think what really scared me is you've always been the one who could have all of me. I have never given that to anyone. I was never ready. I… I remember my mom leaving when I was a kid. Driving away. Never coming back. I have always been afraid I'd lose what I loved, so I always kept a piece of myself back." He took a sharp breath. "Then I lost Becca. It seemed like I was right. I couldn't have you, but in some ways it seemed like that was better. Safer."

"Life is hard," she said. "I can't guarantee anything. But you know that. But hasn't it always been better for us to have each other?"

He nodded. "Yeah."

She could see that there was no wall. Not now. He was exposed. Vulnerable. She kissed him. There above the town, in his car.

"I love you," he said. "It scares me how much. And you are brave. You won't let me get away with giving you just a piece, and I have to dig deep and give you everything, and I'm not even sure I know how to do that."

"It's okay," she whispered. "I didn't either. I learned."

"It makes me feel like I'm twenty, and I want to start over. I want to marry you. I don't think I can ask you that. You're still technically married to somebody else."

"I want that too," she said. "I'm not afraid of it. Because I realized something really really important. I'm not afraid to be alone. But I would rather have you. I could live by myself. But I would choose you."

"I choose you. For all the life we have left to live."

"I just realized something."

"What?"

She smiled. "The book I'm writing. It has a happy ending now."

"You're going to write a book?"

She nodded. "Yes. It took all of this, but I finally know what I have to say."

They made use of the back seat of that car, and she felt no shame or fear.

And when it was over, he held her against his chest, and whispered against her ear. "I wonder where we'll be this time next year."

"I couldn't begin to guess. Because at this point I know… anything can happen."

thirty-one

1959 Chevy Bel Air
One year later
It's a surprise

"Okay," Sam said, smiling as soon as Ethan sat down in the booth at Texas Roadhouse. "Everybody's here."

"Yeah, sorry. My girlfriend wanted to FaceTime."

"You're leaving for school tomorrow," Will said from his position right next to Ethan, across the booth from Samantha. "You're going to see her then. Maybe prioritize spending a little bit of time with your family."

"Dad..."

"What? You're going to see her tomorrow."

"He's in love," Chloe said pragmatically.

Sam and Will exchanged a look, and then she looked at Logan, who was sitting next to her.

"I didn't know you were a romantic, Chloe," said Will.

"When it suits me," she said, smiling at Ethan.

They didn't do this all the time. Though it was becoming less weird.

The kids had taken the news… Well, it was a mixed bag. Aiden had made jokes. ("Who's getting custody?") Jude had been moody and then later had called Sam and been angry. Then called again and apologized that he was the reason they'd had to get married in the first place. Her poor oldest.

Ethan had been surprisingly okay.

All the kids had been home off and on throughout the summer, and she and Will had done their absolute best to make it so they both got as much time with the kids as possible. And sometimes it was just easier for everyone to get together. And with Chloe and Ethan and Aiden headed back to school tomorrow, it seemed like a fair enough idea for them to all get together over steak and rolls.

Right where it had started a year and a summer ago.

Will picked his phone up off the table and looked at a message, and smiled.

Maybe it was a girlfriend. She sort of hoped it was.

But he was on his own journey, and he had to figure out what happiness looked like for him. She couldn't do it for him.

Though there hadn't been anyone serious in his life since the divorce. Maybe he would get there. But he didn't seem in a huge hurry to jump into a relationship.

Sam rubbed her thumb over her engagement ring.

She and Logan had decided to wait for a while before they actually made it legal. Create some space between her and Will's divorce. Give the kids time.

They'd both been certain but this wasn't only about them. It was about everyone they loved.

Even Will.

He was Logan's friend. He was the father of her children.

She'd loved him for a long time, and healing the rift between them had mattered to her.

Chloe had been weirded out for about five seconds, and then

had been ecstatic. But for her, it wasn't a loss. It was just solidifying a relationship they already had.

The boys had struggled with it a little bit. Jude had been philosophical (life happens). Ethan had more questions about the timeline between her and Logan than she liked, but she'd answered them. Aiden hadn't struggled with anything *she'd* done. He'd been angry at his father. He still was sometimes.

That was a tricky one.

But they were managing. And here they all were at dinner.

Logan and Will might not be best friends again, but everyone was cordial. Who could say? Maybe they would be.

Life was so much more complex, wonderful, terrifying, painful and glorious than she'd realized.

"Mom," Ethan said. "When your book comes out, are we all going to be famous?"

"Or infamous," Will said, giving her a side eye.

His side eye wasn't serious. He knew what she'd written.

About their life and their marriage. She hadn't simplified it. The good or the bad. He was also pretty understanding about the fact it was her story, which meant it was her perspective.

It was honest, though. All that honestly she'd been scared of for so long.

He probably wasn't going to read the whole book.

While reading the parts about the two of them had gone a long way in healing some of their wounds, he had been pretty honest about not needing to read about her romance with Logan.

Fair enough.

"No," she said. "Because the odds of more than ten thousand people buying it are low."

"So we'll be niche famous," said Aiden. "Which is more metal anyway."

"The gossip is going to start again," Chloe said cheerfully.

The gossip had never stopped. Chloe just didn't live here

full-time. They were officially a scandal. Sam and Logan ending up together had created a wave of interest and speculation. Sam selling a book about it was even more titillating. (Amy Callahan had an MFA, and was incensed that Sam had gotten a book deal telling her *tawdry story* of *sex* and *infidelity*, or so she'd been told. Especially when Sam hadn't even gone to college.)

The good news about everyone being so interested was that her book was guaranteed to sell a full 2,900 copies at least. In keeping with the population of the town.

There were some personal things in there. But it wasn't really about sex—though she'd written about the sex. It was a memoir about change. About letting go. About living life for yourself instead of a whole town.

Maybe the people reading for shock value could learn something.

But they probably wouldn't. They'd probably go back to their neat homes, with everything in its place, and sleep with men they didn't really love, in the name of not making waves.

Sam could never regret the waves.

They finished eating, talked about the kids' plans, hugged, and went their separate ways. A big, slightly broken family.

This was why she'd written the book. To understand this. To give words to it all.

Not because her pain, her change, her life were unique. But because they weren't.

If another woman read it and saw something of her own life, her own struggle, then that was what the book was for.

Logan took her hand as they walked through the parking lot, back toward their car.

"So the wedding isn't until June, but I feel like we might want to take our honeymoon first."

"*Really?*"

"Yeah. This October."

"Why?"

"Because I thought you might want to spend a month in Europe."

"Seriously?" She stopped walking, and there they were, in a parking lot, bathed in a fluorescent glow.

A mirror of other times they'd been together. Fighting, kissing.

"Yes. Really. I don't want to wait." His voice dropped lower, and it made her giddy.

"I don't either," she said.

Because there was no next time around. There was just this time.

She and Logan were making the absolute best of this time.

It was so funny. She had come to this very restaurant a year and a summer ago, and she had felt like her life had fallen apart.

If she had only known...that she had needed everything to fall apart so she could put it all back together in this different shape.

She started to move to the car, and he caught her, dragged her back to him and kissed her. Hard. Like the first time. Like in Tahoe.

But more. With everything.

With all of him.

He held nothing back. Not with her, not anymore.

They got into the car, and she remembered, viscerally, that first time. That first trip.

She'd been driving into the unknown.

They still were.

But it didn't scare her. Not anymore.

That day, she hadn't known who she was. Apart from her marriage, apart from how people in town saw her. Now she did.

She looked down at her tattoo, which had become a reminder of so many things. But most of all, it was a reminder to be herself. It was a change she'd made that she didn't hide, and didn't want to.

"Just so you know," she said. "You're the love of my life. My real life. I remember once I told you that you, wanting you, wasn't my real life. That it was just me in a crisis, but it was me not able to hide. It was me without my walls. Without denial."

He turned to look at her, and he gave her that smile. She could feel it, all the way to her toes, with no reservations at all.

"And I love you. With all of my heart. It's a hell of a thing. You should look in the back seat."

"Is this a pickup line?"

"It's not. Look in the back seat."

"Our romance is dead," she said, turning and seeing two pieces of luggage sitting on the back seat. "We're not going to Europe now, are we?"

"No. But I thought since Chloe and the boys were leaving, we might as well go on another road trip."

"Where to?"

"You'll see."

They drove for half the night and slept in a cheesy roadside motel—Samantha did use the coin-operated bed, just for fun. There were also mirrors on the ceiling, which she tried to be horrified by. But she liked the view. So she couldn't be too mad about it.

They got up early, and she was cranky and sleep-deprived while they continued on into Arizona. It was amazing, how she felt nostalgia for that time already. There was something she loved about that.

"Where are we going?" she asked.

"I remembered how much you liked that outlook in the Painted Desert. I thought we'd do a bigger one. A grand one."

When they entered Grand Canyon National Park, there was a fair amount of traffic, but she didn't mind. When they stopped at the first viewpoint, and she looked out into the vastness, her eyes filled with tears.

She could remember standing in a place like this, more than

a year ago, feeling so desperately sad at all the wonder she'd never seen. All the lives she hadn't lived.

A year and a summer ago, she had been Samantha Parker, Will Parker's wife. A woman who had gotten married to hide a mistake, to hide her shame. Who had tried to be what everyone around her wanted her to be. Expected her to be.

She'd blown it all to hell.

When she looked out at this view, larger and deeper and infinitely vast, she didn't feel sad for all she hadn't seen. All she hadn't done.

She had the important things. The things she chose.

She was Samantha. Just Samantha.

Her life was enough.

All it had taken to get there was one cruel summer.

★ ★ ★ ★ ★

Samantha's
Cruel Summer playlist

Cruel Summer—Taylor Swift

Good 4 U—Olivia Rodrigo

Misery Business—Paramore

Sugar, We're Goin Down—Fall Out Boy

Your Love Is a Lie—Simple Plan

Mother's Daughter—Miley Cyrus

The Smallest Man Who Ever Lived—Taylor Swift

Heavy—Linkin Park ft. Kiiara

Muddy Feet—Miley Cyrus ft. Sia

Easy on Me—Adele

Pink Pony Club—Chappell Roan

Hope Is the Anthem—Switchfoot

Raise Up—Semler

Drive—Haven Yates

Guilty as Sin?—Taylor Swift

Till There's Nothing Left—Cam

Nothing On but the Stars—Dierks Bentley

my tears ricochet—Taylor Swift

Go Your Own Way—Lissie

Stupid Boy—Keith Urban

Make You Miss Me—Sam Hunt

So High School—Taylor Swift

Kiss Me—Sixpence None the Richer

Die a Happy Man—Nelly

Cruel Summer (Live from Taylor Swift | The Eras Tour)—
Taylor Swift

acknowledgments

I wrote this book very close to my own grief of losing my mother to ovarian cancer. My husband, unlike Samantha's, was very supportive and didn't ask for an open marriage. But in terms of grief journeys, anxiety and surgery, this book bears some similarities to my real life. I even went zip-lining in Skamania right before I wrote that scene.

Like Samantha, I find clarity in writing.

For many reasons, this book was hard-won, personal and challenging. I didn't have to go on a journey to find myself, though, because my personal village rallied around me.

I want to thank Amber, Sheena and Lisa because we went to a pretty awesome drag show while I was mired in the weeds, and that getaway is actually what led to the zip line—and ultimately helped me get this book finished even while it felt like things were professionally falling apart.

I owe my thanks, as ever, to Nicole Helm, Megan Crane and Jackie Ashenden—the best writers I know and the very best friends, who have been there through quite simply everything.

To Flo Nicoll, my amazing editor. How many people are so

lucky to have a brilliant editor who is also a wonderful friend? Not many. But I am.

And finally to my husband, Haven, for being on the journey with me.